Nine New Novellas

Nine New Novellas

By
Jay Dubya

Published by
Jay Dubya
Hammonton, NJ 08037
3462_2

ISBN 978-1-58909-141-2

Printed in the United States of America

iv

Books by Jay Dubya

Adult Fiction

Black Leather and Blue Denim, A '50s Novel
The Great Teen Fruit War, A 1960' Novel
Frat' Brats, A '60s Novel
Ron Coyote, Man of La Mangia
So Ya' Wanna' Be A Teacher!
Pieces of Eight
Pieces of Eight, Part II
Pieces of Eight, Part III
Pieces of Eight, Part IV
The Wholly Book of Genesis
The Wholly Book of Exodus
The Wholly Book of Doo-Doo-Rot-on-Me
Thirteen Sick Tasteless Classics
Thirteen Sick Tasteless Classics, Part II
Thirteen Sick Tasteless Classics, Part III
Thirteen Sick Tasteless Classics, Part IV
Thirteen Sick Tasteless Classics, Part V
Nine New Novellas
Nine New Novellas, Part II
Nine New Novellas, Part III
Nine New Novellas, Part IV
Mauled Maimed Mangled Mutilated Mythology
Modern Mythology
Fractured Frazzled Folk Fables and Fairy Farces
FFFF & FF, Part II
One Baker's Dozen
Two Baker's Dozen
Random Articles and Manuscripts
Snake Eyes and Boxcars
Snake Eyes and Boxcars, Part II
Shakespeare: Slammed, Smeared, Savaged and Slaughtered
Shakespeare: S, S, S and S, Part II
O. Henry: Obscenely and Outrageously Obliterated
Twain: Tattered, Trounced, Tortured and Traumatized
London: Lashed, Lacerated, Lampooned and Lambasted
Poe: Pelted, Pounded, Pummeled and Pulverized
Time Travel Tales
UFO: Utterly Fantastic Occurrences

Snake Eyes and Boxcars
Prime-Time Crime Time
The FBI Inspector
The Psychic Dimension
The Psychic Dimension, Part II
First Person Stories
The Arcane Arcade
13 Tantalizing Tales
PLOTS
PLOTS, Part II
THEMES
Hawthorne: Hazed Hooked Hammered & Hijacked
Hathorne Hacked, Shakespeare Sacked, & Thurber Thwacked
Homer's Ill Iliad
Homer's Odd Sea Odyssey
Homer's Ill Iliad & Odd Sea Odyssey
The Timeless Time Machine
War of the Worlds
The Invisible Man
Parody Paradise
Parody Paradise, Part II
Parody Paradise, Part III
Parody Paradise, Part IV
A Christmas Carol
Bee 17, Short Stories
Bee 17, #2, Short Stories
Bee 17, Part III, Short Stories
Bee 17, Part IV, Short Stories
Bee 17, Part V, Short Stories
Bee 17, Part VI, Short Stories

Young Adult Fantasy Novels

Pot of Gold
Enchanta
Space Bugs, Earth Invasion
The Eighteen Story Gingerbread House

Contents

Introduction

Nine New Novellas is author Jay Dubya's fifth story collection written in the spirit of *Pieces of Eight, Pieces of Eight, Part II, Pieces of Eight, Part III* and *Pieces of Eight, Part IV,* bringing the writer's novella total up to forty-one.

"Friendship" is a unique tale that mixes suspense with a revenge plot, "The Unique Juke Box" is a sci-fi time travel adventure with a surprise ending and "Rock, Paper, Scissors" describes dramatic conflict between groups of doctors, lawyers and Mafia members that dine at a popular New Jersey restaurant.

"The UFO Magnet" is a science fiction thriller that provides a rational explanation for space aliens abducting innocent humans, "Signals" shows a relationship between *ESP* and communication with other dimension spirits and "Drama and Trauma" depicts and explains a hospital patient's strange utterances before the specter of death envelops him.

Finally, "Red, White and Blue America" is a chilling futuristic view of the *United States of America* in 2070 AD, "The Power of Suggestion" has a fascinating hypnosis and reincarnation theme and "June 30, 1956" is an imaginative tale about a man who develops extraordinary psychic powers and then attempts to prevent a great catastrophe from occurring.

"Friendship"

Jeffrey Marsh was quite depressed after reviewing the contents of his *Oakcrest High School 1967 Yearbook*. Marsh's senior year had been a glorious one, all-state New Jersey quarterback in football, president of his senior class, and the handsome young man had also been head-cheerleader Samantha Ross's distinguished escort to the Oakcrest junior-senior prom. 'My entire life's been in a dreadful downward tailspin ever since 1967,' Jeff lamented as he disgustedly slammed his high school yearbook closed and then tossed it into an open desk drawer.

The proud former athlete pondered the nagging source of his melancholy. 'I flunked out of *Rutgers* second semester of my junior year, never was offered the pro football contract I had always wanted, have been divorced from Samantha for the past seven years, and now *she* has custody of Ricky and Caroline. And to top it off,' Marsh concluded, 'I need nine-hundred-thousand-bucks to buy out my incompetent unreliable partner in *our* foundering real estate business. Life's been a real miserable bummer for me since high school, a thorough and total disaster that's for damned sure!'

The doorbell ringing interrupted Jeffrey's disconsolate daydreaming. He rose from his den's most comfortable red leather desk chair and briskly stepped to his modestly furnished Galloway Township townhouse's front door. Frank Donoghue was standing there with a handful of letters, bills and assorted junk mail.

"Hello Jeff," the jovial-but-efficient mailman began, "I have a registered letter for you to sign for."

"I hope it's not another nasty demand or legal threat from my wife's carnivorous attorney," Jeff abruptly answered. "I already pay more than my share of alimony and child support because of that money-hungry vulture."

"I don't think so," Postman Donoghue casually replied. "The registered letter looks more formal than official. I share your conviction about the legal system and I too have little affection for leeching lawyers and their bloodsucking profession."

"Thanks for endorsing my sentiments Frank," Jeffrey Marsh returned as he anxiously signed for the unexpected item. "I'm glad someone else understands my animosity for sue-happy people and their viperous legal representatives. I'm now motivated to see exactly what this important correspondence is."

The resident re-entered his dwelling, waved farewell to his genial visitor and then gently closed the green wooden front door. Jeffrey's restive mind was suddenly filled with abundant curiosity. 'I wonder what sort of letter this is,' Marsh suspiciously considered. 'It's certainly much more interesting than any junk mail or telephone, cable or electric bill, that's for sure!'

The real estate broker quickly tore open the envelope and studied the eight-square-inch card's language, handsomely scrolled in calligraphy, which he immediately recognized as a special invitation from a long forgotten past acquaintance. Marsh's head shook from side-to-side in disbelief as the fascinated recipient examined and then comprehended the interesting letter's content.

> Jeffrey,
>
> You are cordially invited to a party among old friends to be given at my palatial estate situated between Bethany Beach and Fenwick Island, Delaware on Monday, September 8, 2003.
>
> I request that you drive to the Tuckahoe Inn at Beesley's Point where you can park your automobile. I have arranged for my widely acclaimed yacht *Friendship* to be docked at the pier adjacent to the restaurant. Be prepared to board my personal cruising ship at eight a.m. sharp. The captain of my pleasure craft will transport you from the Great Egg Harbor River and down the *Atlantic* from Ocean City, New Jersey to my elegant mansion on the Delaware Coast.
>
> Jeff, I have a big surprise awaiting you. Wear casual attire for your once-in-a-lifetime cruise but please bring along a tuxedo for the formal black tie gala to be held at my mansion afterwords.
>
> I trust that you will be able to attend my exclusive affair. If you cannot, please write and another visit to my vast estate can be scheduled.
>
> Your Oakcrest High School classmate,
>
> Milo Cabot
> 1 Network Road
> Bethany Beach, Delaware 19930

Jeffrey observed the date on his kitchen wall calendar, Tuesday, July 15th. Then he hastily perused his personal agenda book to determine if the Atlantic Coast cruise aboard the *Friendship* interfered with any important business appointments. 'No conflicts,' Marsh acknowledged. 'I'll leave Monday through Wednesday open to accommodate good old Milo. I haven't seen the skinny wimp since high school graduation. Who would have ever thought that the biggest and squarest egghead at Oakcrest would become a prominent American billionaire? Milo really hit it big in the computer networking industry and he's been on the cover of several national business magazines,' the real estate broker recalled. 'Maybe I can convince Cabot to lend me a paltry million bucks to buy out my lazy partner's half of our struggling real estate company. Milo might just be the Godsend I've been praying for to rescue me from a humiliating bankruptcy.'

Marsh opened the freezer compartment door and plunked four ice cubes into a glass. Then after shutting the refrigerator's bottom door, he advanced to the liquor cabinet and generously poured a *Jack Daniels* double. The dreamer sipped the powerful whiskey and contemplated how he would approach Milo Cabot in private and describe *his* unfortunate financial dilemma to the successful and now-famous entrepreneur. 'Milo always had a kind heart in high school back in 1967,' Jeffrey recollected, 'but unfortunately he avoided all class reunions since 1985 when he systematically began accumulating his incredible fortune. He'll certainly help me out of my present difficulty once I convey the simple details. Milo always looked up to me as a role model and as a staunch ally,' the real estate man remembered with a broad grin. "A million bucks is chicken-feed to a rich guy like Milo Cabot!'

Jeffrey very deliberately crossed off each day on his kitchen calendar from July 15th to September 7th. Following a restless night's sleep, finally the morning of his seven-week-long anticipation arrived. Marsh checked the red-number read-out on his alarm clock and sprang out of bed before the object would begin playing an FM station's music at six a.m. 'Only an hour to shave, get dressed and have some coffee and toast for breakfast. I'm glad I already have my tux carefully stashed away in my car's trunk,' the ecstatic fellow remembered.

After packing a suitcase in which he kept a change of casual clothes, underwear and his beige-zippered toiletry case, Jeffrey Marsh donned his black Bermudas and put on his colorful Hawaiian shirt. 'I almost feel like a hormone-driven teenager again,' he wishfully thought as he admired his well-groomed appearance in the bathroom's *vanity* mirror. 'I'm glad I inserted a fresh razor blade into my shaver. Who knows? I might be reunited with a long-lost high school sweetheart at Milo's posh get-together.'

Jeffrey Marsh toted his suitcase to the front porch, locked the townhouse's front door and paced out to his aqua green 2002 *Honda Accord*. He clicked his key chain's remote control and the trunk sprang open. After inserting his piece of luggage, Marsh was ready for his pleasant drive to the historic Tuckahoe Inn. "I'll take *Route 322* to scenic *Route 9*, the highway Bruce Springsteen always sings about. Of course, Asbury Park and the *Stone Pony* are about sixty miles north of Mays Landing,' the blithe man chuckled. 'The *Garden State Parkway* will be more crowded than usual so I'll just relax and take the old Beesley's Point Bridge across the bay to Tuckahoe. I can't wait to board and inspect Milo's yacht. Knowing *his* new reputation, it must be a real dandy!'

The early morning September 8th *Route 9* excursion was indeed pleasurable and soon the aqua green *Accord* was crossing the Beesley Point Bridge, which spanned the Great Egg Harbor Bay. 'It's called Egg Harbor Bay because birds often nest here to lay their eggs. And there are the twin stacks of the South Jersey Power Plant,' Jeff noticed as his four-door vehicle approached the tollbooth situated in the center of the antiquated span. 'Wow, the toll's now a hefty sixty cents! I remember when it used to be a mere thin dime.'

The dual spans of the *Garden State Parkway Bridge* were to the driver's left and Marsh recognized the familiar bumper-to-bumper congestion of tourists motoring south from Philadelphia, New York and Atlantic City down to popular vacation resorts Ocean City, Sea Isle City, Avalon, Stone Harbor, Wildwood and Cape May.

After fumbling in his coin tray for the precise change the traveler then handed the three silver-plated objects to the amiable collector. As soon as the *Honda* continued its transit across the quaint but in-need-of-repair bridge, Jeffrey's keen eyes spotted a glistening object reflecting morning sunlight from the vicinity of the Tuckahoe Inn. 'That must be Milo's sleek vessel!' Marsh marveled. 'It's appearance is somewhere between spectacular and magnificent. Oh my God! The ship has three levels.'

The impressed man next drove his modest *Accord* into the almost vacant Tuckahoe Inn asphalt lot and inconspicuously parked in the rear. After removing his suitcase and his rented black tuxedo from his common means of transportation's trunk, Jeffrey sauntered in the direction of the splendid custom-designed yacht. Upon reaching the gangplank, Marsh was surprised and thrilled to see two former high school acquaintances engaged in general conversation with the *Friendship's* captain.

"Hello Jeff!" greeted Kathy Landis, a friend of Samantha's that had always idolized the Oakcrest Falcons' first-string quarterback. "Fancy meeting you here!"

"Hi Jeff," a rather weak voice added. "Do you remember me from chemistry class?"

"Why if it isn't Richard Daniels," Marsh exclaimed. "I haven't seen you since the last class reunion at the Venice Plaza over in Berlin. You wrote the term paper on Archimedes that enabled me to get out of Oakcrest. And oh yes," Marsh recalled. "Hello Kathy! You were a terrific leader for the school debating team!"

"Jeff, I'd like to introduce you to Captain James," Richard Daniels formally insisted. "He's going to navigate this beauty down to Milo's place, or should I say 'palace' in Delaware."

"Quite a luxury ship Captain James!" Marsh instantly evaluated. "I'll bet with the radar and triple-decks of opulence, this baby probably easily goes for between two and three million clams, even in the throes of a recession."

"Well Mr. Marsh, that's really a humble low-ball figure you have alluded to," the Captain replied with a forced smile. "Mr. Cabot does everything first class, and with all of the *Friendship's* special amenities and fine ambiance, money is really no object to my employer, if you know what I mean!"

"How long will our ocean voyage take?" Kathy Landis asked. "I once got horribly seasick in a rocky rowboat at Lenape Lake Park in Mays Landing."

"About four and a half hours," the navigation specialist returned. "We'll be stopping off at Rehoboth Beach to pick up Mrs. Cabot. She's doing some casual shopping down in Delaware at the clothing mall outlets and should have an extensive new wardrobe to take back to Bethany Beach with her."

"Then Milo is married?" Jeffrey inquired. "I could never picture him in high school having a sound relationship with any female."

"Yes sir Mr. Marsh," Captain James confirmed. "Mr. Cabot married a former *Miss Maryland* finalist seven years ago. The two get along rather harmoniously. Now if you please," the slightly nervous pilot indicated to Marsh, "if you don't mind I'll take your suitcase and tuxedo aboard and temporarily store them in a closet."

"Here they are," Jeffrey offered. "I believe I can trust them to your care," he jokingly added.

When Captain James departed up the gangplank and then stepped into the fabulous white yacht's interior, the remaining threesome struck up an impromptu cheerful chat.

"Tell me Jeff, are you still involved in real estate?" Kathy Landis innocently asked.

"Yes, and are you still working in banking?" her former heartthrob requested knowing.

"I got a recent promotion to branch CD Officer," Kathy indicated, "but I didn't tie the marriage knot for too long. Now that I'm getting older, I do regret not having any children or a faithful husband around the house. I guess I'm really loyally married to my job and *my kids* now are those cherished Certificates of Deposit I sell to appreciative Mays Landing bank customers."

"And how about you?" Marsh asked the usually laconic Richard Daniels. "What are ya' doin' for a blessed living and are you married?"

"I'm single and still playing the field," Richard informed. "I'm a political science teacher at *Camden Community College*. I had taught high school social studies for four years but I got tired and frustrated of all the stupid discipline problems and educational bureaucracy. The college scene is much more satisfying to me than public school education ever was."

Just after Captain James accompanied by a teenage boy again appeared on the main deck and then shuffled down the sturdy gangplank, the high school acquaintances observed a tanned svelte female carrying two new suitcases to where the *Friendship* had been moored. Jeffrey almost swallowed his tonsils when he recognized that the attractive dark-tan woman was none other than his former spouse.

"Samantha, what on Earth are you doing here?" wide-eyed Marsh stammered. "I mean you look so ravishing!"

"Feast your deceitful eyes," the well-built lady replied with an air of contrived sophistication. "You had your chance with me but fumbled the football Mr. Quarterback," the exotic-looking woman cackled as she drew reactive forced smiles from Kathy Landis and from Richard Daniels. "Why Richie! So nice to see you again!" the former Miss Samantha Ross stated. "And Kathy, this is indeed a marvelous coincidence!" the wily female continued. "I still believe that you and Richie would make a terrific couple! And as for my former husband, I think that we'll both try and be old friends simply tolerating each other and we'll fake being genuinely sociable on this particularly pleasant ocean adventure."

Jeffrey Marsh figured that he would change the subject to avoid further embarrassment or conflict from his sharp-tongued ex'. "Who is your young mate there, Captain?" he asked while showing his general inquisitive nature.

"This is Jacob everyone," Captain James revealed. "Jacob is Mr. Cabot's only stepson. His wife Sierra's young lad by a previous marriage."

"Hello and welcome aboard the *Friendship*," Jacob snottily and insincerely announced. "Miss Ross, I believe, I'll take your luggage inside."

"Why thank you Jacob," Samantha answered as courteously as she could. "That was very sweet of you. You seem to be a respectful and mannerly young man. That's a quality lacking in most youth now-a-days," she exaggerated.

"Thank you, M'am," Jacob mechanically replied. "I sometimes enjoy being first mate on this ship and being its only permanent porter. A little common labor once in a while never hurt anyone as my stepfather always says."

"Okay you landlubbers, let's get this ark sailing," the Captain suggested as he waved everyone aboard and then signaled for four workers stationed at the dock to loosen the heavy ropes that moored the *Friendship* to the newly constructed Tuckahoe Inn pier that jutted out into Egg Harbor Bay. "I'll raise the gangplank by pressing a little red button as soon as everyone is safely aboard for departure."

"Oh Richard," Samantha uttered as she ascended the gangplank and attempted to ignore her handsome former husband. "I almost got lost driving here. I keep getting Tuckahoe geographically confused with Tuckerton."

"Actually Samantha," Richard Daniels qualified, "Tuckahoe is a village located right next to Beesley's Point and Tuckerton is a town situated ten miles on so on the mainland above Atlantic City."

"That's what I always admired about you Richie," Samantha Ross falsely complimented. "You know so much trivia that you put the rest of us to shame. Now tell me Captain, how long has Milo owned this fantastic ship."

Captain James explained to his guests that *his* employer had owned the *Friendship* for over a year. "Since as you know Mr. Cabot is partially paralyzed in his left arm, he seldom pilots the ship and has assigned me to perform that task. I was also Mr. Cabot's chauffeur for six years before I obtained my captain's license to navigate the *Friendship*."

"How long have you worked for Milo?" Kathy Landis inquired.

"For thirteen years," Captain James replied. "Thirteen dedicated years of service as gardener, butler, chauffeur and finally as captain."

"Who's maneuvering the ship from the pier?" Jeffrey instinctively inquired.

"Jacob," the captain related. "He's almost as skilled as I am and insists that he must practice the important chore to impress his stepfather." Then the gray-haired man with handsome features continued his standard monologue about the well-appointed ship. "The *Friendship* was custom-manufactured for Mr. Cabot. The Burger Boat Company of Manitowac, Michigan built this nifty ninety-five-foot-long gem. It has an enclosed bridge and as you know it possesses three breathtaking observation levels."

"Isn't *thirteen* years regarded as an unlucky number?" interrupted Jeffrey while referring to the tenure of Captain James' employment with Milo Cabot. "Some of us may be a tad superstitious, you know!"

"Thirteen is a number just like any other number," Captain James diplomatically and objectively countered. "But I must add that Mr. Cabot believed that Midwest boat builders produce a better ocean-worthy product than east coast companies do. That accounts for *his* preference."

"Tell us more interesting details," Samantha implored while again feigning sincerity. "I always like learning new things about the secret habits of the rich and famous."

"And so, this ship was launched in Michigan and I then piloted it from the Great Lakes through the St. Lawrence Seaway and next down the East Coast to its principal mooring just below Bethany Beach, Delaware. It was quite an exceptional adventure and also an honor for me to perform. Now if you all will excuse me," the Captain finished, "I'll climb up to the bridge deck and assist Jacob with his challenging responsibility. I'd hate to have the Coast Guard board this flawless vessel and present me with a nasty citation. Please make yourself comfortable in the air-conditioned lounge. I'll soon dispatch Jacob to service your drinking and eating needs."

As the four guests leaned against the vessel's railing and scanned the bay's shore along with the landmark Tuckahoe Inn, each was thinking of his or her own selfish design for agreeing to be entertained by the renowned and eccentric computer networking mogul, Milo Cabot.

'I know Milo will lend me the cool million to salvage my real estate business,' Jeffrey Marsh considered. 'He'll be happy to aid an old friend.'

'Maybe I'll flirt with Milo and turn him on. He always liked me back in high school,' Samantha imagined, not knowing that Sierra Cabot was just as treacherous and just as vivacious as she was. 'That would make my former husband jealous and perhaps I could have a secret affair and land a very rich husband in the process.'

'I want to quit teaching at the college and then start-up my own computer networking company,' Richard Daniels fantasized. 'Milo will surely give me the seed money I need to fulfill my ambition, and with a little luck, my corporation might grow into the next Cisco Systems or into the next Cabot Enterprises.'

'I need to quit my boring bank job,' Kathy Landis regretfully rehashed in her mind. 'I'll ask Milo for a management position in his wonderfully prosperous company. I'll be a steadfast employee. I feel a personal debt to Milo Cabot for what I had accidentally done to him in high school. I need to heal scars from the past and in the meantime guarantee my future security.'

Everyone's reverie was interrupted by Captain James's distinct voice over the ship's intercom speakers. "The *Friendship* is too huge for us to take the *Inter-Coastal Waterway*. This is an ocean-worthy vessel so we'll proceed south on the Atlantic rather than travel slowly down the bays that separate the barrier islands from the mainland," the licensed operator informatively divulged.

The four captivated guests stood and leaned against the main deck's railing as the *Friendship* gingerly left the marina next to the Tuckahoe Inn and soon Captain James adroitly steered the craft as it majestically glided under the twin spans of the *Garden State Parkway*. Even the huge cylindrical stacks of the South Jersey Power Plant suddenly appeared harmonious with the peaceful nautical and pine barren environments it shared.

"Every time I see that electric plant my mind thinks of some advanced form of Arab-inspired terrorism," Jeffrey related. "I know that violence is an obscure possibility but the threat always seems to haunt my psyche."

"Ever since *9-11*," Richard Daniels said as he stared at the power company's twin towers, "everyone including me is a little paranoid. The safest and most innocent place could suddenly materialize into a mass disaster area. The possibility of sabotage is now present almost anywhere and everywhere in America!"

"I can't wait to see Milo after so many years," Samantha Ross stated off subject. "I wonder if he's still shy and introverted," the woman added as she glanced across at her ex-husband and contemplated *his* strong tan muscular forearms. "I think Milo Cabot was actually cute in his own peculiar way *our* junior year."

"You never know which direction fate will take you," Kathy Landis contributed. "Whoever suspected in their wildest imagination that Milo Cabot would become one of the wealthiest and one of most influential men on the whole planet. Every citizen from Main Street to Wall Street knows and reveres *his* name."

Soon the *Friendship* had gracefully left the tranquility of Great Egg Harbor Bay and smoothly entered the dark blue Atlantic. The Ocean City Boardwalk along with its many food concessions and amusements soon came into view. The four passengers scrutinized and relished the familiar stretch of white sandy beach along with the wide wooden commercial platform's popular pizza, popcorn, salt water taffy and souvenir shop businesses.

Captain James's baritone voice was again heard from overhead speakers. "We'll be cruising down the Jersey Coast at about twenty-two knots. Enjoy the spectacular scenery. The *Friendship* is fully capable of crossing *the pond* to Europe if it had to. It is a most dependable ship and I take great pride in being its captain."

"Look over there to our left," Kathy impulsively requested. "There's the old Flanders Hotel. It's been recently renovated and converted into plush condominiums."

"And there's Ninth Street to our right where the Chatterbox Restaurant is located three blocks down from the boardwalk," Jeffrey Marsh reminisced and reminded his listeners. "Samantha, remember when *we* used to eat at that place during our college year summers while working down there on the boardwalk earning money to pay for our tuition and textbooks?"

"Yes, and what about the Music Pier and Convention Center?" Richard Daniels mentioned and pointed to a familiar structure jutting out into the Atlantic. "The building looks almost exactly as it did back in good old 1967."

'Samantha sure has remained beautiful and alluring after thirty-six years of wear and tear,' Jeff Marsh assessed. 'Maybe I should have given our marriage a second chance like *she* had wanted.' Then the woeful real estate agent contemplated a troubling question his mind had been rehashing. "Say Samantha, who's taking care of Ricky and Caroline?"

"My sister Nancy," the beautiful blonde woman bluntly answered. "She has excellent rapport with both *our* children." And then Samantha had a rather covetous thought. 'I wish I was in bed with

Jeff right now. His biceps and shoulders are looking better and better by the minute.'

"Let's go inside and have a drink," Kathy recommended. "We can review old times and classmates without this wind messing-up our hair."

The four guest passengers entered the ship's spacious air-conditioned lounge area and sat in comfortable green leather chairs around a circular solid oak table. Jacob entered dressed as a formal restaurant waiter. "Would you folks care for anything to drink?"

"Yes, I'll have a double of *Jack Daniels* on the rocks," insisted Jeffrey as he inadvertently licked his lips.

"I'll have a tall Tom Collins," Samantha ordered. 'I wish that Jeff wasn't such an avid alcoholic. That's the major reason why I divorced him,' she recalled.

Kathy Landis asked for a Pina Colada and Richard Daniels requested a Rusty Nail. Then the four reunited classmates engaged in nostalgic conversation. And after a second round of potent beverages, everyone had loosened-up their inhibitions enough to at last be honest about their communications.

"I always thought that Milo Cabot was a trifle peculiar," Samantha honestly admitted. "He was a *nerd* a full two decades before the terminology ever became part of the American pop culture scene. Milo was definitely somewhere between an egghead and a common fink back then!"

"Milo and I competed for the honor of being the best academic student in the graduating class," Richard recollected and mentioned. "He was much smarter than I was but I somehow managed to be his staunch rival throughout high school. Boy, now I wish he and I had been closer friends than we actually were. Milo was always a little aloof and distant," Daniels bluntly stated. "I believe he had additional eccentricities, but I suppose I'll never be privy to what those specific quirks might be."

"Richie, I absolutely concur with your on-target impressions," Kathy agreed. "Milo was a bit timid when it came to dating girls. But now I regret not having an affair with him. I mean I did marry Steve Hart and we stayed together for two years," she related, "but then we didn't hit it off and my life ever since has been one plagued with lonely drudgery and dreadful aggravation."

"You know what you should do, Samantha," Jeffrey Marsh playfully proposed to avoid hearing any more of Kathy Landis's grievances with life. "You could give us one of those old Oakcrest

High fight cheers for old time's sake. You were one helluva' head cheerleader."

"I'll be ready, willing and able after another round of drinks," the gorgeous woman promised her flattering admirer. "It'll be easy once I warm up to the occasion."

Captain James very skillfully guided the *Friendship* along the enchanting Jersey Coast. The ship seemed to be gliding along as if the eternal sea was a continuous sheet of wave-less navy-blue salt water. The four passengers exchanged fond memories as they sat in the lounge around the impeccable circular oak table. Meanwhile the vigilant skipper kept the vessel on a parallel path about a mile off the irregular Jersey coastline.

"Why do you think Milo invited the four of us to his mansion?" Kathy Landis boldly asked her fellow passengers.

"Actually, I believe he's looking for some sort of closure to an ugly chapter in his life," Jeffrey theorized and replied. "He's now looking for our acceptance. In his heart Milo craves to gain the lost prestige that he had missed during his formative years. Only the four of us, being the most popular kids in his high school class could satisfy his dire emotional need."

"What gives you that strange impression?" Samantha challenged while demonstrating her typical domineering attitude. "How can *you* even pretend forming such a strong opinion about someone we all hardly ever knew?"

"I suspect there's a giant void in Milo's life," Jeff Marsh summarized. "He simply desires filling that vacuum with us giving him his lost recognition. I mean we were the four envied class officers and poor Milo was basically a non-entity," the former quarterback and class president hypothesized and shared.

"I believe Jeff's correct in his theory," Kathy Landis concurred. "I was vice-president, Richie was class treasurer and Samantha, you were the senior class secretary."

"Holy cow!" Richard Daniels exclaimed. "How time flies! I had forgotten that we were the four class officers forty-three years ago when Oakcrest High was brand new!"

"And now that Milo has gained international notoriety," Jeffrey Marsh continued, "he has to reinforce that new-found domination by validating himself to us. It's his way of making a proclamation that he's made it big in the real world. It's Milo's way of obtaining tribute and honor from those that had overshadowed him in high school. Milo was what you might call a late-bloomer!"

"I now agree with my haughty ex after listening to *his* persuasive argument," Samantha reluctantly confessed. "I think Jeff's right on the money," she begrudgingly acceded. But then the conniving woman surreptitiously kept her secret thoughts to herself. 'Jeff is intelligent and physically alluring, but Milo's got the heavy-duty bank account. I'll try to use my feminine charms and entice *him* to buy me a new *Mercedes*. If I remember correctly,' the cunning woman speculated, 'Milo had a mild crush on me in high school. I don't care if he's now married to *Miss Universe*, or whatever she is. I'm gonna' get that expensive white convertible if it's the last blessed thing I ever do!'

The *Friendship* soon passed the coastal town of Strathmere and now several high rises from Sea Isle City could be seen to the southwest from the immaculate ship's spotless pane windows. The resort town was mostly residential and not nearly as commercially oriented as Atlantic City or Ocean City. Nevertheless Sea Isle's ocean frontage sold at a premium price as did most limited but in demand land did along the heralded and enticing New Jersey Coast.

Five minutes later Jacob again rather awkwardly entered the ship's lounge and appeared with a tray having a coffee pot, four cups with saucers and a delicious-looking already-sliced cheesecake. After the encumbered junior waiter distributed plates, forks, knives and teaspoons and then poured four cups of the freshly brewed java, the guests indulged in consuming the delectable dessert by devouring two cheesecake slices each.

"This boat is almost as well-equipped as an ocean liner," Jeffrey Marsh mentioned to Jacob. "I'll bet it'll be yours some day when your stepfather buys a *Cunard* ocean ship for himself and takes off to the Mediterranean."

"Oh Jeff, just look at those expensive mansions in Avalon and Stone Harbor!" Samantha jealously shouted as she pointed out the ship's windows. "They go from anywhere between three and five million each. An acre of beachfront property sells for a cool million at bargain basement prices," the gorgeous woman elaborated. "Some rich people buy an old ocean front house for two million, have it demolished and then they effortlessly construct a five million dollar palace in its place."

"Big deal!" a somewhat perturbed Jacob snottily declared. "My stepfather's mansion cost fifteen million to build and now he's tired of the dump and plans to have a bigger and better beach residence erected. He's already discussed the details with his architect."

'I'm definitely going for an Ocean City condo' in addition to the white *Mercedes* convertible,' Samantha Ross decided. 'I now know I should have flirted with Milo back at Oakcrest. I was too into myself and into my vain popularity to seriously realize *his* great potential!'

The ship's ever-trusty propellers churned the outstanding sea-worthy vessel past Wildwood, and the four travelers led by Jeffrey Marsh sang a dissonant version of Bobby Rydell's classic pop hit "Wildwood Days," which celebrated the glorious joys of spring and summer high school escapades at the amusement-laden boardwalk featuring sensational carnival-ride piers having mammoth water-slides. Richard Daniels thought about his college fraternity taking over the flashy town and *its* honky-tonk venues, Kathy remembered her friend's wild bachelorette party at a downtown Wildwood 50s'-style art deco motel, and Samantha and Jeffrey mused about their first experience at lovemaking underneath the expansive boardwalk while hundreds of unwary vacationers promenaded on wooden planks eight feet above *their* passionate embraces. Soon Jacob appeared with another round of potent drinks and after setting the tray on the sturdy oak table, Milo's egotistical stepson dutifully began cleaning-up the dessert plates.

"My stepfather demands that I learn life as he did from the bottom up," Jacob mildly complained to his audience in a melancholy tone of voice. "Someday I'll be sitting in the chairman-of-the-board driver's seat and giving similar commands to my eldest son just to keep Pop's stupid slave tradition alive."

"We'll be cruising by Cape May in about half an hour," Richard observed and stated. "I just love all of the colorful Bed and Breakfast places. It's the most Victorian resort town on the entire East Coast."

"It's certainly an expensive tourist trap," Samantha opined. "But the town has lots of character, charm and history too to balance things out! A visit there is like taking a swell journey into the past. Sometimes the tour guides dress-up in turn-of-the-century costumes and you get the feeling that you're actually living in the 1890s."

"Anything in Cape May is a dump compared to my stepfather's castle," Jacob arrogantly interrupted, "and that's the plain simple truth without any bragging. One-day Pop will buy the dumb town and change it into something modern. He's the only person that I know of that could pull that maneuver off without a hitch!"

The picturesque Cape May Victorian edifices soon faded from view, the exquisite and historic lighthouse on New Jersey's southern peninsula was speedily passed, and without hesitation the *Friendship* was soon beyond the Cape May tip of New Jersey and crossing the mouth of the Delaware Bay.

"Look, there's the old concrete ship that sunk just off the inlet," Richard said while using his right index finger. "It was an experiment that was a dismal failure to conserve steel for army use during *World War II.*"

"And there's the Cape May-Lewes Ferry on its way to the Delaware shore," Kathy perceptively noted. "From a distance it looks like it's going to rendezvous with the ferry coming in the opposite direction from Lewes."

"I've been on several deep-sea fishing expeditions out of Cape May," Jeffrey Marsh informed his listeners, "and the Baltimore Canyon is about ten miles or so from here out in the Atlantic. It's a haven for serious anglers!"

'And *you* always came home from charter-boat fishing drunker than an Irish sailor,' Samantha concluded and kept to herself. 'That's when *your* erratic behavior was a total embarrassment to always have to explain to Caroline and to Ricky.'

"We'll be docking in about an hour and fifteen minutes at Rehoboth Beach to pick up Mrs. Cabot," the Captain announced over the intercom speakers. "All passengers can relax on chaise longues out on the sundeck if you'd like. There's a whirlpool spa running for your convenience."

The *Friendship* cut across the seventeen-mile-long mouth of Delaware Bay as if it were a knife severing through a sea of soft butter. Jeffrey, Samantha, Richard and Kathy frolicked about on the wooden sundeck like school children exploring their first playground experience. All of their immediate world appeared innocent, carefree and full of gratifying luxuries as the foursome dangled and splashed their feet in the spa's swirling water.

When the streamlined yacht docked at the northern end of Rehoboth Beach, the four guests ceased their playful romping and dried off using towels that had been generously supplied by their wealthy absent host. It was now time to put on their shoes and sandals and formally meet the very stunning Mrs. Sierra Cabot.

A tall tanned radiant woman was standing on the side pier holding six bags of newly acquired apparel. "Over here Jacob!" she yelled to her apathetic spoiled son. "Come and help me with these horribly heavy packages!"

The boarding plank was lowered and Captain James reached out to assist the temporarily overwhelmed lady onto the yacht. "Welcome aboard Mrs. Cabot!" he courteously greeted. "May I introduce you to Jeffrey Marsh!"

Sierra Cabot took a glimpse at the man's handsome face, pearly-white teeth and powerful body and a sudden broad smile beamed just above her chin. The now-dazzling-looking auburn-hair woman suddenly abandoned her usual sarcastic demeanor. "And this is Samantha Ross, a fellow high school classmate of your husband," Captain James stated to Mrs. Cabot.

The two glamorous women jealously stared at each other, both instantly recognizing a rival's charm and grace when those distinct qualities suddenly confronted each of them. The two lovely ladies feigned brief smiles as their suspicious eyes made direct contact.

"And here are Richard Daniels and Kathy Landis," the Captain introduced the pair to Sierra Cabot. "They also had graduated Oakcrest High School with Mr. Cabot in 1967 back in New Jersey."

"Glad to make your acquaintance!" Sierra nonchalantly declared with a false degree of etiquette. "Now if you'll all excuse me, I'll retire to my stateroom. I'm completely exhausted from that ghastly shopping spree. And that bus ride to the dock with all those nasty tourists was rather atrocious and quite pedestrian to say the least. I should have gotten my husband's chauffeur to wait and drive me back to Bethany Beach but Milo insisted that Paul had to drive *him* to Salisbury to close an important legal transaction. At any rate," Sierra Cabot protested in an exaggerated sophisticated manner, "here I am. Jacob, please be so accommodating as to carry my new belongings to the master cabin."

"Okay everyone, you may return to either the recreation den or to the sundeck spa area!" Captain James bellowed to his four original passengers. "Mrs. Cabot is fatigued from her lengthy shopping ordeal and requires her rest. We should be shoving off in about five minutes and are scheduled to arrive at South Bethany Beach in about one hour. Enjoy the beautiful Delmarva peninsula viewed from the ocean."

The four travelers retreated to the sundeck where they discussed their various appraisals of Sierra Cabot. Opinions were flying around like bullets at the infamous O.K. Corral.

"Sierra is certainly a beautiful woman," Richard began his honest analysis, "and she could probably win the Mrs. Delaware Beauty Pageant right now if she was a contestant. Next to Samantha, she's the most stunning creature I've ever seen."

"Thanks for the nice very polite compliment," Samantha Ross answered. "But it is quite obvious Milo's wife has a haughty

16

disposition that won't quit. I can see where Jacob gets his ugly self-centered conceit. If my son Ricky ever acted like Jacob does, I would smack him across the face so hard that his teeth would rattle. That snooty kid needs his jaw fractured at least once!"

"Perhaps you're being a little too judgmental of Sierra and of Jacob," Kathy Landis cautioned her opinionated acquaintance. "Samantha, you don't know enough about either of them to even begin writing the preface to their biographies."

"True," Samantha defensively replied, "but I'm a devout believer in first impressions being accurate, and I think that Milo's snobby wife and *his* bratty stepson are ambitious parasites bent on exploiting Milo's extraordinary wealth."

"Samantha, I can't believe that you feel so damned threatened and insecure because of the presence of another formidable heavenly female in our midst," Jeffrey criticized. "The two of you stared at each other like two felines about to claw each others' eyes out. And neither of you was openly acting out your hostility either! The animosity between the two of you was quite palpable and easily felt. It's a good thing Sierra retired to her cabin or else a vicious cat-fight between you and her was bound to occur."

"You should have been a child psychologist," Samantha sarcastically remarked and ridiculed. "You don't have the capacity to ever satisfactorily psychoanalyze adults," the sharp-tongued woman finished in one of her predictable classic put-downs.

"Enough personality assassination! Let's change the topic to something more relaxing," Richard intelligently suggested. "I don't appreciate conflict in real life. I prefer vicariously encountering and experiencing it in the movies."

* * * * * * * * * * *

Milo Cabot stood still as a statue peering-out from a window in his fabulous mansion's north tower. A faint white object was barely visible glistening like a white diamond floating on the calm-but-shimmering sea. The computer-networking tycoon's eyes were transfixed on the inimitable *Friendship* as it strategically approached its South Bethany Beach destination. Hatred gradually swelled in the wealthy man's normally cold heart.

'All I loathe and despise on this Earth is now sailing on my yacht,' Milo imagined. 'I hate you Sierra for cheating on me with that avaricious scoundrel Martin Jamison, alias Captain James, my disloyal yacht meister! Your little love affair has not gone unnoticed,' Milo angrily recalled. 'Yes Sierra, you have attempted stealing my vast fortune right after you succeeded in stealing my heart, but your scheming evil black soul is destined to soon meet its demise.'

Milo Cabot paused for a moment to avoid acting too hastily and prematurely. He very methodically wiped some cold sweat from his forehead despite the good air-conditioning system inside his private "Tower of Meditation." 'And to you Master Jacob, my greedy and craven stepson, you want a fortune without working for it as I had diligently done. You are a dangerous nefarious punk ingrate dreaming of ways to eliminate me and making your mother and you my exclusive heirs. Yes Jacob, you and your greedy mother are identified as principal heirs in my recently written will, but I shall survive the both of you and then gleefully modify my last testament!' Cabot mentally predicted. 'Your vile spiteful conspiracy against me will be a total failure!'

Milo Cabot's diabolical heart was pounding loudly inside his frail chest cavity. The thin-but-tenacious man breathed heavily while garnering the required audacity and the resolute inspiration to perform his premeditated heinous misdeed. 'You three vile vipers have seriously wronged me. Captain James and Sierra, you shall pay for your infidelity and for your reckless scheming and you too Jacob shall be swiftly punished for your lusty covetous ambitions!' paranoid Milo Cabot thought in an almost maniacal trance.

And as the fabulous *Friendship* came within a mile of Milo's resplendent ocean estate, more wicked thoughts surfaced from the networking tycoon's turbulent soul up to the man's now-livid consciousness. 'And you four high school classmates had grossly violated my good intentions in the past,' the madman recollected. "You Samantha Ross had crushed my ego when you refused to go to the junior-senior prom with me. I have carried this lingering grudge for forty-three agonizing years, and now is my chance at obtaining retribution!" the highly irritated insane lunatic internalized and then mechanically whispered to the tower's window. "And you Jeffrey Marsh, class president and fearless football quarterback, you used to taunt and pick on me in the halls and push me around for the amusement of your muscular jock friends. I have never forgotten your mean-spirited cruelty or the extreme humiliation that your insensitivity had caused me to suffer," Milo uttered in a lucid tone of voice. "Your perpetual browbeating and your incessant belittlement have not escaped my memory! Soon revenge will be mine! All mine you despicable bully!"

18

And after a sobbing interval of self-pity, Milo proceeded with his demented muttering. "And oh yes Richard Daniels, cunning Oakcrest fellow graduate. You had stolen Mr. Jenkins's final physics exam' and at the end of the school year beat me out by a tiny infallible fraction on grade-point-average. You cheated and became class valedictorian while I had to settle for salutatorian. I have never forgiven you for depriving me of my justly deserved academic distinction. I had to live with the disgrace of being second best after dedicating my whole high school life to being the top honors' student in our class," Milo muttered to the window and also to the timeless sea in a state of self-imposed hypnosis.

Milo Cabot's bloodshot eyes were now bulging right out of their sockets. His right fist was clenched and the man's long fingernails were penetrating his white-sweaty-palm. The vengeful gaunt genius had one more individual to indict in his self-proclaimed dictatorial prosecution. "And finally Kathy Landis, I loved you when we were in eighth grade, but you always gave me your cold shoulder. I hated being ignored and I had to live eighth grade and high school as a rejected subordinate and as a social isolate. And then the week after the high school prom, you and I were involved in that terrible automobile accident!" Milo Cabot cried. "I have been paralyzed in my left arm ever since that fateful collision. I know *you* claim it was an accident, but to me I have had to live these past four plus decades with physical injury added to painful emotional insult! You should have never recklessly sped through that stop sign Katherine Priscilla Landis. And yet I have managed to overcome all those immense obstacles and through much sacrifice and trial and error, I've ascended to the great societal height I have achieved with steadfast determination and with focused perseverance!" Milo angrily panted and pouted.

The eccentric billionaire then very slowly and meticulously opened the center drawer of his fancy handcrafted semi-circular dark cherry-wood desk. His thumb gently touched a red button that had been cleverly concealed inside. Just as the *Friendship* came within a half-mile's range of *his* superb ocean-side mansion, the jaded aristocrat firmly pressed the remote control button. A powerful bomb detonated aboard the gliding yacht and a distant flash followed by a booming explosion was evident upon the sun-kissed shimmering Atlantic.

The *Meditation Tower's* door swung open and the chief butler appeared in the portal, the servant having a pallid alarmed expression upon his countenance. "Excuse me Mr. Cabot, but did you just hear a loud booming noise!" the startled butler gasped.

"Yes Simms, I believe there are scattered thunderstorms in the vicinity and lightning must be approaching South Bethany. Be sure to have all windows shut in case of an unexpected cloudburst."

"Yes Mr. Cabot, I'll see that your instructions are carried out immediately!" Simms vowed as he deftly closed the secluded tower's sole means of entrance and exit.

'It's a good thing I shrewdly had the *Friendship* insured for only a third of its actual value,' Milo contemplated in a more rational and calculating state of mind. 'Oh well, I really need a new yacht anyway.' Cabot paused for a moment to collect his next thoughts. 'And besides, I have effectively and simultaneously eradicated all of my enemies from the present and all of my harassers from the past. I'll testify to the authorities that I believe that misguided Arab terrorists were conducting an economic jihad against an eminent American capitalist and that *their* fundamentalist beliefs have been responsible for the shocking sea explosion,' Milo Cabot schemed. 'Naturally the unscrupulous Arab terrorists had miscalculated that I would be entertaining some innocent guests on my luxury yacht with *my* illustrious presence on board. I can't wait to give my already-rehearsed deposition. I'm certain that the police will accept my practical theory as being both plausible and valid. Hello future! Goodbye *Friendship!'*

"The Unique Juke Box"

Friday, July 4th had arrived in Hammonton, New Jersey and Eddie Palmer had dutifully taken his wife and three children down to Bellevue Avenue to watch the annual patriotic parade. As the small contingent of *VFW* survivors slowly marched by the Central Avenue viewing area, Eddie had a very selfish thought parade across *his* mind while standing next to the town's "Reagan Rock." 'Tomorrow Kim is taking Jenna, Tommy and Joey to vacation for a whole week at Long Beach Island,' Palmer contemplated. 'Then I can use *my* vacation time to paint my newly constructed recreation room, to cultivate the tall weeds out in the vegetable garden, to mow the lawn and to pick up my new juke box.'

Eddie was a '50s fanatic, such an addicted '50s fanatic who never fully evolved out of that glorious memorable decade. Palmer still wore long greasy hair, had Elvis sideburns and on weekends sported a black motorcycle jacket along with blue denim jeans when he wasn't selling new and used automobiles for a local car dealership up on the White Horse Pike. Eddie Palmer took great pride in being the vice-president of the Hammonton Classic Car Club, himself owning a bright red 1958 Chevy convertible with an impressive Continental wheel attached to and extending from the back.

The following Wednesday Eddie gave his closest friend Jack Nelson a call. "Say Jack," Eddie said from his often-used cell phone, "I need a big favor from you tomorrow morning. Do ya' think you can help me out?"

"Are ya' gonna' finally replace that faulty distributor in your '58 Chevy?" Jack Nelson curiously asked. "I'm a jewelry store owner and I'm not too talented as a greased monkey!"

"No Jack, I'm plannin' on havin' Anthony and Louie over at A.T. Auto Clinic on the Pike do that specialized maintenance for me," Eddie revealed. "It's a tough job and I only want expert mechanics workin' on the project. But I need ya' to perform a much more challengin' duty with me."

"Well then Eddie, what did ya' have in mind?" Jack instinctively inquired. "I could be available on Thursday morning. Like you, I'll take a day off from the office for mental health reasons. *Christmas* time is really my busy season in the retail jewelry business."

"Great!" Palmer instantly responded. "I need ya' to accompany me over to Bristol, Pennsylvania. I traded in my old Seeburg juke box and have upgraded to a colorful rainbow Wurlitzer. It's a real beauty, Jack! I'm gonna' use my pickup and I've arranged to borrow a dolly from Richie over at Chester's Hardware. We'll use boards as a tailgate ramp to get the heavy juke off the truck and into my den," Eddie anxiously informed. "Two men can easily handle the job. But Jack, we have to be exceptionally careful. I don't want to damage that baby! It's a priceless relic!"

"What was wrong with the old Seeburg?" Jack Nelson automatically questioned his excited pal. "That thing was also a collector's item. I would have bought it from you if I had known that baby was on the market!"

"Jack, you oughta' see this out-of-this-world Wurlitzer," Eddie eagerly answered. "It's been re-conditioned and is just like brand new. I reluctantly traded in the Seeburg and got a premium price for it. Only problem was that the Wurlitzer came equipped with 33 rpm records and I preferred to have '45s specially installed."

"Well Eddie, do we have to transport the Seeburg up over to Bristol?" Palmer's pal asked. "You said you had traded the Seeburg in for the Wurlitzer, didn't you?"

"No," Eddie tersely replied. "The Liberto Juke Box Company had already picked the Seeburg up last week."

"Then why can't they simply deliver the new Wurlitzer just like they picked up the Seeburg?" Jack reflexively wondered and inquired.

"Because the company won't be able to deliver it until after *Labor Day* but I want to have that beauty in my possession right now!" the '50s fanatic disclosed. "Jack, now do you understand all of the pertinent circumstances?"

"And you're getting '45s inserted to replace the bigger records?" Jack wanted to know. "I would have preferred '45s too! Is that what you're tellin' me?"

"Exactly Jack!" Eddie confirmed. "The Wurlitzer I purchased had to be sent out all the way to Connecticut to be completely refurbished to allow for *that* particular custom-change. The freight bill alone to ship it back and forth from and to Bristol has been astronomical."

"Why didn't ya' just have it shipped from Connecticut directly to your home rather than back to Bristol?" Jack Nelson interrupted. "That maneuver would have saved you money and saved *us* both plenty of time and labor!"

"Because the Liberto Juke Box Company over in Bristol wanted to check over all systems to make sure the Connecticut modifications had been satisfactorily performed," Palmer explained to his best buddy. "I've paid a pretty penny for the Wurlitzer despite the

Seeburg trade-in and I need to know that it is in perfect condition before it ever reaches Hammonton.”

“How much did this investment cost you?” Jack inquisitively probed. “I’ll bet more than the average diamond wedding ring!” the gem expert remarked and giggled.

“More than the week-long vacation house Kim had rented at Long Beach Island,” Eddie informed his friend. “Eight thousand bucks after the trade-in. The only way Kim has allowed me to purchase the Wurlitzer was for me to compromise and spend an equal amount of money on the family for *our* annual big vacation. That’s how I’ve pulled the incredible juke box acquisition off!”

“My wife would divorce me in a New York second if I did a similar impractical thing like acquiring an exotic juke box for my own selfish happiness. Say Eddie, what time do ya’ want me at your place?” Jack enviously asked.

“Be here at nine tomorrow morning,” Palmer indicated. “And thanks Jack. I really appreciate your loyal assistance. I’ll buy you lunch sometime next week.”

“Any time Eddie,” Jack Nelson replied with a mild chuckle. “I have to give you an A in courage and an A+ in shrewdness! Why not make it breakfast tomorrow morning and lunch sometime next week? Bye now!” Click.

Eddie Palmer diligently finished his personal domestic responsibilities in the yard by Wednesday night. He enjoyed two cold beers that evening and watched a *Phillies* baseball game on television. Then Palmer took his standard long hot shower, called Jack to remind him of *his* “Bristol commitment,” hopped into his lonely bed and eventually fell asleep forgetting about his wife and kids vacationing on Long Beach Island while exclusively dreaming of his special about-to-be acquired refurbished Wurlitzer juke box.

At nine a.m. sharp Jack Nelson appeared at the front door of 345 Liberty Street just as he had promised his good friend. “I parked my *Mazda* in your cluttered back yard,” Nelson disgustedly related to his disorganized pal. “Ya’ never know about mindless vandalism with kids being the way they are nowadays. It’s a whole different ballgame since the time *we* were growing up.”

“You’re perfectly correct in taking that precaution,” Eddie commiserated. “Either teenagers will steal your car for joyriding or they wanna’ sell it to chop shops to get money to buy drugs. Occasionally,” Eddie went on complaining, “punk rebellious kids even take delight in atrociously demolishing a random vehicle with sledgehammers for their own destructive gratification. There are more punk juvenile delinquents around in 2003 than there ever were back in the late '50s when we were growin' up. Teenage defiance has certainly taken on an entirely new dimension."

"You're absolutely right on target!" Eddie's amenable companion concurred. "Insolent kids today rule the roost at home. Many of 'em boss their wimpy doting parents around, smoke marijuana instead of cigarettes, don't respect adult authority and don't give a hoot about their future," Jack pontificated. "They only live for today and that's their entire motley existence!"

"And they all look like urban ghetto hip-hop wannabes'," Eddie elaborated. "The boys nowadays wear earrings and have five pounds of metal punctured onto their faces. They're like young jungle cannibals practicin' body mutilation, wearin' baggy pants that make 'em look like rag-pickers and talkin' jive inner city nonsense rather than plain formal English. They're an absolute disgrace! What's this world comin' to Jack?"

"It's really not comin' to anything," Eddie's alert listener mused and then declared. "The world just keeps circling around the sun each year and eventually winds up precisely where it had started out from!" Nelson joked.

"Well regardless of astronomy," Jack's trapped-in-the-'50s pal commented. "Forget about teenage drugs and AIDS. Those problems were non-existent back in the nifty fifties. Let's change the subject. We're on our way to Bristol to get my mint-condition Wurlitzer, and right now that's all that really matters with me. We'll stop at the Red Barn on *Route 206* for a nourishing breakfast. Then it's off to the Liberto Juke Box Company on Mill Street."

"Sounds acceptable and almost plausible to me," Jack affably admitted. "I can taste those delicious blueberry pancakes, hot coffee, home fries and eggs-over-light right this very second. Evelyn's a terrific cook over at the Red Barn. I wish my wife knew *her* kitchen secrets."

The men enjoyed their sumptuous breakfasts at the popular and cozy Red Barn "kitchen restaurant." Eddie felt compelled to clarify several salient points to his loyal comrade. "The restored Wurlitzer comes re-done with flashing lights inside the rainbow circumference. And besides Jack," the avid '50s memorabilia collector said, "I had an option to get a hundred modern CDs in the Wurlitzer but I chose to have 100 classic '45s instead. Oldies sound better on vinyl, especially Little Richard, Fats Domino, Elvis, Chuck Berry and Jerry Lee Lewis. The Wurlitzer will capture the original music without any artificially added studio track overdubs."

"I wish I were you," Jack enviously stated. "Helen won't even let me buy a new engine for my black '53 Mercury coupe. She says I gotta' save every extra penny for our kids' college educations," Nelson lamented. "To what remote solar system has all the world's justice disappeared? It's like I'm trapped in an endless economic nightmare! Whatever happened to smart kids getting scholarships?"

"How was the breakfast' guys?" Evelyn asked as the Red Barn owner scurried to the men's table. "I prepared the eggs special for you two connoisseurs."

"Just great!" Eddie exclaimed. "Jack's accompanying me over to Bristol to pick up a beautiful Wurlitzer juke box. When playing, the object pulsates like a flashing spectrum!"

"Terrific!" Evelyn sincerely answered. "Next time you have one of your famous '50s parties be sure to invite me. I'd rather be there than be square! Sorry guys but I gotta' scoot. I'm short a waitress this morning."

Eddie paid the bill, left a hefty tip and then he and Jack departed the Red Barn establishment, hopped into Palmer's shiny black pickup having "Dealer" tags and soon pulled out onto *Route 206*. Twenty-three miles up the two-lane state highway Palmer took *County Road 541* at the Slumberland Motel to bypass Mt. Holly, and twenty minutes later the truck was crossing the Delaware River into Pennsylvania over the ancient but well-preserved *Burlington-Bristol Bridge*. After a mile on *Route 413* Eddie made a right turn onto Pond Street, which soon led to Mill. Three blocks east down Bristol's one-way main street was the aforementioned Liberto Juke Box Company.

"Isn't this Wurlitzer a work of art?" Dave Liberto pointed out to his ecstatic New Jersey customer. "It's one of the best I've ever labored on. It's a collector's dream come true!"

"Are you certain all systems have been checked out?" Eddie questioned the confident proprietor while showing an excessive amount of obvious concern. "This item is putting a definite crimp on my family budget and my squawky wife will be looking for even the most minor flaw."

"It's been checked over three times by my competent staff," the juke box merchant informed. "I assure you everything is functioning perfectly. Did you bring along the quilt to wrap it up in so that it can be safely transported back to Jersey without any highway dust or bugs smacking into it?" the businessman asked. "The elements can be brutal at times to an exposed jukebox's many seams and crevices. Even an errant mosquito or moth could mess up the coin slot or tarnish a noticeable piece of the exterior."

"Yes," Eddie astutely stated. "I'll get it right now so that your shipping department can wrap the quilt up around the Wurlitzer and tie it with rope or twine. I trust that your 'competent men' will carefully load the apparatus onto my pickup."

"Certainly," Mr. Liberto guaranteed. "And your final payment is three thousand dollars!"

Eddie Palmer eagerly signed the check and handed it over to Jean Liberto, David's crackerjack accountant/wife. Ten minutes later he inspected his wrapped-up precious cargo, hoisted the tailgate and drove his Ford pickup with Jack Nelson riding "shotgun" back to Hammonton. The forty-mile return drive seemed three times as long as the trip to Bristol had for the enthralled '50s collector. The purchaser's anticipation at utilizing his new acquisition was quite emotionally overwhelming. "Well Jack, looks like we're gonna' make it back to Hammonton just in the nick of time. Check out the bleak-looking sky!"

"Those black storm clouds to the west look rather ominous," the other occupant observed and stated. "We have to get this baby moved into your den before there's a wicked downpour. I hope we don't get drenched!"

"I hear thunder rumbling and see lightning flashing over to the west near Berlin," Eddie said. "It's a good thing we'll be on Liberty Street in about five minutes once we pass the *Route 30* light."

The men wasted little time in strapping the quilted Wurlitzer onto the borrowed dolly and then together gradually wheeling the horizontal cart down the tailgate boards serving as a convenient ramp. In five minutes the prized juke box had been gently deposited inside Eddie's '50s-themed den. After using wire cutters to sever the twine, the quilt was gently unraveled, removed, folded and placed in Palmer's cluttered cellar. Eddie wasted little time and immediately plugged in the renovated juke to ascertain if the electrical system was in good order.

"Eddie, it's goin' to pour in a minute and I wanta' rush home and make sure all my windows are shut!" Jack pleaded. "I'll have to request a *rain-check* on fully appreciating the Wurlitzer, no silly pun intended!"

"Thanks for your capable assistance," Eddie answered. "Stop over tomorrow morning after the storm's passed and I'll demonstrate this rare machine to you. My '50s den is now finally complete with its most treasured decoration!"

"Great Eddie! Lots of luck with it!" the same street neighbor hurriedly agreed. "See ya' manana!"

After Jack Nelson quickly exited the ranch home to dash to his *Mazda*, Eddie Palmer delighted for several moments simply enjoying the mere touch of his magnificent juke box. 'This is a major upgrade from the old Seeburg!' he thought while completely ignoring the savage storm that was approaching the usually somnolent South Jersey' community. 'I'm very tempted to play an oldies song!' he mused as the man admired his latest possession and then studied the tunes that had been listed on the extensive menu. "Hey, here's "Stormy Weather!""

A lightning bolt crackled and collided with a nearby telephone pole, temporarily knocking-out all of the electric in the house. 'I'd better unplug the juke box and wait for the storm to pass,' Eddie prudently realized. 'It's not worth the risk to try and play this thing during a thunder and lightning display. I'll have to exhibit some patience and hold my horses for a couple of hours. This thing might be just as vulnerable to torrential rain electric storms as the sensitive modem in my computer tower is.'

Three minutes later the house's power came back on, but true to his commitment Palmer waited until after supper to operate his superb mechanism. He even watched the *Weather Channel* to determine that all showers had reduced to a passive level in the Hammonton vicinity. When the '50s enthusiast was certain that all atmospheric inclemency had passed, the proud man entered his recently painted '50s den and read the song titles listed inside the Wurlitzer. 'Now that the storm threat has sufficiently subsided, I can examine and experiment with my new fabulous toy,' Eddie reckoned. 'I can't wait to hear the quality of the speakers.' The blithe owner inserted the plug back into the wall socket, and after the rainbow lights illuminated he then again analyzed the menu's song selections with keen attention.

'I guess it's now safe to give it a try!' Eddie reassured himself. 'I already changed all of the house's blinking clock readouts back to their appropriate times. Now I gotta' find out if the tempest did any damage to my new juke.'

The Wurlitzer's menu contained an eclectic array of colorful '50s and early '60s oldies renditions ranging from Bill Haley's 1955 sensational hit single "Rock Around the Clock" to the Supremes 1964 Motown smash chart-buster "Baby Love." 'What song do I want to hear first?' the enamored fellow wondered. 'Hey, here's 'The Bristol Stomp' by the Dovells. I remember that vibrant song from back in '61. Jack and I had just been in Bristol, and that's precisely where the song originated.'

But soon Eddie saw another item on the prodigious menu that made him change his mind. 'Here's 'At the Hop' by Danny and the Juniors. I remember that big hit from 1958 when I was still a young high school stud. I'll simply press buttons A-9 and listen to a rock and roll classic.'

Eddie's nervous fingers pushed 'A-9' and then the '50s authority watched the jukebox's selector locate the designated disk. After the machine's arm gracefully dropped the selected '45 onto the rotary, the needle arm lowered and began scraping against the spinning record. Palmer then closed his eyes and imagined his glorious youth. The opening notes and upbeat tempo of 'At the Hop's' first bar began. Eddie Palmer opened his lids and was astounded to find himself' situated in time and space at a familiar nostalgic 1958 record hop.

As the amazed middle-aged man glanced around he witnessed to his right three girls giggling like crazy. "Oh my God!" Eddie gasped. And then Palmer became aware of *his* public exhibition of awkwardness and covered his mouth in awe. 'It's my old high school sweetheart Barbara Smidillo and her two girlfriends Judy Sacco and Gabrielle Attanasi and they're all wearing poodle skirts. They're all laughing and making fun of my strange clothes!'

Eddie looked down at his designer sneakers, yellow tank top shirt and blue denim summer Bermudas and immediately felt mortified. 'I feel like a fish out of water!' Palmer embarrassingly thought.

"Say Mister, where did you ever get those crazy threads and those boss bony knees?" Barbara Smidillo asked the elderly gentleman, whom she never for one second recognized because of the very apparent vast age differential. "And I think your knobby knees are so cute!" she added with mild ridicule. "I'll bet you were handsome when you were a teenager!"

"Look girls, I don't know exactly what has happened," Palmer tried explaining while sucking up his rotund beer belly, "but this record hop seems so very familiar. And 'At the Hop' is still my favorite oldies song."

"What do you mean by *oldies*?" high school prom queen Judy Sacco questioned the hop newcomer. "The song's brand new!"

"And how come an old geezer like you is crashin' a teen record hop?" head cheerleader Gabrielle Attanasi demanded knowing. "Don't you have any friends your own age?"

"Hey old-timer, let's cut a rug!" Barbara Smidillo insisted as she grabbed Palmer's already trembling right palm. "Judy and Gabrielle, you two can join in and share my new man if ya' want to!"

The three attractive girls took turns jitterbugging with the thoroughly confused new arrival. When Barbara tapped Gabrielle on the shoulder signaling that she wished to again dance with the totally baffled Eddie Palmer, her jealous boyfriend David Noto accosted the Danny and the Juniors' fan and the antagonist instantly exhibited *his* ever-mounting animosity.

"Look Mister, Barbie's my chick and I resent you foolin' around and makin' time with her!" David Noto emphatically stated. "Just for that I'm gonna' give ya' a beatin' you're never gonna' forget, old man or no old man!"

The "At the Hop" tune ended precisely at the moment when Eddie Palmer was the unfortunate recipient of an on-target powerful right cross originating from the angered high school linebacker. The next thing Eddie knew he was holding his throbbing jaw while lying on his den's tan carpet next to the magical Wurlitzer.

'That young guy's fist must have been made of iron!' Eddie concluded as he wiped a trace of crimson from the right corner of his mouth. 'Luckily no teeth are broken! How would I have ever explained what had happened to Kim when she gets back from Long Beach Island with the kids? This amazing juke box can have very serious consequences!' Palmer realistically assessed. 'I better be more deliberate in how I use it! I'm gonna' have to experiment and determine if what I had just experienced was a fluke!'

Despite the apparent blood drops on his left hand and his aching swollen lip, the '50s devotee's mind still was a degree skeptical of the Wurlitzer's remarkable powers. It required a full hour of rest on the couch and a glassful of *Southern Comfort* on the rocks for the '50s collector to fully regain his composure, courage and his sanity.

'I was back in 1958 for a little longer than two minutes,' Eddie deductively determined. 'That's about how long the song 'At the Hop' is. I'll bet I stayed in the past the exact length of time as the song allowed. I gotta' test my theory on another less hazardous number. Let's see here!' Palmer speculated as he studied the jukebox's extensive menu. 'Here's 'Alley-Oop!' by the Hollywood Argyles. I really like the Dante and the Evergreens version better, but I just have to learn exactly how this marvelous machine works. Perhaps the electrical storm and the power outage had something to do with the time warp I just experienced. At any rate, I'm not closing my eyes this time. I wanna' see everything that's happenin!'

Eddie pressed down 'B-7' with his left and right index fingers. The Wurlitzer's selector arm found the programmed disk and soon "Alley-Oop!" by the Hollywood Argyles began resonating from the jukebox's powerful internal sound system. 'This is a song about a comical cartoon-character caveman!' Palmer recollected as all of the room's furniture began eddying around. A dense blur filled the enchanted den and before Palmer could synchronize his senses to accurately perceive reality the time traveler heard a distinct grunting noise. Turning to his left in what appeared to be a tropical setting, Palmer recognized the approach of a muscular short hairy Neanderthal Man carrying a heavy club. The antagonized caveman was loudly snorting and grumbling in what sounded like very primitive gibberish.

Eddie bent down and stepped backwards to avoid detection but his left foot accidentally crushed a fallen twig that had been situated on the ground. The discernible crunch made the caveman's eyebrows slant downwards as *he* perceived the existence of some possible enemy hiding in his midst. The very real anachronism cautiously approached the rock behind which Palmer had been hiding.

The man from the future bolted from his stationary position and took-off down a narrow jungle trail. Soon the hungry and incensed prehistoric hunter was actively pursuing Eddie Palmer. 'I hope he's not cannibalistic!' Eddie worried as he dashed forward.

A vicious saber toothed tiger was startled by the intense jungle chase and aggressively fled in the opposite direction to evade the unpredictable screaming human and the equally bizarre growling humanoid giving pursuit.

The last refrains of the novelty number "Alley-Oop!" permeated the jungle atmosphere as Eddie Palmer was wildly sprinting for his life. 'Thirty seconds until the song's last note!' Eddie estimated as he sped with all his might past lush green bushes down the winding trail. 'I hope this ancient lunatic doesn't pass through some weird time portal and then manages to crazily chase me around my den and all over my house!'

The 1960 music finally stopped and Palmer suddenly emerged out of his smoke-filled hazy time vacuum and found himself' stupidly scurrying in circles around his comfortable den furniture set. He stopped in his tracks, took ten deep breaths and wiped away what seemed like a half-pound of sweat that had accumulated on his brow.

'I can't believe it!' Eddie concluded as he plopped down on his green cloth recliner and then critically doubted his own veracity. 'I can't keep this phenomenon a secret any longer. I'm gonna' give Jack a call so that he can come over and share some of this ongoing inexplicable adventure. I have to see if the extraordinary device will work the same with two people.'

"Jack, I finally got my Wurlitzer workin' and I'd like to invite ya' over to see it goin'!" Eddie conveyed over the kitchen's land-line phone. "What time can ya' come over!"

"How about after supper at around eight!" Nelson suggested. "Helen plans to stay home and do some *Internet* surfing and the kids will be almost ready for bed. I'll tell my skeptical wife that you need me to help fix a loose part in your new juke box. Little white lies come in handy sometimes."

"Okay Jack, but please be prompt and punctual!" Eddie genuinely requested. "You're gonna' have the absolute time of your life buddy! I assure it!"

"Just have a couple of delicious thirst-quenching cold beers and some tasty pretzels ready," Jack healthily laughed. "That's about all the excitement that my fragile weak heart can sustain! I'm no young pup anymore!"

Jack arrived at Eddie's place at the specified time. After some light conversation about forthcoming joint Caribbean vacations, classic car shows and the improbable prospect of the *Phillies* making it to the *World Series,* the host shifted the focus of discussion to the reason for Jack's visitation. Palmer drew his guest's attention to the wonderful Wurlitzer juke box.

"This dandy has a most excellent sound system," shrewdly began Palmer, "and it has several remarkable features that no other brand or model possesses."

"Like what?" cynically responded Jack as he looked for a convenient place to put his empty brown beer bottle. "I didn't come over here and leave my nagging wife and demanding children just for a tiny bit of sentimental fun!" the visitor facetiously continued with a wry smile. "This better be something special or I'll have to protest by writing my congressman!" The visitor then crunched his teeth down on a salty hard pretzel.

"This listening experience is literally out of this world!" Eddie Palmer promised his comrade of forty years. "Just relax, enjoy your freedom and appreciate the speaker differentiation after I select a fast-paced song."

"What are ya' goin' to play?" Jack phlegmatically asked. "I can't believe that this juke box sounds better than my four speaker stereo sound system I bought myself' last *Christmas*! I'll wager there's no comparison!"

"Here's a blast from the past! I'm gonna' select 'Boogie Woogie Bugle Boy of Company C'!" Eddie decided and relayed to his companion. "I really like the rhythm and the tempo!"

"Say, wait a darn minute!" Jack strenuously objected. "That's a 1940s *World War II* tune. I think either the Fontane Sisters or the McGuire Sisters recorded it! I thought you specialized in early fifties and sixties pre-acid rock and roll!"

"Normally I do," Palmer honestly admitted, "but Bette Midler recorded a more modern version of 'Boogie Woogie Bugle Boy' in 1973. For some obscure reason," Eddie related, "that song is mixed up on this oldies' juke's listings with '50s and early '60s numbers. Bette Midler's interpretation has tremendous sound and voice modulations. It's a classic presentation with a great instrumental background."

"Okay maestro," Jack reacted with a forced grin before taking another swig from his new beer bottle. "Let's hear what's so dynamic about your new Wurlitzer."

"Jack, I recommend that you put your second beer bottle down on the table and completely swallow your pretzel so that you can get the machine's full effect," Eddie seriously directed. Palmer then very dramatically pressed down keys 'E-5', and after the selector placed the disk on the rotating wheel and the needle subsequently descended, a visual whirlwind suddenly encompassed and soon quickly enveloped the two eyewitnesses.

"Hey, what's goin' on?" yelled Jack. "This must be some psychological illusion! What's with all the visual effects? Are we in some sort of time travel movie? Does *that thing* come with a disco?"

"Just about!" Palmer affirmed. "If my assumption is accurate, we're on our way to 1973. If we're lucky, we'll get Bette Midler's autograph!"

As soon as the incomparable voice of Bette Midler sang the initial words to "Boogie Woogie Bugle Boy," the cyclonic atmospheric surroundings diminished and then soon vanished into thin air. The two time itinerants were standing in a restricted area in front of a large auditorium's stage, and people sitting behind the new arrivals were shouting for them to locate seats and to stop blocking *their* view. The music was so fantastic and so loud that it drowned out the many vociferous complaints coming from irate people sitting in the audience's first row.

"This is some sort of trick or hallucination! It's gotta' be a mirage or something!" Jack screamed into his companion's ear. "Don't try and tell me that your juke box sent us on this fantasy time excursion and that we're really livin' right this minute in 1973!"

"Just savor the great song's lyrics!" Palmer replied. "I'll try and tell you everything when we get back to my house! It's all way beyond being remarkable! I suppose it's more like a supernatural miracle than anything else!"

"When will that be?" inquired the still-awed Jack Nelson. "How long does this incredible spell last!"

"It's about maxed-out right about now!" Eddie alertly noted as he detected three burly security guards heading down a side aisle in *their* direction. "We'd better scamper the heck out of range or else we'll soon be clobbered and then physically abused and mauled."

The two men bolted across the theater in front of and beneath an oblivious Bette Midler, who was preoccupied wailing away on a stage with her popular song rendition. The men scurried up the opposite aisle as four additional theater guards and ushers joined the hunt and gave pursuit. The entire chase scene represented only a mild distraction to a portion of the enthusiastic and boisterous hand-clapping audience.

The two frenetic escapees skittered out of the theater's swinging back doors and ventured into a mezzanine sales counter section. They next sprinted and tripped down fourteen steps and then fled down a richly carpeted corridor until they quickly exited the premises through heavy leather-padded doors onto New York's Fifth Avenue.

"Please tell me what's goin' on?" a bewildered Jack Nelson asked as the two time voyagers scampered south in the direction of *Times Square*. "Are you some kind of space alien or something?"

"I can't believe that the music can not only change our time into another decade but it also can transform the city we're bein' sent to!" Eddie yelled as his throat struggled to inhale more oxygen.

"What in the world are you babbling?" Jack criticized and panted with total astonishment. "You're makin' me a candidate for the loony bin!"

"Only about thirty more seconds to the song!" Palmer declared. "Then we'll be back in Hammonton in 2003 and I'll be happy to give you all the pertinent details! Say Jack, you run better than my refrigerator does!"

* * * * * * * * * * * *

After the rotating whirlwind finally decreased to a cessation, Eddie Palmer took ten deep breaths and then conscientiously educated his amazed spellbound dizzy listener of the unique jukebox's special characteristics and abilities. Jack Nelson sat on the soft couch totally flabbergasted and quite mentally disheveled.

"You mean to say that your juke box has the power to transport us to the time and place of the recorded song!" Nelson marveled after polishing off another cold beer. "Are you sure your name isn't Rod Serling, that '50s *Twilight Zone* announcer I still watch on the *Sci-Fi Cable Channel?*"

But after the juke box owner told his friend about Alley-Oop and about David Noto giving him a swollen lip at the high school sock hop, Jack Nelson again lapsed into his dubious state of mind. "Did I hear you say that a caveman and a saber-toothed tiger were chasing you through a jungle in around 100,000 BC?" Eddie's close chum incredulously asked. "And that your high school nemesis punched you in the chops for flirting with luscious Barbara Smidillo! Where's the nearest insane asylum? I think we both require professional help! Say Eddie, that Mrs. Barbara Noto is still a very lovely woman!"

"I can't state for sure what the year was," Eddie clarified, "but I can claim that the experience and the ultimate pursuit were real for the duration of the song. I actually met and interacted with a fictional historic figure named Alley Oop!" Eddie reminded his baffled neighbor. "The saber-toothed tiger became frightened and took off into the jungle. But only the Wurlitzer knows the exact answer to *our* most recent quandary!"

"This juke box makes weird seem like normal!" Jack rationally maintained. "And your lip is still swollen with a blood clot on it even though your honest account defies all regular logic. I guess *that* fact could be construed as proof. And yet," Jack conceded, "Bette Midler seemed as real as the pounding headache I'm now feeling. Eddie, that 1973 concert was both real and surreal at the same time. I'll tell ya' what. Let's have another time transition to see if your crazy hypothesis is really bona fide."

Eddie advised that Jack examine the Wurlitzer's array of songs and then select another tune in order to verify Palmer's rationalization. Nelson rubbed his bearded chin and then verbalized some of the selections, reading each one aloud. "I sorta' like 'Peggy Sue' by Buddy Holly and the Crickets. And then there's 'Rockin' Robin' by Bobby Day and here's 'Little Darlin' by the Diamonds."

"Those three numbers are from '57 and '58, the Golden Age of rock and roll," the '50s expert confirmed. "I like all three. And Jack, here to the left is 'Come Go With Me' by the Dell-Vikings. That's one of my all-time favorites. And to the right we have 'The Great

Pretender.' That golden oldie' Platters' tune happens to describe each of us perfectly!"

"Here's one of my favorite '60s picks!" Jack gleefully exclaimed. "It's 'California Girls' by the Beach Boys. That choice seems pretty safe and tranquil. How could we go wrong lookin' at beautiful young ladies in bikinis for two and a half minutes or so? Let's get the show on the road!"

"I think you've convinced me on that one," Eddie happily agreed. "Kim and Helen don't look half as good in bikinis now as they had back in the mid-sixties when that song was the rage."

Without initiating any further exchange of dialogue, Eddie Palmer emphatically pressed ruby red keys' 'D-3'. The standard and expected cyclonic effect transpired when the juke's needle touched the disk, which incidentally was turning at the precise rate of forty-five rounds per minute. The den then gradually dimmed and in an instant the voyaging men were standing in their blue denim Bermuda cutoffs on a hot California beach crowded with gorgeous buxom girls scantily clad in two-pieced bikini bathing suits.

"Jack!" Eddie merrily yelled. "There must be at least ten thousand fabulous dolls with great bellybuttons on this crowded beach and we're the only two guys. I'm gonna' play California girls on the juke box until the record decays and finally disintegrates."

"And look!" the stunned companion hollered back. "Six luscious young ladies are coming up to introduce themselves to us. This has gotta' be the most magical moment of my life!"

"They're probably wonderin' where the loud Beach Boys' music is comin' from without us havin' any powerful radio," Eddie speculated and then related.

The six comely young ladies began touching the two men's arms and chests and the receivers of the overzealous caresses began to worry about the females' very amorous intentions. And then a dozen other affectionate tanned chicks paced over the hot sand to duplicate what the six knockout girls were doing. The California time-visitors began getting intensely nervous at being conspicuously situated at the center of the male fantasy universe. The duo's wildest dream soon transformed into a bizarre nightmare laden with a vast contingent of beautiful aggressive promiscuous young women.

"Let's make a run for it!" Eddie loudly insisted. "We'll never be able to satisfy all of these lusting ladies in a thousand years. An excess of anything including sex can be detrimental to our health! Neither of us has enough hormones for this outrageous challenge!"

The pair of neurotic time journeyers desperately ran down the California beach, zigzagging between exotic females lying on assorted beach towels and blankets. Other thin and trim fair damsels observed and heard the men's distress and soon took up the chase from other locations, and the frantic fellows had no alternative other than to leap into the surf and begin frenetically splashing their way out into the Pacific.

The highly motivated girls followed the panicky men's awkward example. Many of the female aggressors were stellar swimmers and were shortening the distance between them and the extremely frightened males, whose arms were now churning through the choppy waves like swirling windmill blades. A score of hysterical curvaceous girls happened to be riding surfboards and were deftly using incoming waves as an additional method of also harassing the delirious male swimmers.

Fortunately, the song "California Girls" terminated and Eddie and Jack instantly discovered themselves in a frenzy rotating their arms and flipping their legs on Palmer's tan den rug. They abruptly stopped their unnecessary behavior and stared disbelievingly into each others' eyes.

The embarrassed duo then got to their knees and finally managed to stand upright. The fact that they were both soaking wet from head to toe supported the notion that their encounter with the over-stimulated California females was definitely not a figment of their imaginations. Eddie advanced to the ranch home's bathroom and obtained two towels for Jack and him to dry off.

"I never realized that such romantic pleasure could turn into a life-threatening situation," Jack concluded and remarked. "Those young horny girls would have torn us to shreds if they had a little more opportunity to do so. I'm sure glad Helen has gone through menopause."

"Let's discuss what to do next over another cold brew," Eddie intelligently suggested to his exhausted chum. "I still have two more bottles in the 'fridge. I'm really thoroughly fascinated with the Wurlitzer's astounding ability. I want to have one more time-trip tonight. Are you game Jack?"

"Well sort of," Nelson hesitantly replied in a very evident puzzled tone of voice. "I still can't figure out how an electrical storm could change your ordinary juke box into a musical time machine. It all defies accepted scientific laws, you know!"

"That's what makes it so damned interesting!" Eddie bellowed with a lusty laugh. "It's an exceptional device indeed as long as it doesn't get us killed. It's certainly adventurous to say the least. I mean it really proves that the hunted generally experiences more thrills through fear than the hunter does all through the violence of the chase. My new extraordinary juke box really gets rid of the boring aspects of everyday life, that's for certain."

"Sometimes I think you need the services of a good psychiatrist that specializes in exorcisms," Jack joked in an effort to camouflage his own haunting consternation. "You could even convince the Pope to switch religions and become a Muslim! You certainly have that strange knack! Let's drink to the female libido!" The two fatigued men then returned to the '50s den.

"Hey, this song listed here has gotta' be an awesome choice!" Palmer triumphantly uttered to his still very bewildered friend. "Love Me Tender," he reverently read. "I always wanted to see Elvis performing in person. If we're lucky, we'll get up close to the stage just like we had done with Bette Midler."

"I think you don't have enough limbs on your tree," Jack vehemently protested. "I mean you almost got us apprehended by security guards in 1973 and then you virtually had us pulverized by swarming females in skimpy bathing suits in 1965. I just don't know what danger will happen next!"

"That's the fun of it all Jack!" Eddie effectively argued. "I'm fascinated by the unknown! And now tell me, how detrimental can 'Love Me Tender' really be?" Palmer questioned.

"But just the song title is written in on the menu without any artist being provided," Nelson countered. "I'm mighty suspicious of *that* detail! Maybe it will be sung by the Devil in hell for all we know!"

"No one else has ever sung 'Love Me Tender' as a #1 smash hit' single except Elvis Presley," the '50s whiz persuasively volleyed. "And besides Jack, you once told me that Elvis was the greatest singer ever!"

"Okay, I'll concede that fact," Jack reluctantly acknowledged. "Let's go back to the '50s and see Elvis on stage somewhere in the world before I sober up and change my mind."

The intrigued juke box owner anxiously pressed 'F-2' for "Love Me Tender" and when the dependable selector located the appropriate disk, the room again became a hazy cyclone of whirling furniture and lamps. When the needle lowered to the spinning '45, an open field scenario crystallized all around the two anachronisms time traveling into the past from the year 2003. Soldiers in gray uniforms were firing cannons to Eddie and Jack's left while army men clad in blue were blasting cannonballs from cannons to their right.

"Holy smokes Eddie!" the almost-petrified Jack Nelson shrieked. "We're in the middle of the *Civil War!* I'm not stickin' around to figure out exactly what battle we're involved in!"

"We just have to survive for two minutes!" Eddie nervously answered. "Love Me Tender" is a very short song. I hope the Wurlitzer's needle doesn't get stuck!"

"There's a dense woods on the other side of that ravine," Nelson informed his colleague as *he* pointed to the right. "Let's make a dash for it! It's our best chance to escape doom!" Jack yelled as a blast exploded to their right and a lone sturdy elm tree next to them instantly snapped in two.

The pair zipped along as fast as their legs would carry them towards the ravine and woods that Jack Nelson had perceptively identified under intense and extreme pressure. The two hundred yard exodus was augmented by gunshots and screaming coming from the hoarse throats of determined military personnel on either side of *their* valiant hustle.

"You might know plenty of details about the 1950s but you don't know squat about American history!" Jack puffed as the two bolted across the open field.

"What's that supposed to mean?" Eddie defensively asked. "How could I ever have known we would wind-up on *this* wicked battlefield? And Elvis isn't singing the lyrics to 'Love Me Tender'! Listen, it's an instrumental version playing instead!"

"The song 'Love Me Tender' is really a re-doing of a tune popular during the *Civil War* era called 'Aura Lee'," Jack gasped and shared. "The notes and melody are identical," Nelson shouted as he wildly ran parallel to Eddie, "and 'Aura Lee' was then changed to 'Love Me Tender' in the '50s and the new lyrics were written especially for Elvis!" Palmer's companion yelled, huffing and puffing all the way.

"Now you tell me!" Palmer panted just before he tripped and tumbled to the ground. Jack assisted Eddie to his feet, and as the horrified pair was about to continue their desperate race to the woods, a loud blast exploded nearby. Both men collapsed in agony to the dusty ground.

* * * * * * * * * * *

Jack Nelson found himself lying wounded in a pool of blood on the tan rug in Eddie Palmer's den. He had the presence of mind to dial *911* on the table touch-phone before lapsing into unconsciousness. A Hammonton Rescue Squad ambulance was immediately dispatched to the Liberty Street residence. The local police broke open the door, and Eddie's closest friend was given first aid and then swiftly transported to Kessler Memorial Hospital.

Jack Nelson had suffered multiple broken bones in his arms and legs along with first and second degree burns on all his appendages. Although seriously injured and afflicted with amnesia, Nelson's vital signs remain strong and he is expected to survive his severe bodily damage and is now listed in "Critical Condition." The victim however does fade in and out of consciousness and does not remember anything pertinent from the past, ranging from his own name to that of his closest friend.

As for Eddie Palmer, he has mysteriously disappeared from the face of the modern-day Earth. The Hammonton Police are investigating a possible "house robbery attempt and aggravated assault case," but local detectives are completely baffled by the existence of only "weak circumstantial evidence" and by the lack of a motive for the dual crimes.

Kim Palmer returned from Long Beach Island with her three children in a state of shock and the aggrieved wife sadly conveyed to area newspaper reporters and to the assembled television media, "I will not play my husband's new Wurlitzer juke box until Eddie finally returns back home. I sincerely request that the abductors who had kidnapped my husband from our home and who had hospitalized Jack Nelson will have the decency to release Eddie."

The New Jersey Crime Fighters Chapter has offered a fifty-thousand-dollar reward for information leading to the capture of Eddie Palmer's kidnappers and Jack Nelson's assailants. So far there have been no takers.

"Rock, Paper, Scissors"

Every area epicure of fine food from Cherry Hill to Vineland knows about Vianna's Restaurant on White Horse Road in Voorhees, New Jersey. The establishment's six-page menu offers the most palatable Italian, American and seafood selections at very reasonable prices and the clientele consists mostly of professionals including eminent doctors and lawyers. Since Vianna DiAngelo speaks fluent Italian, her restaurant is widely reputed to be a haven for local Mafia members. Usually everyone entering the beveled glass door (including an occasional suspected hit man) dresses formally in business suits and exhibits refined aristocratic manners.

Several minor fracases have sporadically surfaced at Vianna's, which tended to sully the place's otherwise stellar culinary reputation. Earlier in May of 2003 the main chef quit when Vianna refused to fire two obnoxiously snooty waiters that continually taunted the kitchen headman. On another busy night in July one of the waitresses became so frustrated by the fussy chef's demanding disposition that she first imitated *his* heavy Italian accent and then threw a handful of forks and knives into the air during a fit of rage, accidentally gouging a chunk of skin out of an unsuspecting customer's bald scalp. Before the waitress could officially announce her quitting to Vianna, the man's wife got into an altercation with the already indignant waitress and two-reputed Mafia figures in pinstriped suits then had to skillfully separate the combatants, providing the remainder of the patrons with "the night's entertainment." Other than those trivial incidents, Vianna's is generally regarded as a "tranquil civilized business serving very excellent cuisine."

The restaurant does not accept 'Entertainment Book Discount Coupons" on Tuesday nights because on that special evening tables at opposite corners of the main dining room are reserved for three incompatible contingents: doctors, lawyers and Mafia. On Tuesday evening August 12th, 2003, a gathering of four prominent surgeons was preoccupied discussing "shop gossip" at *their* reserved table.

"I have a very funny story to tell you," Dr. James Burke of Cherry Hill's Kennedy Memorial Hospital related to his three distinguished colleagues seated at the physician's weekly round table. "This story happens to be a real gem!"

"What is it?" pleaded Dr. Phillip Campbell of Vineland's Newcombe Hospital. "I could use a healthy chuckle to cancel out my mild indigestion! And I haven't even been served tonight's supper yet!"

"Yes, give us the scoop!" implored Dr. Thomas Wagner, veteran head surgeon at Hammonton's Kessler's Hospital. "I hope your story is funny. I could use a good laugh."

"Don't bark it too loudly!" insisted Dr. Robert Layton of Our Lady of Lourdes in Camden. "This place is a cultured refined restaurant and not a disorganized chaotic operating room!" the surgeon jovially bantered.

"Okay gentlemen, here it goes," Dr. Burke suavely continued his story. "In *our* x-ray department at Kennedy we have a new doctor, a callow radiologist named Harold Dexter. He's getting married to a very lovely lady next Saturday." Dr. Burke paused to determine if he still had everyone's undivided attention. He was well-aware that his introductory remarks had generated a great deal of interest amongst his three critical and sometimes hypocritical friends.

"So what's so extraordinary about that commonplace event!" objected Dr. Campbell. "So far your tale is the typical dog bites man back-page newspaper story. What about giving us some man bites dog fodder?"

"Really Jim," interrupted Dr. Wagner. "We have a young radiologist over at Kessler who's also tying the knot next month. Radiologists get married all the time the same as internists, neurologists and nose and throat specialists do. So far your story is rather nondescript."

"I see you were all intensively listening to my eloquent preface," Dr. Burke giggled and then laughed before sipping from a potent whiskey sour. "Now if you'll all just be a trifle more indulgent, I'll proceed with my little anecdote."

"Don't bore us to *death*," Dr. Layton sarcastically advised. "Your captive audience is too young and ill-equipped to enter the hereafter right this moment!"

Dr. James Burke waited for the levity to subside before advancing to phase two of his narrative. "Anyway," the speaker resumed in a whisper, "this vernal radiologist Harold Dexter had to get married because he knocked-up his bride-to-be!"

"What was she, a prostitute?" cackled a half-inebriated Dr. Campbell. "One must really be careful how he distributes his sperms in this day and age, now doesn't he?"

"You'll never believe this crazy yarn in a million years," Dr. James Burke replied with a rather stern face. "The woman that Dr. Harold Dexter made pregnant before marriage happened to be a gynecologist at my hospital. Isn't that one of the funniest ironies you ever heard? A gynecologist gets knocked-up and the real victim is the overzealous radiologist! If anyone should know any better about averting pregnancy, it's gotta' be the impregnated female doctor! Ha, ha, ha!"

"It sounds like a definite case of entrapment to me!" Dr. Wagner opined. "I'm laughing so hard at that ludicrous story that I think I'll have to use the facilities soon! That delightful tale really takes the cake, icing and all!"

The table of stoic lawyers in the opposite corner of Vianna's had noticed the doctors' levity and were curious about what exactly had caused it. The four attorneys shrugged their shoulders in response to the surgeons' "undignified public behavior." Several of the men in three-piece suits found the doctors' boisterous deportment abominable.

"I wonder what's so funny with those emergency room sawbones," Richard Harper, Esquire cynically commented. "You'd think those scalpel-wielding professionals were grade-school children cavorting out on the playground during recess!"

"They're more like scalpel butchers than scalpel professionals!" Attorney Seth Ruberton chimed-in. "No wonder why so many of them are sued by innocent patients suffering operation complications. They're acting like a cabal of raucous alcoholics having a bad humor convention!"

"I fully concur with Seth's accurate assessment," the famous trial lawyer William Davis promptly agreed. "Irresponsible surgeons are to blame for thousands of lucrative malpractice cases all across America. They bring them on themselves by being negligent, incompetent or inebriated. Thank God for tort cases to keep the fools in check!"

"Seth and Bill are right on target," stated Attorney Dennis Martin. "Those medical lunatics are becoming more and more boisterous every Tuesday night. You'd think that David Letterman, Johnny Carson and Jay Leno were sitting at *their* table. They ought to be optometrists because they're making a real spectacle out of themselves!"

The assembled surgeons were fonder of their exotic desserts and their imported coffee than they were of their professional counterparts seated in the opposite corner of the popular dining room. The doctors were soon aware of *their* loud conversation when the rest of the room's diners suddenly became silent. So becoming more self-conscious, the physicians then engaged in more docile and hushed exchanges that centered upon how most politicians in state government and in the *United States Congress* were "greedy lawyers" that made legislation mostly to benefit the success of themselves and of their "ignoble profession."

"I'm not too enamored with any pathetic lawyer," Dr. Burke maintained. "They're all devious scoundrels and quick talkers looking for technicalities to affect the outcome of a case in their favor. As you gentlemen know," the eminent physician added, "lawyers and costly lawsuits are to blame for the colossal medical malpractice insurance *we* annually have to pay. And the more language and the more pages that exist in a Congressional bill, the more lawsuits that can be generated by the vile scoundrels!"

"I know a surgeon on Long Island that converted himself' into a corporation and then he shrewdly made his wife and his children the principal stockholders," Dr. Campbell informed his very astute listeners.

"Why did he ever do such a terribly foolish thing?" Dr. Wagner challenged. "I would never consider having my wife and children having economic dominion over *my* destiny. It's preposterous even to consider such an absurd idea."

"It's not quite as ridiculous as you might have believed upon first impression," Dr. Campbell politely responded. "The Long Island surgeon refuses to pay malpractice insurance, period. If any patient's lawyer ever sues him, he owns absolutely nothing. His wife and children control all *his* assets and give him a modest salary of thirty-five thousand from the dividends in their shares of *him* being the corporation."

"I see definite merit in what Campbell is suggesting," Dr. Robert Layton seriously declared. "I pay over three hundred thousand dollars a year for malpractice insurance. That's money out of *my* pocket and taken away from my expendable income all because some greedy parasitic lawyers promote the practice of generating patient grievances against doctors. I don't know of any doctor who deliberately injures a patient," Layton emphatically insisted. "And yet *we* all must pay steep sums before taxes for the wrongful actions of a few derelict physicians and for the lust for easy money by the nation's leeching settlement-grubbing lawyers."

"Layton for Governor! Layton for President!" Dr. Wagner jested and then saluted with his wine glass. "Just look at those cavalier attorneys sitting over there all smug and complacent with their corrupt lot in life. They're hungry fleas out looking for dogs to feast off of!" the disgruntled doctor cited. "Shakespeare was no dummy when the bard supposedly proclaimed that the first thing a new government should do is eliminate all the country's lawyers. And Old Honorable William used a less polite term to dispose of the rabble than the benign word *eliminate*."

But Dr. Robert Layton was a brain surgeon that also often outspokenly despised paying for exorbitant malpractice insurance. Presently Layton needed to ask pertinent questions to obtain relevant answers. "Now Phil," the skeptical doctor said to Campbell, "can that Long Island specialist avoid being directly sued by making himself' into a corporation and having the company's profits divided among the lucky shareholders in his family?" the medical guru rhetorically asked. "I don't know if I could ever trust my wife and kids to handle *my* earnings! They would squander every cent that I had and would make me into *their* personal slave until age ninety or death, whichever came first! I think I'd rather take my chances with malpractice insurance!"

"That's exactly the point!" Dr. Campbell indicated. "The Long Island fellow hasn't to my knowledge been sued yet to determine whether or not his insurance-evasion strategy would work. Maybe he just buys the minimal insurance allowed in his state just like a driver gets the highest deductible on his car insurance policy to lower the rates. And also," the loquacious doctor stressed, "I understand that the corporation pays him the meager $35,000.00 up front and then quietly gives him the quarter-million savings he has reaped from not paying for the maximum malpractice insurance, which represents a quarter of the corporation's earnings."

"Phil may have introduced a pretty significant argument tonight," Thomas Wagner injected into the forum. "You have to be more devious than either the lawyers or the Mafia to make a sizable disposable income nowadays. The whole idea behind malpractice insurance that the bloodsucking lawyers use as their trump card is that each individual is responsible for his or her actions," Wagner pointed out. "If the doctor's wife and kids own all stock in the man's corporation, they are probably exempt from being liable for the Long Island surgeon's prospective negligence lawsuits."

"I predict things are about to change for the better," James Burke prognosticated to his highly concerned colleagues. "The time for procrastination has passed and soon surgeons will be retaliating. I know of a growing conspiracy and I'm going to reveal some of it to *you three* geniuses in a few minutes," Dr. Burke confidentially shared with his closest loyal friends.

The gray-haired well-respected heart surgeon then whispered a general introduction of his incredible conspiracy scheme to his associates, all of whom were shocked-but-supportive of the general theme. "Next Tuesday night I'll review for you gentlemen the exact nature of the reprisal against malpractice lawyers. But first before I become more specific," Dr. James Burke articulated with sparkling eyes accentuating his forceful language, "I need the three of you to take a pledge of loyalty to *our* fraternal brotherhood of surgeons. Is this agreeable to everyone at this table?"

The three other medical doctors conferred briefly amongst themselves and then unanimously assented to Burke's extraordinary proposition. Then while the other medical men were finishing-up their scrumptious Banana Foster desserts, Dr. Burke conveyed in a low voice to his fellow healers more details of his secret knowledge involving operating room procedures being conducted at certain Philadelphia and New York hospitals. The essence of Burke's amazing revelation would be sufficient enough to make Hippocrates's skeleton turn over in its grave.

* * * * * * * * *

The following Tuesday night at Vianna's the connoisseurs seated at the corner Mafia table seemed quite cheerful along with the doctor delegation, but the three lawyers present appeared rather visibly disturbed. Attorney William Davis, a chronic smoker had undergone a scheduled cancer surgery at a major Philadelphia hospital, but he unexpectedly died shortly after the intricate lung operation had been performed. Davis's funeral had been arranged for Thursday and the three listless attorneys sat somberly at *their* table and were not nearly as animated or as convivial as they usually were. The lawyers used that Tuesday night's dinner at Vianna's to sadly reminisce about and grieve their dearly departed friend.

After Dr. James Burke nonchalantly ordered his standard surf and turf entrée, the instigator whispered several preliminary sentences designed to inform his fellow surgeons the relevant details concerning William Davis's untimely death. Burke then respectfully read the elderly attorney's impressive obituary, which had been published in that morning's edition of the *Philadelphia Inquirer.*

"What happened during the lung operation?" Dr. Thomas Wagner insisted on knowing while feigning a degree of sympathy for the deceased. "Was there a problem with the anesthesia? Did Davis suffer a heart attack or stroke during the operation?"

"Remember now, last week you good men swore your allegiance to a medical fellowship fraternity," Dr. Burke reminded his dearest comrades. "Well my most trusted colleagues, cooperative teams of surgeons at Philadelphia and New York major hospitals are systematically putting an end to *their* profession's ugly malpractice woes. Attorney Davis's passing represents the mere beginning of the overall solution."

"Could you please be more specific?" Dr. Thomas Wagner requested while almost choking on his fresh garden salad smothered with French dressing. "It sounds like you're evasively speaking in zany riddles."

"Yes, please elaborate on this arcane conspiracy/fraternity business," Dr. Phillip Campbell also demanded. "I hope its subject matter is above and beyond tabloid publication!"

Dr. James Burke divulged over dinner in the then crowded main dining room the particulars of his disclosure. His audience of three sat spellbound listening to *his* astounding-but-solemn rhetoric. .Six eyes at the table focused on every syllable uttered from the acrimonious-and-vengeful heart surgeon's mouth.

"Operating room doctors in Philly' and New York hospitals have begun eliminating malpractice trial lawyers when *they* come in for either routine procedures or for delicate organ operations," James Burke objectively conveyed without a trace of guilt or emotion evident in his tone of voice. "Now *they're* calling on other doctors in *our* profession to join them in abolishing malpractice lawsuits by virtually eliminating greedy trial lawyers. Our fraternal duty is to reciprocate with *our* esteemed colleagues. It's come down to the survival of our noble profession versus the avaricious nature of *theirs*!"

"Exactly how does this *termination* process work?" asked an intrigued Robert Layton. "To tell you the truth, It sounds a little too Arnold Schwarzenegger-like to me."

"Yes, and how did Davis expire? What were the specific circumstances?" Dr. Phil Campbell asked. "He's been a real thorn in many doctors' rear ends for over three decades now. His name had to be high-up on the hit list. Davis wasn't too revered by the medical profession in the Greater Philadelphia area!"

"Well gentlemen," Dr. Burke methodically proceeded as if *he* was mentally preparing to adroitly perform a triple bypass, "Rule Number One is that a surgeon never murders a lawyer that *he* has had conflict with in the court room. Other doctors in other hospitals do it for him. Each team in every operating suite affected works together to make sure that the patient dies in recovery by screwing up *his* or *her* vital organs and his or her immune system. It's all connected with the administration of a secret non-traceable chemical injection that is virtually foolproof and undetectable."

"How does this retribution involve *us* suburban surgeons?" a now-very concerned Dr. Thomas Wagner asked while wiping some sweat-beads from his wet brow. "Some doctors might prefer paying out-of-this-world malpractice insurance rather than be active accomplices to obvious criminal acts. Felony acts if I might add! How about first degree murder?"

"The doctors only dispose of lawyers that have given other surgeons severe financial difficulty," Burke dispassionately reiterated. "Now they want us suburban sawbones to get into the battle arena and join the crusade. Eventually the clandestine revenge scheme will be widespread and implemented all over the country."

"Won't all of the random attorney hospital deaths trigger a wave of police investigations and courtroom litigations?" Dr. Robert Layton incisively argued. "This revenge conspiracy indeed sounds like a very precarious business to me."

"Maybe," James Burke calmly answered. "But that's the only way to get rid of the plague of malpractice attorneys and the scourge of malpractice lawsuits. Eventually the lawyers will become so afraid of dying that they'll cease bilking honest money from dedicated doctors and then prey on some other vulnerable professions like pharmacists, accountants or even other lawyers. It's essentially Darwinian ethics gentlemen. Only the strongest species survive, only now it's professions and not species! The parasitic lawyers will soon find weaker targets to exploit once *they* totally fear the secret medical retribution factor."

"What else do you know that we aren't yet aware of?" Dr. Phillip Campbell anxiously inquired. "I mean Jim, surely you can tell us more important facts about this bizarre scenario than you already have. You've successfully stimulated my curiosity."

"Yes Phil, I have two pertinent things I can reveal right now," Dr. James Burke announced in a quiet-but-strong bass voice. "Number one is that Attorney Dennis Martin is going into a North Philly' hospital for a routine arterial stent insertion. I don't think you'll see him comfortably sitting over there at his customary table next Tuesday evening!"

"What's the second relevant thing you want to tell us?" asked a fascinated-but-apprehensive Dr. Thomas Wagner.

48

"We'll be finishing dinner tonight way before Martin, Harper and Ruberton get done theirs," James Burke observed and related. "Then we'll saunter over to their table and express our condolences to the three predator barristers for William Davis's unexpected death before *we* casually depart from the premises."

"Anything else?" Dr. Campbell asked Dr. Burke. "Jim, you have the charismatic characteristics of a dictator. You could have given Hitler serious competition."

"Yes, and be sure to wave at the grim-faced Mafia guys on our way out of Vianna's," Burke aptly suggested. "You never know when we might need the cooperation of notorious South Jersey thugs like Tony Valentino, Frankie "the Assassin" Scardino, Carmen Campanella and Nicky Tassone."

The next seven days elapsed rather slowly for Drs. Phillip Campbell, Thomas Wagner and Robert Layton with each of the restive surgeons awaiting news of Attorney Dennis Martin's demise. All local daily newspaper obituary pages from the *Camden Courier-Post* to the *Press of Atlantic City* were thoroughly scrutinized. The trio had been assiduously scanning all regional papers like possessed men endeavoring to obtain physical tangible verification of James Burke's rather disturbing prediction. On the following Monday morning the prominent lawyer's lengthy obituary appeared in the *Trenton Times.* The three researching physicians quickly notified one another of the shocking article's publication.

On Tuesday evening Dr. James Burke elucidated on the Dennis Martin sudden death situation. "You plainly see my dear friends, Dennis Martin is officially dead by all newspaper accounts and as you can presently observe, the viperous malpractice villain is not now seated at the corner lawyers' table. In fact, the damned table is completely empty tonight."

"I now believe that your conspiracy group's tactics are already showing significant positive results," Dr. Campbell complimented his wily mentor. "The attorneys are either overcome with grief at losing another key associate or the remaining two malpractice case prosecutors are home fearing for their very lives. My friends, it's no fun being a duck floating inside an active shooting gallery!"

"Don't worry!" Dr. Burke confidently boasted. "Their day will come sometime in the future. We doctors must stick together and thwart those lecherous bandits that legally rob us blind with mammoth unjustified malpractice settlements, all granted by naïve sympathetic juries. It is ironic that we doctors must exterminate an undesirable element of the public to keep society-at-large healthy.

Harper and Ruberton fully know that *they* are white-collar crooks, just like their legal profession cronies, the nation's judges and justices. The corrupt vermin have the privilege of robbing us blind without ever using handguns."

"The Mafia men sitting over in the other corner of Vianna's don't seem too disconsolate about Dennis Martin dying or about the attorneys not sitting at *their* familiar table," Dr. Thomas Wagner objectively noticed and contributed. "I've seen more melancholy at New Year's Eve parties!"

"Now my dear friends," Dr. James Burke said in a firm-but-low manner, "I understand that Richard Harper is scheduled to go to a downtown Philly' hospital for analysis of an irregular heart rhythm. His examiner was an old college friend of mine, and we're both graduates of the *University of Pennsylvania*. The diagnosing physician will definitely recommend a quadruple bypass. I've been recently contacted at my home and I was happy to hear from my old med-school dorm' roommate," Burke qualified and smiled. "He wants *me* to assist in performing Harper's unneeded "precautionary bypass operation." Of course for *us* to escape suspicion, the patient, or shall I say *victim* will die in the recovery ward several days later from a mysterious delayed lethal injection administered just before *we* begin our routine procedure."

"Are you sure you want to get involved in murder?" a worried Dr. Robert Layton challenged his mentally-possessed colleague. "I've known you for a long time Jim and think you've gone absolutely overboard on this one."

"I assure you," James Burke answered with resolute blazing eyes, "I'm quite adamant about this direct threat to *our* profession. If it weren't for having to pay malpractice insurance, all of us would be happily retired in San Diego or Fort Lauderdale, and the biggest problem we would be having would be where to navigate our million-dollar fishing yachts. Murder is what you do to another human being," Burke argumentatively defined. "Killing is what you do to an animal. And let me make it perfectly clear that these despicable covetous trial lawyers are nothing more than extremely dangerous carnivorous scavenging human animals disguised in three-piece-suits!"

"And by disposing of parasitic malpractice case lawyers," Dr. Robert Layton cleverly theorized and stated, "we would all be *specialists* in the strictest sense of the word. Congratulations Dr. Burke on enlightening us about *our* great civic duty as practicing American surgeons doing business in a most complicated free-enterprise economy!" The brain surgeon raised his glass of Merlot and he, Campbell and Wagner all showed praise for the presence and the audacity of the venerable Dr. James Burke. Everyone seated at the reserved doctors' table clicked their wine glasses in unison and then gulped down the vintage liquid.

No sooner had the three other doctors celebrated their endorsement of Dr. James Burke's sagacity that the glass front door to Vianna's Restaurant violently swung open and in stepped five sinister-looking characters wearing well-tailored pinstriped suits with matching color-coordinated shirts and ties. The five formidable-looking newcomers immediately caught the attention of all the elite unsuspecting diners sitting inside the establishment. A sudden and distinct five-second hush resulted from *their* unexpected appearance inside the main dining room.

Then, much to the alarm of most all in attendance the five nefarious henchmen pulled out revolvers and began firing their pistols at the four stunned still-seated surgeons. Everyone else in the room hopped off their comfortable green leather chairs and sought shelter from the ricocheting bullets as the customers frantically ducked under dinner tables and wildly overturned others for protection. After thirty seconds of savage carnage, the shooting stopped and the five vigilante intruders left the place of business and next speedily fled the scene in a waiting get-away white Lincoln.

Tony "the Bonebreaker" Valentino was the first person to arrive to render assistance to the dying Dr. James Burke. "Is there a doctor in the house?" the Mafia don ironically yelled at the top of his lungs. "Someone call an ambulance right away! The other three guys are dead but this one is still breathing a little! Call an ambulance I said!"

* * * * * * * * * * * *

Five Mafia diners inconveniently met the following Tuesday night at Sugar Hill Restaurant and Bed and Breakfast in Mays Landing on the northern bank of the Great Egg Harbor River. Tony Valentino presided over the impromptu thug conclave. His demeanor was as harsh and as gruff as usual.

"Look you punks," Tony "The Bonebreaker" imperatively began, "we had to switch to Sugar Hill until Vianna's can get back into business. There's lots of glass shards and also broken furniture all over that place. And a big police investigation is in progress, too."

"Tell me Boss," Carmen "the Eliminator" Campanella piped-up in his squeaky staccato voice, "why did Rocco's gang wipe out that table of nice doctors. Who's gonna' operate on *me* now if my ticker goes out of whack?"

"Relax Carmen baby," Tony Valentino recommended. "Rocco's gang from South Philly' was assigned to the job. Our gang and his gang have been getting extortion money from the area lawyers for around ten years now. Since they pay us and line our pockets with all the extra greenbacks we need, the Mafia owes the attorney fraternity a little favor when *they* ask for it!"

But something additional was perplexing Frankie "Fingers" Scardino's delicate cerebrum. "But Tony, why did the rub-out happen at Vianna's? I happen to like that place very much! No more lobster-tail there for me for a while!" he verbalized.

"Because numbskull," the Bonebreaker rankled as he brushed some random dandruff flakes from the right shoulder of his black pinstriped suit, "the cops ain't gonna' blame *my* boys for killin' the MDs. How can the Mafia be at fault when the Mafia was in the restaurant dinin' and actin' civilized and tryin' to save lives? Ya' get where I'm comin' from you dumb Sicilian grease ball!"

Tony's three subordinates all slouched down in their chairs and lowered their chins to show their subordination to their boss's nasty temper. But then Nicky "The Fish" Tassone gathered up the courage to ask a salient question.

"But Boss," the Fish cautiously interrupted the general silence at the table, "who spilled the beans on the MDs? How did Rocco's gang get the go-ahead to make Vianna's place look like Mussolini's headquarters after the U.S. Army demolished it in the big war my Pappa used to talk about?"

"Stop actin' like a stupid scooch-a-mensa!" Tony Valentino loudly balked in the exclusive private dining room overlooking the river. "Can't ya' figure the gig out Nicky? Richard Harper was a big shot lawyer goin' in the hospital for a heart examination and stress test. He's got a buddy named Jason Dixon that's got both a degree in medicine and a degree in law. This Dixon jerk became a practicin' lawyer instead of a practicin' doctor. So then Dixon decides"....

"I get the gist now!" Frankie "Fingers" Scardino enthusiastically exclaimed. "Dixon found out about the doctor conspiracy to knock-off the lawyers and told Harper. Harper got wise to the pattern after his two pals Davis and Martin bit the dust. So naturally Dixon ratted to Harper about Burke and his fellas' havin' *their* contract out on the lawyers and then"....

"And then the climax to the stupid drama happened at Vianna's," Tony non-eloquently finished. "Rocco's gang really did a number on the docs', didn't they boys? The lawyers were legally extortin' big money from the doctors with their handsome malpractice lawsuit commissions, and the Mafia was illegally extortin' *insurance money* from the lawyers. The lawyers appealed to the syndicate, so we had no alternative other than to get rid of Burke and his high falutin' chums to keep our revenue-flow goin'."

"How much dough did the rub-out cost the court jockeys?" Nicky Tassone asked. "I like it when lawyers get ripped-off! And the more doctors there are, the more *we* get to make from the lawyers!"

"Two million bucks!" Tony Valentino proudly announced to his avid and impressed listeners. "And it was worth every penny to 'em to terminate the crummy docs'!"

American kids often play a silly simple hand game called Rock, Paper, Scissors. A closed fist represents a rock, a flat hand signifies paper and two moving fingers thrown-down indicates scissors. Paper covers rock and it wins when the opponent has a closed fist. Scissors cuts paper so it prevails when the other player shows a flat hand. In the case of the traditional Tuesday night patrons of Vianna's Restaurant, the greedy lawyers were the rocks, the covetous doctors were the paper and the avaricious final-word Mafia was the inevitable lethal scissors.

"The UFO Magnet"

Professor Conrad Emery had taught literature for thirty years at the stately *Rutgers University* New Brunswick main campus. The scholar retired with dignity at the top of his game in 1990 and now that *his* New Jersey state pension was secure, Dr. Emery could spend the remainder of his time academically investigating the existence or non-existence of his avocation, Unidentified Flying Objects. The literature authority also was fascinated with the decoding of cryptic messages, and Dr. Emery was inspired to pursue that second hobby after once again reading Edgar Allan Poe's imaginative classic novella, "The Gold Bug."
'Laura died of cancer in 1986 and her death really left me emotionally devastated,' Conrad Emery recollected about his wonderful wife. 'And now that my only son Justin is an astronomer working for the *University of California*, perhaps he and I could collaborate on some future UFO project,' the good professor thought in the spring of 1991. 'I strongly doubt that UFOs have visited Earth, simply because the distances between solar systems that could produce intelligent life are so vast. It would require thousands of years to journey from one planet with smart life technology to another. Warp speed exists only in science fiction books and movies,' the dedicated professor concluded and believed up until 1997. It was then that Emery started his UFO investigations as an armchair researcher doing cursory *Internet* studies to fill a giant void in his life left by his dearly departed wife's passing and by his own retirement.
Much of Conrad Emery's rather extensive exploration of the mysterious UFO subject was also conducted at various libraries at *Rutgers University,* including the *Cook College Library* near the Douglass College Campus and at the *Livingston College Library* over on the other side of the Raritan River. The retired professor decided to finally limit his inquisitive study to the area of alien abductions because a plethora of information on the UFO phenomenon had been cataloged in myriad books and magazines and also cached in various popular *Internet* search engines. The social philosopher's personal computer's memory had to be upgraded to one hundred gigabytes to fully accommodate the three thousand lengthy UFO files the thorough investigator had very meticulously accumulated.
One of Professor Emery's most controversial inquiries was into the sensational case of Janet Weston of Milford, Delaware. Janet was

alone at home one spring night since her husband had been away in Kansas on a two-week-long company business trip. A bright light had appeared in the sky over Milford at three a.m. and after the illumination ceased pulsating, a male alien inexplicably entered Janet Weston's locked house, hypnotized her by use of some heretofore unknown mental power, lifted the woman's paralyzed limp body out of bed and carried her listless-but-still alert brain and form to a nearby saucer-shaped spaceship. A ramp slid out of the craft's circular hull and after the alien and *his* captive were fully inside, the ramp ingeniously retreated into the ship's interior without a seam or crack ever showing.

The petrified-yet-paralyzed woman then was deposited on a cushioned examination table. Next Mrs. Janet Weston's clothes were gently stripped and it was then that she had an opportunity to fully perceive her abductor, whose face possessed enlarged insect-like eyes, a small mouth, recessed nostrils and a hairless round head. According to Mrs. Weston's original oral statements, the most remarkable aspect of the bizarre-looking creature was that the gray-skinned space visitor stood nearly seven-foot-tall, its sinister face never exhibiting any hint of expression or emotion.

Dr. Emery placed little credence in such alien abduction "tales" and his initial motivation was to discredit and attempt to disprove all of the various victims' "irrational accounts." His bias was not evident however in the bland manner that he conducted his telephone interviews with the flying saucer "contactee." The astute delver first had to win the abductee's confidence through preliminary phone calls that were empathetic with the human's personal plight. After that introductory phase had been completed, the person claiming the interaction with an alien or aliens would loosen-up and then answer virtually any question that the curious researcher presented.

"Tell me Mrs. Weston," Conrad Emery soothingly asked over the telephone, "what do you suppose was the motive of this alien that had almost-magically removed you from your bed? Was he hostile in any way towards you?"

"I believe he or it desired to rape me from the outset," Janet Weston sobbed. "He was so utterly grotesque in appearance and yet so gentle in his manner. His powerful mind could control my instincts and all my thought patterns through some sort of very advanced mental telepathy. I was vulnerable and had no alternative other than to submit to his or its intentions. The mental force he or it exerted was quite irresistible. And he or it carried me onto the ship by means of some kind of gravity erasure method! I was weightless at that moment. At least that's what my memory vividly recollects!"

"Very interesting! Did he or it converse with you in English?" the professor turned UFO buff perceptively inquired. "Did he speak with you at all?"

"He communicated in English but not by speaking words from his mouth," Janet regretfully recalled and stated. "I can't even remember if the thing had a tongue or voice-box. It was like his mouth was merely some sort of decoration or ornament on his face without any specific function. I now remember that I had mentally asked him about *that* exact same thing."

"And what did the humanoid disclose without speaking?" the interviewer objectively asked. "I want to determine if *your* answer is consistent with other interviews I have conducted with other victims, er, I meant to say people!"

"Its mind transmitted to me that once the scientists of his or its race the Galdeans had evolved to the point where they developed their current superior intelligence," the interviewee said, "the new-breed aliens could then use brain waves to communicate ideas much the same way as an earth radio transmitter or a television tower uses sound waves or microwaves to beam-out signals. But Zama's powers far superseded any human's ability I've ever seen at a mentalist's or at a magician's show. Zama was truly phenomenal, to say the least!"

"You say this Galdean creature had the name Zama?" Emery asked, showing mild interest in what he dubiously had assessed and recorded as 'non-logical non-scientific information.' Could you verify that name for me?"

"That is correct," Mrs. Weston uneasily replied as she squirmed in her bedroom chair. "The incident was definitely not a hallucination or any illusion. Honestly, it was a very real experience that I just dread remembering every time the traumatic crisis surfaces in my mind."

"And exactly where in the *Milky Way* is this mysterious planet Galdea?" Emery asked the emotionally distraught Janet Weston. "Is it anywhere near *our* solar system?"

"Zama mentally communicated that Galdea is in what we earthlings call the Orion Constellation," the cooperative subject clarified. "It revolves around a sun that is the middle star in Orion's belt as seen from Earth."

"And I hate to get personal," Conrad Emery cautiously forewarned, "but did this humanoid Zama attempt to have any normal or abnormal sexual contact with you? You don't have to comment on that if you're too upset to do so. I just need to see if your verbal response will be compatible with the testimonies I've documented from other recent alien abductees."

Janet Weston paused momentarily to gather her composure. "Somehow I trust you Dr. Emery and I must share my terrible nightmare with someone besides my husband before I'm ready for admission into a local mental hospital," the woman sincerely and somberly remarked. "First of all, the horrible-looking creature unskillfully fondled my breasts and then he or it awkwardly inspected me in my most feminine part. He or it next took pleasure in massaging and caressing my genitalia. It was most degrading and most disgusting for any lady with any sense of morality or decency to endure!" Mrs. Weston commented between intermittent weeping and labored breathing.

"I realize that you're under extreme stress," the interviewer compassionately conveyed, "but I must fulfill my responsibility and establish whether or not this space alien tried having sexual intercourse with you?"

"Yes he did," Janet coughed while softly crying over her bedroom land-line telephone. "But that's what's so absolutely absurd about the entire ordeal. The seven-foot-tall alien had an ugly erect reproductive organ that was smaller than my little finger. My first reaction was to laugh but I couldn't because I was under his or its powerful mental influence, besides being totally petrified from the duress of my ongoing ordeal."

"Did this Zama creature feel a need to account for his tiny reproductive organ?" Conrad Emery asked. "Did he have a plausible explanation for it?"

"Yes he did," Janet Weston vividly recalled. "Zama mentally told me that all males of his race have small genitals because when the Galdeans evolved into advanced mental beings with enlarged heads, their need for physical reproduction conversely diminished. The Galdean males still have the biological urge to procreate but since all of their' offspring are genetically engineered by combining sperms and eggs in test tubes and then grow from a zygote into a fetus by virtue of an artificial placenta," the interviewee attested, "their species' male organs have shriveled over six millennia from a foot-long down to a tiny inch and a half. I mean I hardly felt any penetration during the entire horrible dilemma. Thank God for that!"

"Weren't you afraid of becoming pregnant?" the knowledge explorer curiously asked. "Perhaps you might have been carrying a new type of humanoid hybrid in your womb!"

"No Professor Emery!" grim-faced Mrs. Janet Weston abruptly responded between sobs. "The males from Galdea are all impotent. They can achieve small erections but their fluids contain a very low sperm count. At least that's the telepathic message that Zama had transmitted to me. Any sex they have is basically inconsequential in terms of reproduction."

"Yes, I see," Professor Emery empathized and replied as he feverishly jotted-down some relevant applicable notes. "It's analogous to the human appendix Mrs. Weston. At one time the appendix must have served a valid digestive purpose with our ape ancestors but as modern man evolved and gradually changed his diet," the professor casually lectured, "his digestive tract had to make a radical transformation as well. That's why the appendix exists but no longer serves any real beneficial function in the human anatomy. It's all a result of ongoing evolution, you know! Now tell me Mrs. Weston, is there anything else of any significance you'd like me to add to my documentation on your rather strange encounter?"

"Yes," the distraught woman bluntly answered. "Dr. Emery, is my story consistent with those you hear from other females that were space alien abductees? I think I need to join a support group where we could all have a sort of sharing and then bond with some kind of mutual identification."

"I think I can arrange that type of forum for you," the UFO investigator revealed. "I know a particular woman in Pennsylvania and also another one in Maryland that both have had similar experiences to the one that you've just so graphically described. I'll send you their addresses and phone numbers so that the three of you could correspond."

"Were they also abducted by Zama from Galdea?" Mrs. Weston asked.

"No they weren't!" Professor Emery paused and then lied. "Their molesters came from the Capricorn zodiac constellation and not from Orion the Hunter. Thank you Mrs. Weston for your valuable contribution to a noble cause. I'll try to talk to you again over the phone in about a week or so with some follow-up questions. Goodbye for now." Click.

'Another quack! Another pathetic charlatan!' Dr. Emery mused as he placed his antiquated desk phone inside its almost-obsolete cradle. 'Now I'll contact Mr. Carl Jensen of Tarrytown, New York. According to tabloid reports he claims to have been abducted while camping-out near a woods close to his home. The unique aspect of Jensen's story is that two amorous space females had heterosexual sex with him before they released Jensen back into human civilization.' Then Dr. Emery thought some more on the topic. 'I wonder why these abominable alien encounters always happen far away from shopping centers, stadiums, universities and cities where thousands of people could independently witness the events,' Emery imagined and chuckled. 'Instead of calling Carl Jensen, I'll make it a point to meet the impostor in person instead.'

Dr. Emery had already made arrangements to dine with some former *Rutgers* colleagues at the New Brunswick campus's main cafeteria and then he planned to motor up to Paramus and meet Carl Jensen at a designated Charlie Brown Steakhouse and have a "non-campus real meal." On the way up the *New Jersey Turnpike* from New Brunswick to the *Garden State Parkway* Exit 11, the UFO analyst hypothesized what kind of "peculiar tale" his next testifier would present.

At 4:15 pm, Conrad Emery had successfully employed the directions Jensen had provided and pulled his Chevy Blazer into the franchise restaurant's asphalt parking lot. Over sumptuous grilled steak dinners, the two men became better acquainted. Finally, just before the franchised restaurant's very famous fudge-brownie sundae dessert was served, Jensen and Emery got down to brass tacks.

"Carl, you say that two heterosexual female space aliens jointly molested you," Conrad Emery began his inquiry. "That sounds like a man's dream come true down here on planet Earth. What was responsible for their strange compulsive action? Did the lady aliens have time to tell *that* detail to you?"

"These two space women were positively gorgeous and either one of them could easily seduce any earth-man at will at any bar or on any beach," Carl Jensen matter-of-factly prefaced his remarks. "The promiscuous lady aliens claimed that they habitually get aroused after watching filthy X-rated videos shown from Earth satellite transmissions. I know it sounds entirely too crazy to believe but that's what *they* related to me."

"Did the attractive alien females speak to you and relate those facts or did the aggressive lady abductors use mental telepathy to express their odd ideas and sexual behavior habits?" the professor directly questioned.

"How did *you* know that they didn't talk?" Jensen returned in an amazed tone of voice. "Dr. Emery, I had neglected to mention that fact. At any rate, the space women took turns manipulating my mind and toying with my feelings as if they were accomplished control freaks. It was the most abnormal extraterrestrial-like and most emotionally devastating experience of my life!" Carl Jensen indicated. "It was sort of ethereal or heavenly but also hellish at the same time, you know what I mean Professor?" the middle-aged bald-headed funny-looking victim answered.

"I can perfectly identify with your rather common case Mr. Jensen," the interrogator deliberately deceived his listener. "Many other victims describe similar bizarre circumstances and situations that happen to coincide with yours. Now please tell me Carl, how tall were these sex-starved interstellar ladies?"

"I know you're not going to believe this," Carl Jensen embarrassingly relayed, "but both vivacious females were around seven-foot-tall. I hate to tell you *that* weird statistic because the height factor seems like a gross exaggeration."

"Not at all," the distinguished former literature instructor convincingly fibbed. "I've heard of human-like space aliens that are ten-foot-tall. Did the two amorous females abduct you inside their space ship?"

"Why yes they did!" Jensen exclaimed. "They did it all in some mystical-like exotic bed that gyrated and crazily spun all over the metallic chamber the three of us were in."

"Did the luscious lady aliens tell you why they have to have sex with earth-men and why they don't prefer having it with males of their own species?" the good doctor asked.

"They both used telepathy to inform me of their reason before I was ravenously raped. The female aliens communicated that the males of their species have very tiny reproductive organs," Jensen embarrassingly explained. "Since they're rather enamored and fascinated with American and European pornography films, the space women soon become very excited and then go into a kind of estrus cycle and need to have sex with strong handsome well-endowed Earth guys like me."

"I see," Professor Emery acknowledged as he hastily scribbled down a few summary sentences onto his personal notepad. "And from what planet were the two female aliens from? Did they reveal that pertinent information to you?"

"They *thought* and communicated the word Galdea several times," Jensen instantly recalled with certainty. "But I can't recollect what constellation it was located in. I think it started with an O and I believe it's the same one we down here on Earth call 'The Hunter'."

"How do you spell, or excuse me Mr. Jensen, how did *they* spell the noun Galdea?" Emery asked. "Did they mentally share that Earth spelling with you?"

"Yes, it was spelled G-a-l-d-e-a, and the star grouping that I can't right this minute pronounce is spelled O-r-i-o-n," the odd neurotic gentleman proudly and emphatically articulated between spoonfuls from his all-too-delicious Charlie Brown sundae. "Those exotic space gals planted those two facts so deeply inside my subconscious mind that the answers suddenly surfaced and I just recalled them in a flash."

"Have you ever met or spoken on the phone with a woman named Janet Weston?" Emery quite earnestly wanted to know. "Her story sounds much like yours."

"Is she from Colorado?" the baffled man inquired. "I don't recognize that name at all. The lady from Ft. Collins I spoke with had the name Laura Roberts. I'm quite certain of that. Do you mean to say Professor Emery that this Janet Weston had sex with two space women too?"

"Thank you Mr. Jensen very much for your valuable time and help," the befuddled Professor stated in an effort to terminate the highly irregular restaurant chat. "You've been an immense help to my research and I'm indebted to you for your valuable contribution to my important study. And don't worry Carl, I'll pay the bill. The fabulous meal and delectable dessert are on me."

On the long drive from Paramus to his home in Princeton, Dr. Conrad Emery was intrigued with the most recent exceptional parallel stories. 'Carl Jensen and Mrs. Janet Weston don't know each other and yet both subjects stubbornly indicate that they've been molested by seven-foot-tall space aliens from the planet Galdea in the Constellation Orion,' he considered as he maneuvered his auto' in and out of congested five-lane southbound traffic. 'I'd better give Justin a call tomorrow morning and see what my son knows about Orion. The hunter's name sounds like an Irish guy to me,' Dr. Emery mused and then smiled. 'The name really needs an apostrophe and a capital *r*. Maybe I'll wait until noon to phone him. California time is three hours later than ours is here in the east.'

The retired lit' professor turned UFO cynic contacted Justin the following afternoon and after the customary exchange of pleasantries and sharing of family gossip, Dr. Emery asked his son what *he* knew about the Constellation Orion.

"Dad, first tell me what *you* know about Orion," Justin insisted. "This way I can be more selective and not get into any redundant details that would only duplicate given facts already in your knowledge base."

"Well," the father casually began his narrative, "I know about the mythological origin of all the zodiac constellations. I often touched upon them when lecturing my *R.U.* Ancient Literature classes. In mythology Orion was a great Greek hunter. He was a son of Poseidon and the sea-god gave Orion the ability to walk on water and to wade through the sea with impunity. Soon the hunting goddess Artemis fell deeply in love with the brave young handsome hunter."

"Well Dad, I only know the scientific aspects of Orion," the young astronomer admitted. "Give me more specifics about the Greek myth. I'm more into astronomy than into astrology. That pseudo-science is more relative to *your* academic domain."

Conrad Emery proceeded to relate that one morning Orion was energetically swimming in the sea a mile offshore when Artemis accompanied by Apollo strolled by. The god of music was jealous of Orion's daring and *that* evil impulse inspired Apollo to challenge the hunting goddess to hit a distant target floating in the sea to determine exactly how accurate her highly reputed bow and arrow skills were. Artemis did not know the object in the distance was her earthly lover Orion and she accidentally mortally wounded the muscular youth. "This accident caused Artemis to be sorrowful for many centuries," the former *Rutgers* literature professor concluded and disclosed.

"That's a pretty fascinating myth," Justin complimented, "but how did Orion become a constellation in mythology? I remember the part that he exists in the night heavens standing alongside his faithful dogs Canis Major and Canis Minor."

"That is correct," the professor praised in a raised voice. "The dogs were put there by the gods to hunt Taurus the bull in the night sky. But another Greek myth contradicts the one about Apollo and Artemis," the father then pointed out.

"How is the second myth different?" Justin asked. "Dad, I must say your mind is really cluttered with a lot of minutia."

"Orion falls in love with Merope, one of the sisters in what we know as the Seven Sisters or Pleiades star grouping," Dr. Emery lectured via the telephone. "Merope rejected Orion's advances. The great hunter then inadvertently stepped on Scorpius, the huge scorpion. But the ending to the second myth remarkably coincides with that of the first," the father indicated. "The Olympian gods felt pity for Orion. They placed the bowman in the sky so that *he* could have a second chance at slaying Scorpius, which coincidentally is the star grouping we call Scorpio, which is located right next to the mythological hunter in the night sky. That just about consummates my knowledge about Orion. Now *you* can fill me in on some more meaningful scientific data."

The young astronomer had recently been transferred from the *UCLA* campus to the *University of California* Santa Cruz facility and was stationed at the Licks Observatory, where a team of dedicated scientists was performing sky charting using the 120-inch telescope at nearby Mt. Hamilton.

"Dad, first of all the only form of life on planets anywhere near the Earth would have to be bacteria, algae, fungi or some type of primitive microorganisms," Justin maintained. "That's what most of my colleagues here at Santa Cruz along with myself think."

"Well, I'm glad you didn't get transferred to the *Cal' Berkeley Campus*," Conrad Emery kidded his only son. "Those teachers there are entirely too liberal for us stay-the-course professors that have taught here in the conservative east. Justin, what are the individual names of those bright summer stars I see every clear night in Orion?"

"Well Dad, as you might well know Orion sort of parallels the Earth's celestial equator. The bright star Bellatrix is situated on the hunter's left shoulder. The brilliant red star on the right shoulder is identified as Betelgeuse, and I'm not referring to the goofy ghost movie either," Justin joked. "Rigel is the glowing sun in the huge hunter's elevated left foot."

"Do you know the names of the three linear stars in Orion's belt?" Conrad Emery asked his erudite son. "I'm interested in the middle one in particular."

"Yes, and I'm delighted to speak astronomy with you," the young scientist proudly acknowledged. "The three stars' names are Alnitak, Alnilam and Mintaka. They form a straight line and Earth observers interpret the three stars as the hunter's belt. But as you know it's only a coincidence that *it* looks like the hunter's belt."

"How do you spell the middle star's name?" the elder Emery anxiously asked.

"It's Alnilam. A-l-n-i-l-a-m," Justin slowly enunciated each letter. "You can look it up in any standard encyclopedia or on the *Internet* search engines."

The UFO investigator inquired if there was anything else he should know about Orion. His son amiably obliged.

"Funny you have mentioned that," Justin Emery answered, his voice turning a trifle defensive. "I'm been assigned to do some government research for the military on the Constellation Orion. I can tell you some other non-classified information about it. For instance, a sword is shown dangling from Orion's belt, and a cloudy area that can vaguely be perceived by the naked eye is known as the Great Orion Nebula with the famous Horseshoe Nebula in close proximity," Justin elaborated in a more serious tone of voice. "These unique space-dust areas probably mark the creation of new stars being formed but the lengthy process requires millions and millions of Earth years for the individual sun births to actually materialize."

"Thanks Justin," Dr. Emery quickly commended. "You really know your stuff! You've afforded me a wealth of information to ponder. I'll provide you with more odd stories I've heard from wacky space alien adductees the next time you visit Princeton."

"Pop, please realize that space travel is virtually impossible," Justin politely admonished. "The distances between star clusters are too vast and the technology is too primitive to accomplish any practical form of cosmic transportation. The speed of light is around 186,000 miles per second," Justin diplomatically reminded his father. "It would require nine minutes to reach our sun at the speed of light and then it would take thousands of years to finally locate a planet in another solar system, let's say somewhere in Orion that supported intelligent life. And that's if a spaceship could impossibly travel at the speed of light!"

"Thanks again Justin! Goodbye for now Son. There's no doubt in my mind that your very convincing closing argument is correct." Click.

The following week Professor Emery temporarily abandoned his UFO pursuits to do something he always also wanted to do, study the Greek letters and the Egyptian hieroglyphic symbols on a model of the Rosetta stone that a teaching colleague had fondly given him as a retirement gift. 'I'll learn all about Egyptian picture writing and this should add to my aptitude for decoding encrypted messages,' the good doctor conjectured. 'I can now spend all the leisure time I want academically studying my second hobby. I wonder if the ancient Egyptians were into pornography like human abductees claim the perverted space aliens are?' he wondered and then grinned.

The following week the UFO researcher received a phone call from a former interviewee named Timothy Olander of Naples, Florida. Olander, an office manager for a national insurance firm had had a second alien encounter and desperately needed to convey his "tale" to Professor Emery, who enjoyed UFO investigating because *he* had a certain penchant for myths, for legends and for imaginative human exaggeration.

"I'll be in Trenton to clear up some family inheritance business next Thursday," the caller divulged over the phone. "Professor

Emery, can you meet me for lunch somewhere in the Princeton or the Burlington area?"

"Mr. Olander, I'm free next Thursday," Emery answered after checking his personal calendar book for any potential conflict. "I need a break anyway from some decoding project I've been sidetracked on. We'll meet at the Old Columbus Inn in Columbus, which is a small town just off *Route 206* not far from Bordentown. The restaurant's got a quaint colonial atmosphere and the place serves excellent lunches. How about 1 p.m. next Thursday at the Columbus Inn."

"Great idea Dr. Emery," Timothy Olander replied. "I'll rent a car at my Trenton hotel and I promise I'll meet you there at that colonial tavern you just mentioned in Columbus. I've heard of that place. Goodbye." Click.

The week went by and Dr. Emery and Timothy Olander met 1 p.m. at the designated historic Columbus Inn as they had mutually scheduled. After ordering sandwich platters and frosted mugs of beer from the lunch menu, the men had a dialogue about Timothy's latest alien confrontation and ultimate capture.

"What's so highly irregular about your latest contact with space aliens?" the professor asked while effectively disguising his extensive skepticism. "First of all Tim, was the abductor male or female?"

"Without a doubt it was a most horrific experience!" Olander very emotionally declared. "I was terrified being abducted and horribly raped by two weird-looking male aliens. I am a straight heterosexual Dr. Emery, and just the notion of same sex sodomy is entirely repugnant to me. I cringe, hyperventilate and almost become hysterical whenever I rehash the wretched incident in my mind. It was despicable! Totally deplorable!"

"That's very odd," Professor Emery courteously interrupted. "I just received a call yesterday from a certain Mrs. Cynthia Wilson of Spokane, Washington. She claimed that female aliens from a planet somewhere in Orion had molested her. She too is a heterosexual and deplores any kind of lesbian activity and found her reprehensible misadventure quite emotionally debilitating and disturbing as well."

"I'm glad I'm not alone in my misery!" Olander strangely commented about his personal perplexity.

"Where were these male homosexual aliens from?" Conrad Emery asked. "I want to see if the planet is the same as that of the female aliens that had assailed and raped Mrs. Wilson."

66

"I'll tell you what! It's definitely in Orion," Timothy uttered. "I have an idea. We'll both write down the name of the planet on our paper napkins and then compare the results. Not that I don't trust you Professor, but if the planet's name is the same on both napkins then both of us will have confirmed *that* truth and will obviously share a mutual surprise."

The men jotted-down the Orion planet's name and then traded paper napkins. "Well I'll be a gorilla's brother!" Professor Emery replied in a heightened voice that got the immediate attention of several other seated diners. "It's exactly what *I* had written down, Galdea!"

Timothy Olander then in a low tense voice retold his extraordinary tale in a ten-minute monologue. His exposition included the familiar facts that the aliens had indeed been seven-foot-tall, had insect-like eyes, communicated by mental telepathy without moving their mouths or lips, possessed recessed nostrils, had pointed ears and bald-heads and had an affinity for appreciating graphic Earth pornography.

"That sounds incredibly comparable with other alien encounter stories I've recently been privy to," Dr. Emery informed a quite relieved Olander. "Now Tim, do you have anything else you'd like to divulge before I pay the bill?"

"Well Professor, now that you've completely won my trust and confidence and since I also know that you're an expert code decipherer," Timothy explained, "I wish to present you with this!" Olander reached into his sport jacket's pocket and the handsome mustached executive gingerly removed a metallic sheet the size of a paper usually found in a spiral memo' pad. He carefully handed the shiny object and accompanying inscription to the astonished professor.

"What is it?" Emery incredulously asked. "It's fantastically light yet exceptionally flexible and durable."

"I stole it from the UFO and slipped it in my dungarees while the aliens were undressing to perform their repulsive act," Olander reported. "Somehow my mind was able to deflect receiving the full brunt of their preliminary hypnosis and I still possessed moderate control of my faculties. Their second mesmerism was much more powerful and soon I was totally under *their* wicked influence. When Hensa and Ludi dressed me after their heinous immorality had been completed," Timothy Olander very seriously stated, "they never detected the lightweight memo'-size sheet slickly concealed in my back jeans' left pocket."

"This is absolutely phenomenal!" Dr. Emery marveled and declared. "I see several symbols repeated on this metallic plate and if I can scrutinize it more in detail with a clear mind at home, I might be able to translate its exact content. Your little theft might turn out to be just as significant as Napoleon's French soldiers discovering the Rosetta stone during an important Egyptian military expedition!"

"I'm glad *you* want to study it further," Olander enthusiastically exclaimed. "Dr. Emery, please let me know if I've found anything indispensable that might prove the existence of space aliens and UFOs. I'm tired of being shunned and mocked at the office and being called 'a weirdo'!"

Conrad Emery ecstatically returned to his secluded Princeton residence and energetically studied the metallic memo' sheet in the privacy of his computer room. The recognizable recurring symbols were isosceles triangles, spirals, double spirals, backwards sevens, horizontal parallel lines, wavy vertical parallel lines and side-way X's. 'If only I had another alien text with six or seven more matching symbols in it,' Emery contemplated and lamented, 'then I could probably crack this enigmatic cryptogram as if it was a common everyday walnut.'

Several weeks later the intrigued professor received an urgent phone call from his now-excited son. At first the objective-minded recipient thought that Justin was involved in an emergency and needed help, but then the professor calmed the enthusiastic astronomer down to a level where the researcher's statements were more lucid.

"Dad, I'm callin' you from a random payphone at a shopping mall," Justin neurotically informed his father. "I don't want to use my home phone, cell phone or use my computer to e-mail you because I don't trust the government's motives. The *FBI* or the Army might have a wire-tap on my line since *my* secondary study team at Santa Cruz has made the recent great discovery."

"Be more specific and stop talking in generalities," the father nervously demanded. "Exactly what *great discovery* has inspired all of this euphoria you're exhibiting?"

"Yesterday my office staff had intercepted space transmissions and some detailed video pictures," Justin exuberantly related. "I believe that this new fantastic information is what you've been in quest of in your UFO research!"

"I thought you maintained that interstellar space travel was impossible!" Dr. Emery instinctively chastised. "How do you know that this new find of yours isn't some enormous hoax? What about the standard bacteria and the microorganism arguments?"

"Well, there are such forces out there in the universe between galaxies known as worm holes, black holes and the like," Justin Emery logically answered. "Although *their* distinct functions are just theoretical, some scientists think that the space anomalies might represent galaxy shortcuts from one star cluster to another!"

"Very interesting hypothesis indeed!" the elder and calmer Emery conceded. "But how do *you* know that this transmission you have obtained is not some sort of quack trick or fraud?"

"I assure you Pop, it's definitely authentic and valid!" Justin panted. "The transmission we had intercepted is coded of course, but our sensors have reliably determined that the communication was between two alien spaceships because there appears to be measurable time separations between sending and receiving messages," the son informed. "Now please permit me to give you the precise evidence! I'm sending a computer disk copy I have smuggled out of the university's astronomy office to you in New Jersey via *Federal Express* next day delivery. You'll receive it sandwiched between two music disks in a package tomorrow before noon. Whatever you do Dad, don't leave the house until you sign for the package."

"Okay Justin, I'll get right on the project tomorrow afternoon the minute after I receive the package," the father promised. "I hope I'll be able to sleep for an hour or two after the late night movie. Take care Son." Click.

Conrad Emery tossed and turned in his bed all night, imagining and conjecturing about the essence of the CD's qualitative and quantitative significance. He ate a small breakfast of toast and raspberry jam with coffee and then munched like an anxious chimpanzee on a ripe banana. After signing for the *Federal Express* delivery item precisely at noon, the receiver thanked the courteous driver, closed the front door of his secluded country home and very methodically unraveled the package. Concealed in between a Fleetwood Mac compact disk and a Doobie Brothers CD was the object the professor had been nervously anticipating. He stepped briskly into his computer room, inserted the compact disk inside his tower and then pressed the appropriate button to turn the device on. His extreme passion for learning was not disappointed.

Emery first viewed the entire document for a full hour from beginning to end and closely examined the ten photographs that had been programmed into the partially encrypted "space transmission." Color pictures of American pornography stores were shown along with photos' of popular smut video titles. 'Sex makes the world go around!' the former literature professor imagined. 'Apparently the urge and need for sex also drives the intelligent biological universe, at least all the way to Orion.'

After Emery viewed and classified the ten random photos', he then very industriously began analyzing what appeared to be the language captions found under each picture. He next compared them to the words that had been electronically etched onto the metallic memo' sheet that Timothy Olander had so generously provided. Finally several discernible patterns and combinations were established and the alien word rhythms soon converted into the expressions for "woman, girls, men, sex, objects, stores" and "pornography," all of which were eventually decoded and translated. From the acquired data Professor Emery was now capable of interpreting and ascertaining all of the previously arcane symbols represented on Timothy Olander's metallic sheet.

'The metal sheet literally says,' the Professor thought as he adjusted his bifocal glasses, 'Be careful in your atmospheric escape maneuvers and remember what almost happened at Roswell.'

The astounded retired professor then double-checked the alien symbol-letter language equivalents, which ironically had been communicated across space in English by the reckless mimicking interstellar space visitors. Next the very preoccupied Professor considered the 1949 saucer disaster at Roswell, New Mexico and believed that the collision might not have been an accident at all. 'Maybe those two flying saucers had been shot down by some maniac maverick alien,' Emery theorized, rubbing his chin. 'I'll have to search for more tangible information in Justin's duplicate disk he had sent me before I can affirm or disprove my outlandish speculation!'

Carefully separating the pornography pictorial representations Dr. Emery soon discovered series of coded words that signified a certain *close to earth* space transmission between an alien from Galdea named Sutari and another voyager in another spacecraft. Further delineation of the coded symbols indicated that Sutari was sending the message from a quadrant of *our* solar system near Neptune and that the *Milky Way* traveler receiving the "warp speed space mail transmission" (as Dr. Emery described it in his notes) was a creature named Murga. It required Dr. Emery a full month to adequately translate the entire space missive exchanges.

'Now I understand the whole fantastic matter,' the captivated professor concluded while sitting in his swivel gray-cloth computer

70

chair. 'A super-race of aliens had evolved on the planet Galdea in Orion. In time the super-race used their brains more than their appendages and after numerous centuries of evolution the need for *other* body muscles such as internal organs, reproductive organs and a strong anatomical bone structure to support defense from attacking creatures became obsolete to this hybrid form of *short* aliens,' Dr. Emery realized.

The Professor slowly poured himself a glass of blackberry brandy to savor all aspects of his great discovery. 'And Sutari and Murga were tiny Galdeans making a space odyssey to Earth. Actually, they are Orion-style vigilantes, or I should say assigned bounty hunters coming to Earth to ferret-out and destroy the taller culturally inferior and morally bankrupt renegade Galdeans that come in three distinct varieties: heterosexual males, heterosexual females and homosexual male and female Galdeans.'

Dr. Emery took another sip from his delicious blackberry brandy glass. 'And the smaller, smarter more scientifically advanced aliens are asexual creatures and don't have any dominant sexual urges,' he surmised. 'They're not sexually inquisitive as the decadent seven-foot-tall Galdean voyeurs are that come in three varieties to visit Earth for basic sex and for pornography.'

The professor gulped down some more of the very rich-tasting black liquor. 'The smaller Orion aliens periodically come to Earth to conduct some sort of moral cleansing of their own aberrant species,' the good doctor logically speculated. 'According to the extraordinary space transmission that Justin and his fellow researchers had intercepted, Sutari and Murga are two space policemen seeking-out and eliminating seven-foot-tall indecent sexual perverts voyaging from their own planet. *Their* pledged objective is to exterminate the three immoral classes of *their* distant-relative species. The shorter advanced Galdeans believe that *their* civilization should not interfere with activities or events on any foreign planet including the Earth,' Dr. Emery deducted. 'Their genes are preserved in laboratories from past centuries and the smaller-bodied more intelligent Galdeans are much like traditionalists or conservatives are here on Earth. The three more decadent classes of deviate Galdeans are more like seven-foot-tall liberals or social revisionists, all three branches, in their own separate ways, desiring absolute freedom and a more hedonistic way of life free of rules and behavioral restrictions!'

The Professor happily quaffed-down the remaining blackberry brandy from his glass. And then the fatigued truth explorer had several final thoughts. 'To the shorter moral-oriented hybrid aliens, sex is not even a vicarious experience. It is regarded as sort of a mortal sin of the greatest magnitude. The conflict between the small and the tall Galdeans has been ongoing and perpetual. Sutari and Murga along with their dedicated comrades will diligently pursue the evil sex violators' all over this sector of the *Milky Way*. That's why the Earth, with all its abundant decadence, is a genuine magnet for frequent UFO visitations!'

The fully satisfied man placed his left elbow on his computer desk and his arm's fist was then raised-up to his jaw to pensively assess one additional revolutionary idea. 'UFOs are for real and the federal government indeed has been covering up *their* clandestine activities,' the thinker evaluated and professed. 'Here's what the scenario probably was in Roswell back in 1949. Two small space officers similar to Sutari and Murga were pursuing a Galdean sex violator in another spacecraft from opposite directions. The hunted craft managed to successfully employ evasive tactics and it luckily out-maneuvered the two smaller alien attack saucers, which then impacted and exploded over the arid New Mexico desert.'

Before the professor could satisfactorily finish his deep meditation, the telephone and the doorbell both rang simultaneously. 'Caller ID tells me that's Justin on the phone,' the Professor keenly noticed. "I'll call him back as soon as I get rid of this nuisance person incessantly ringing my doorbell. How do traveling salesmen ever find this isolated rustic Princeton home out in the middle of nowhere right next to my sacred pristine pond?'

The perturbed professor finally answered the doorbell ring and was stunned to see two short space aliens pointing their shiny ray guns directly at his face and chest.

'Dr. Emery, I presume. You were expecting maybe a visit from Henry David Thoreau?' the first miniature humanoid mentally transmitted. 'Your home's setting here next to the small lake is very much like that which had been described in that wonderful book *Walden Pond!'*

'Okay Professor Emery,' the second small creature cerebrally communicated. 'Hand over the metal memo' sheet and the computer compact disk right now. We've been monitoring all of your surreptitious activities and all of your electronic phone conversations ever since you became a self-appointed authority on space visitors to this very fascinating small planet,' the second diminutive Galdean disclosed. 'And after you provide us with the requested memo' sheet and the vital computer disk Dr. Emery, we're going to completely erase your memory of flying saucer matters and then you'll have to start your most difficult investigative task all over again from square one to prove that Galdea, Sutari and I really exist!' Murga imperatively stated.

"Signals"

Wednesday, April 2, 2003 started-out as an ordinary day. I rose from the king-size electric bed, put on my slippers, fed and walked the family Chihuahua, had breakfast with my moody wife and then sauntered out of the house in my bathrobe. I waved to a neighbor and ambled down my long asphalt driveway to retrieve the morning newspaper. The *Atlantic City Press* was not in the paper box situated next to my highway mailbox as expected. Instead, at the mouth of the driveway was a folded-up newspaper with unique letter fonts. I inspected the date on the front page and it was indeed Wednesday, April 2, 2003.

'The Weekly Chronicle!' I dubiously read. 'Never heard of the idiotic publication.' My curiosity compelled me to further examine the main headline. 'Deadly Snakes Invade Area' was read in large print right under the masthead, which coincidentally disclosed 'Published in Hammonton, New Jersey.' I was very intrigued by the strange feature article so I further perused the unsolicited edition of the *Weekly Chronicle* as early morning traffic whizzed by on busy *Route 30*, the White Horse Pike.

My fancy scrutinized other front-page articles and they too all dealt with snakes, lizards, amphibians and reptiles. I had my misgivings. 'This must be some kind of very sophisticated practical joke,' I impetuously speculated. 'The only newspapers published locally are the *Hammonton News* and the *Hammonton Gazette,* and they are both printed on Wednesday but are delivered by the mailman's white Jeep on Thursday.'

My interest being thoroughly stimulated, I thumbed through the front section to find the mysterious edition's editorial page. Anonymous authors had written twelve opinion columns on lizard and snake conservation and there were no standard "Letters to the Editor" on the page nor was there any customary address listed for the publisher. My next inclination I immediately honored and that intention was to toss the 'practical joke' into the garage's blue Atlantic County Recycling Trashcan. 'Who would go to such extremes to play an expensive prank like this one on me?' I wondered with great curiosity. 'This must be some sort of belated *April Fool's* ploy,' I reckoned as I checked the day's date on my trusty wristwatch.

On Wednesday, April 9th I stepped out to my *Atlantic City Press* newspaper box, waited for the speeding traffic to pass and reached into the object's interior. I was more than a little surprised when I discovered that another undesired edition of the *Weekly Chronicle* had been stuffed inside in substitution for my regular daily *Press* subscription. The main headline read, "Dangerous Snakes Terrorize Hammonton."

I intensively scanned all the pages and every single article and advertisement again had to do with lizards, snakes, amphibians and reptiles. 'Well, at least alligators, crocodiles and Gila monsters are not trespassing into this part of New Jersey. We've always had snakes living in the nearby pine-barrens and in the local deciduous mixed forests,' I considered with deep reflection. 'Someone is going to great lengths trying to rattle my confidence.' I demonstratively threw the 'trick item' into the blue Atlantic County Recycling receptacle and thought, 'I won't even give the sender any satisfaction and won't even keep the *Weekly Chronicle* as a silly souvenir. Is my *Press* news-paper man part of a perverted prank conspiracy?'

But a week later my aggravating quandary became ever more stressful. On Wednesday, April 16th I ventured out from my property in my merlot-colored *Nissan Maxima* to the Fairview Avenue *WaWa* convenience store to purchase a loaf of square-cornered sandwich bread, a half-gallon of milk and a chocolate candy bar. I saw a headline in the morning *Philadelphia Inquirer* that instantly caught my attention: "Three Hammonton Town Officials Indicted For Mafia Ties." My hands picked up the reputable Philly' paper and the portly genial clerk tabulated my bill on his computerized cash register that sounded like slot machine bells and featured clanging sounds whenever the drawer opened. The accommodating attendant neatly placed my four new acquisitions into a white *WaWa* plastic tote bag and thanked me for my loyal patronage.

Upon arriving home, I entered my two-story white colonial house and methodically removed the purchased items from the plastic bag. The milk was placed inside the refrigerator and the bread was laid in the top pantry cupboard. The candy bar I left on a counter to consume at my leisure. My irritable wife was upstairs taking a shower so I figured that I would read the juicy town article in the *Inquirer*. To my astonishment the all-too-familiar and very perplexing *Weekly Chronicle* was between my hands instead of the anticipated Philadelphia newspaper. The main headline shockingly read: "Hammonton Infested With Black Snakes."

I disgustedly ripped up "the tabloid" and chucked the fragments into the kitchen garbage disposal, turned the plastic dial and crushed the *Weekly Chronicle* into the other trash that already was inside the waste container. 'That paper isn't even good enough for the Atlantic

County Recycling Trashcan!' I angrily discriminated. 'How could the newspapers be switched? Perhaps the *WaWa* cashier is in on the practical joke too just like the *Atlantic City Press* newspaper man?' I suspected and theorized. 'On the other hand I don't even know either *their* first or last names!'

At 4:37 p.m. on Wednesday, April 23rd I was viewing a cable newscast when I heard a gentle rapping at my residence's front door. An amiable *UPS* deliveryman handed me a small brown cardboard package. 'Working late today huh!" I greeted the nameless familiar face. "Take it easy! Looks like rain out to the west towards 'Philly!"

"Have a good one!" the regular driver answered. "I still have fifteen more stops before I can call it a day! It's my wife's birthday and I still have to buy her a gift and then take her out to dinner!" the driver informed, indicating to me his propensity for procrastination.

After the exchange of pleasantries with the harried driver, I stood for a moment and watched him maneuver his big brown truck out of my U-shaped driveway and then zip west on *Route 30*. 'I don't remember ordering any product from Amazon.com!' I suddenly thought. And after I tore open the rectangular cardboard box with the Amazon logo on it, I was very alarmed to discover another reprehensible edition of the *Weekly Chronicle*. The main headline ominously read: "Venomous Vipers Plague Isolated South Jersey Community." I was determined to ascertain exactly who was responsible for initiating the very elaborate-but-frustrating 'roguish newspaper mischief.'

The advent of May proved to be even more confounding and haunting than April had been. My annual horoscope personality profile suggests that I am very superstitious by nature and that I strongly believe in signs, omens and the sensational powers associated with *ESP* as an extension of a primeval human early warning system. Joanne was at the hairdressers on that late Thursday May 1st afternoon, when the telephone annoyingly rang. I was writing checks for due utility bills and looked at my portable phone's *Caller ID* readout. 'No name or number!' I immediately realized. 'Why should I pay the phone company money for an extra service I'm not receiving. This better not be one of those irksome telemarketers!' I effortlessly picked-up the portable land-line phone and said "Hello!"

A rather weird-sounding dial tone was followed by a very undeniably familiar voice from the past. "Giovanni, you had better do the right thing," the recognizable baritone with the Italian accent cautioned. "Your grandmother and I want you to make sure no one gets hurt, injured or killed. Please listen to my wise advice!"

"Who is this?" I wildly demanded with my head swimming in awe. "This is a very cruel and vile prank you're playing, whoever you are!" I yelled into the bottom of the telecommunication device. "Don't call me again or else I'll have the phone company trace your number and then I won't hesitate to prosecute you!"

"I'm warning you Giovanni," the eerie deep hollow voice remarked as if it were originating from another entirely different dimension. "Pay attention to everything that you do!" Click.

I was too perturbed and too exasperated to later tell Joanne of the 'peculiar disturbing and most obnoxious crank phone call. I could not think of any unscrupulous enemy that would be so diabolical as to pretend to be my deceased grandfather's ghost. 'Grand-pop died in 1973,' I recalled. 'And whoever has committed this atrocious outlandish deed should burn in hell for all eternity! That couldn't be my maternal grandfather beckoning me from the hereafter! No way!' I rationally concluded.

On Thursday May 8th Joanne was visiting a half-mile down the highway over to her sister's home when I had another inexplicable arcane experience. I was checking my e-mail when an unanticipated letter flashed-up on my computer monitor. "My Dear Nephew," it strangely and ominously began. "Uncle Leo and I wish only the best for you. Be on the lookout for any unexpected treachery or danger looming on the horizon. Love always, Aunt Vera." The message then slowly faded off the computer screen before I could print it.

I was in an absolute state of mental disarray as ideas and emotions collided and deflected all throughout my head. I could not satisfactorily account for the wretched phenomenon. Aunt Vera and Uncle Leo were both killed in an automobile accident in September of 1972 while traveling to Uncle Al and Aunt Elsie's summer place in Virginia on the Potomac River. 'And besides that,' I worried, 'my father's sister is buried alongside Uncle Leo in a Baltimore cemetery a hundred and twenty miles away. I know because I had attended *their* very sorrowful dual funerals.'

Then my muddled mind considered a few other ideas. 'How come these friendly spirits aren't using direct and specific references when they're benignly contacting me?' I pondered. 'Why must they always communicate in general language that sounds more like a series of riddles than like lucid comprehensible communication?'

I felt myself languishing in emotional torment. My spirit needed rejuvenation. My mind decided to relax, contriving that my imagination was causing me to become "stupidly paranoid." I inserted an easy listening CD into my computer room's stereo system and believed that the inspiring music would liberate me from my mental dilemma. 'I'm depressed and simultaneously suffering from mild anxiety,' I decided. 'Joanne's probably right when she cutely diagnosed me last week as being bipolar!'

My mind had an instantaneous premonition that the stereo would betray me and soon I discovered the validity of my suspicion. A very distinct voice with a Baltimore accent was discernible and it was coming from the unit's twin wall speakers. "Cousin John, this is your late Cousin Joan," the distinct-but-hollow voice vociferated. "Listen Babe, even though I am drifting about in the after-world, I am still fond of you and must look out for your earthly welfare. Heed the previous signs that have been intentionally beamed towards you. We'll meet again when your time has finally come. Take care, John. The finite sand in the hourglass is gradually falling."

I was so flustered and so neurotic that I hurried to the downstairs liquor cabinet, opened the doors, removed a quart of *Southern Comfort* and swallowed the remaining contents in less than an hour. When Joanne returned from her visitation at her sister's home, she blasted me for being intoxicated.

"What's wrong with you!" my wife sarcastically hollered. "I leave you home alone for three hours and then I have to come back to a drunken fool!"

"I'm sorry," I genuinely apologized in a very disconsolate mood, "but I'll never be able to explain the situation to you in a million years, and if I could Joanne, you would immediately have me tested for admission into an insane asylum."

"Well, at least you realize you do have serious mental problems, even while you're drunker than a fish swimming in vodka!" my mate sharply criticized. "Go up to the bedroom and sleep it off while I prepare a late supper. I hope that you're somewhat sober by seven-thirty!" Joanne sarcastically finished.

On Thursday May 22nd the voice of my maternal grandmother (who had passed away in 1987) contacted me on my private cell phone number and on Thursday May 29th I had heard my deceased father's singular raspy voice warning me of perilous future events over my *Maxima's* stereo radio. 'I only wanted to push a button and hear some seventies music,' I nervously thought. But my heart sank almost into my abdomen since I realized I had missed my father so very much. 'Dad died of a heart attack on September 10th, 1974!' I sentimentally recalled. 'I can't figure out how or why these bizarre events are happening. If I tell Joanne, she'll want to divorce me and live with her aged mother. I'm really going to have to carry this heavy almost-unbearable burden all by myself!'

Early Friday morning, June 13th I exited my home's white laundry room door and proceeded into the two-car garage to drive to the local *Dunkin' Donuts* and then buy several morning treats. I had noticed that my wife had not sufficiently pulled her green *Nissan Altima* inside the night before because the *Altima's* garage door had not fully descended and had stopped against my spouse's back bumper. 'She probably had pressed the electronic garage button, entered the house, closed the mudroom door without becoming aware that the electronic garage door had never touched the cement,' I concluded.

I entered the thirty-three-year-old house and vehemently scolded my companion for her "gross oversight." Joanne became antagonistic upon being "disciplined like a child" and defended her ego by firing back wild accusations in what resulted in a rather major boisterous disagreement between us. We both were livid and stubborn.

"A vagrant-turned-criminal could have rolled his body under the raised door, entered the house and suddenly become greedy while we were sleeping," I imprudently argued. "Or maybe an itinerant band of Mexican farm workers might have walked by on the highway, have seen the partially open garage door, got an idea of grabbing some easy money and then would storm into our bedroom at midnight wielding knives and threatening our lives," my accusative lips loudly indicted.

"You're always hypercritical and too quick to blame others, you chauvinistic hypocrite," my wife acrimoniously snapped back. "Nothing really happened because of the garage door, did it John? I made an honest inadvertent mistake and then *you* try to arraign me in your arrogant court of perverted justice. I'm sorry Husband, but I'm not quite as perfect as *you* are!"

"And besides that, the garage door made a dent mark on the back bumper-area of your new green *Altima*," I caustically blamed my spouse. "You don't respect property enough to be more careful when you haphazardly do things. You should pay more attention to what you are doing, especially when you drive your new green *Nissan*," I nastily rankled. "Money doesn't grow on trees ya' know!" I yelled. "Try to be more careful next time!"

"Just for that I'm going grocery shopping with *your* new red *Maxima*," my wife angrily volleyed back. "Maybe I can dent *that* car up too!"

"Now wait a minute!" I countered. "I'm not going to have you go to the chain store in *my* mint-condition *Maxima*. You always park too close to the front of *ShopRite's* or *Wal-Mart's* main entrance because you're too lazy to walk another hundred feet and get some needed exercise. Some person in a rush is liable to slam their shopping cart into the *Maxima* and cause a needless dent without *you* doing it yourself!" I bellowed. "And besides that, my car's color is merlot and not red!"

"What if I park *your* precious vehicle further away from the store and then some punk idle kids with nothing better to do savagely key the paint on both sides?" my wife loudly returned. "You can't spend the rest of your life worrying about every possible little thing that might happen or might go wrong!"

"Just like in the winter two years ago!" I argued back, showing a very nasty temper. "You came into the driveway, approached the house too fast and then skidded into the left garage door. There are still two big dents on the door showing exactly where you had impacted the automobile. Sometimes Joanne, your absent-mind both acts and looks like you're on drugs or something! You must learn to always be more alert!"

My resolute high-strung Italian wife was not-too-enamored with my critique of her lackluster driving ability. "That was just a minor accident you're alluding to and you have the very bad habit of magnifying every little deviation into a major catastrophe," she very effectively maintained.

"And what about the time last year when *you* anxiously hopped into your last car and started up the engine without realizing that the garage door had not been raised," I reminded Joanne. "You backed up your old gray *Sentra* into the closed door and caused considerable damage. We had to purchase two new automatic doors and then *you* insisted on buying a new vehicle and that's why we acquired your *Altima* because the gray *Sentra* had two gigantic dents in the trunk bumper area from the unnecessary accident. Remember Joanne," I scoffed, "accidents just don't happen; they are caused by human error, and in this case it was *your* human error!"

'I'm leaving right now to go shopping!" my wife shouted in frustration at my continual faultfinding. "I hope you're more sensitive and objective when I return. Be ready to carry all of the grocery and shopping bags inside when I pull into the driveway. And don't go to that silly doughnut place," she tyrannically barked. "You're getting entirely too fat! You're beginning to look like a huge inflated sausage!" the woman venomously assessed while effectively getting in the last word in her typical flight retreat mode.

No sooner had Joanne exited the laundry room door and entered the adjacent garage that she let out a most hideous and spine-chilling scream. I rushed into that section of the house to determine the cause of her hysteria. "Ahhhh!" she shrieked in extreme alarm. "There's a long black snake that just slithered into that corner behind those empty boxes and metal cans."

"Great!" I exclaimed in a true moment of awe. "How long was the reptile?"

"Around three feet!" Joanne yelled back as she was too petrified to move an inch either left or right. "But it was skinny and not that big around!"

I honored my sense of self-preservation, reverted into my survival mode and instinctively picked-up a long flat-bottom shovel. I apprehensively moved several stacked boxes from the corner and scared the already frightened creature from its place of hiding. The black snake slithered out in a flash, lashed out at me and I was skillful and lucky enough to lower the long shovel's flat blade directly behind the snake's head. It lifted its mouth in agony and then began hissing through its opened fangs as my shovel applied more weight and downward pressure. The garden tool had eventually punctured the reptile's skin and blood squirted out its back.

"Hurry John! I can't stand watching this happening! Please hurry and kill it!" my terrorized wife implored in a delirious state of total pandemonium.

Like a crazed barbarian I raised and lowered the shovel a half dozen times and finally severed the creature's scaly neck from its still wriggling body. In another moment I ceased my mania, realizing that I had successfully decapitated the innocent animal and that it was now dead.

"It's probably only a non-venomous snake," I said to Joanne as I felt my heart wildly palpitating inside my chest. "I wish I was as courageous and as trained as one of those Australian animal capturers I see on the *Discovery Channel*. Steve Irwin would have simply stooped down, picked the snake up by the neck and then safely deposited it into the field next door."

"I'm glad you killed it!" my wife commended me in a rare display of appreciation. "I hope it doesn't have a lair inside one of our walls. This horrible event was traumatic enough!"

"No Joanne, it probably got in here because *you* failed to observe that *your* garage door was not closed last night!" I accused. "The cold-blooded snake was obviously seeking warm shelter and a pleasant place to spend the night and you had absent-mindedly provided it to him!"

Joanne seemed relieved and paused for a moment to regain her sensibilities. After taking a deep breath, she amazingly asked a rather plausible question. "Where did you get the idea of using the shovel as a killing tool? That was pretty inventive on your part. You do have a practical imagination after all!"

"Last May a few hours before your father died a large black snake appeared in your mother's driveway," I answered while still breathing heavily. "Your Uncle Dick bolted into your mother's tool shed and obtained two blunt-ended shovels. He handed me one and instructed that I should keep the huge snake's head down against the asphalt while he repeatedly sliced the thing's back and spinal cord to shreds with his shovel's flat edge!"

"You never ever show good discretion!" my spouse quickly admonished. "You're so insensitive! You didn't have to remind me of Dad's passing. You're just too honest for your own good! Maybe you could have been a little less graphic and used a trifle more good judgment by keeping *that* particular information to yourself! That's why you've made so many enemies in your life!" Joanne alleged. "You don't think of the other person's feelings before you impulsively say something they consider offensive!"

"Why don't you just drive over to the shopping center while I scoop the remains of this snake up and then bury the pitiful black creature in back of the house near the woods?" I answered as pragmatically as I could. "Sometimes absence makes the heart grow fonder!" I finished.

After disposing of the long skinny snake, I drove the green *Altima* a quarter of a mile east on *Route 30* to the wonderfully quiet and serene Oak Grove Cemetery. The new Hammonton High School had recently been constructed across Old Forks Road on the east edge of the old graveyard and the modern-looking contemporary architecture represented a stark contrast to the cemetery's tall oak trees and general soothing tranquility.

I usually trek all of the cemetery's asphalt lanes, which amounts to a little more than a mile of beneficial cardio-vascular exercise. The daily early morning ritual always proved to be good healthy therapy for both my body and my mind. My brain cells are then energized, my emotions become stabilized, and I could once again bravely face my wife with a cordial disposition and deal more diplomatically with her mercurial snide rancor.

'I'll just ease my tensions with this satisfying daily trek,' I imagined. 'Soon the notion of evil black snakes will dissipate and fade from being important. It was too bad Joanne's father died several hours after her uncle and I had killed the larger black snake in her parents' driveway. Ever since *that* event happened, I have always regarded the horrible occurrence as a precursor of his death!'

Nothing irregular occurred during my morning hike around all of the various loops and bends of beautiful Oak Grove. Natural beauty and things that are placid tend to feed, to positively charge and to pacify my psyche. The cemetery's stately oak, elm, tulip and pine trees have a definite beneficial remedial effect upon my mental state of being. 'I always seek asylum here to avoid being institutionalized in a state asylum,' I mused. 'And I enjoy periodically stopping and reading inscriptions etched on tombstones dating back to the nation's *Civil War* era when the graveyard had been established. Many of the original headstone epitaphs have almost eroded and are hardly legible.'

My spirit reconstructed, I felt compelled to return home and attempt to peacefully coexist with my flamboyant and sometimes nasty wife. I am a *CPA* by profession and prefer the company of numbers and statistics on a sheet of paper in a quiet room rather than be exposed to the nuisance of bothersome human beings prattling their shallow commands, complaints and trivial grievances in my face. That is why I prefer having an office downtown on Bellevue Avenue rather than be pestered by continual marital interruptions and quarrels at home while trying to concentrate on my work. I basically abhor harsh verbal conflict and endeavor to avoid it whenever I can. A docile moderate life has always been the ideal pursuit that my heart has striven to attain.

Invigorated by my "morning constitutional", I rested for a half-hour on a cemetery bench and contemplated the meaning of life and the significance of my lackluster existence. Then I drove the green *Altima* back to 699 North White Horse Pike to reunite and bond with Joanne. 'It's now Saturday, June 14th and nothing sinister or malicious had occurred the day before,' I gratefully thought. 'I've safely made it through another unlucky Friday the thirteenth,' I imagined. 'I see that Joanne is home from doing her light shopping.'

When I stepped through the garage portal into the tan tile-floored laundry room, I found my wife to be in an extremely aggressive and prosecutorial mood. Regretfully I did not honor my first impression and abandon her rancorous diatribe before she made her vicious scathing incrimination.

84

"Look John, I'm not a witch so stop thinking that I am!" she instantaneously reprimanded.

"I am not insinuating that you are one, although sometimes that particular thought does enter my mind!" I cautiously replied to camouflage the true belligerence I was feeling toward my spouse at that moment. I tried getting by her nagging mouth into the main part of the house when "my significant other" felt motivated to lambaste me some more.

"And stop thinking that I am bossy, spoiled and arrogant," my wife imperatively squawked. And as if she were accurately reading my tender mind she next bellowed, "And yes John, you must trim the bushes, mow the lawn and weed-spray before you decide to watch television, drink your *Southern Comfort* or take your predictable afternoon nap."

'She's undeniably reading my mind!' I quickly concluded. 'She *is* a damned witch after all and I don't even live anywhere near Salem, Massachusetts!' I defensively decided but kept to myself. 'I'll remain quiet and see what caustic rhetoric she'll verbalize next!'

"And besides," my incensed wife adamantly uttered in a ridiculing tone of voice, "you can't go to Atlantic City and gamble your hard-earned money away while drinking more *Southern Comforts* at the poker tables. Do as I say or else I'll live with my mother and you'll soon be hearing plenty from my lawyer!" the crazed lady yelled with bulging brown eyes.

'Joanne's apparently become psychic and possibly even clairvoyant!' I strongly suspected. 'She was actually reading my mind word for word and idea for idea in the exact sequences I had thought them, or was it just a series of coincidences dealing with known circumstances in my daily household responsibilities and in my predictable personal amusement interests?'

I obediently changed into my work clothes, put on my orange work gloves and conscientiously trimmed the bushes, mowed the lawn and weed-sprayed around the property's flowerbeds and trees. I am not henpecked, but my wife could definitely be a miserable shrew so my compromising disposition often judges that it is better to get along rather than to perpetually do battle, for I pride myself on being judicious and civil-minded. My zodiac sign is Libra and I naturally am constantly in quest of balance, truth and beauty in all life experiences.

On Sunday morning, June 15th I was perusing the thick *Philadelphia Inquirer* I had purchased at *WaWa* and my horoscope read: "Dear Libra, today's your lucky day. Don't be afraid to take some risks you ordinarily wouldn't attempt. Whatever you endeavor today will certainly have a fortunate conclusion."

I eagerly exited the house without consulting my wife, skipped my morning cemetery jaunt, had a quick high-calorie snack breakfast and coffee at *Dunkin' Donuts* and then anxiously drove thirty miles east on *Route 30* toward Atlantic City. I parked my immaculate merlot *Maxima* in a casino concrete high-rise garage, took the elevator to the appropriate second floor and meandered my body through the crowded gaming hall.

My first inclination was to play poker or roulette, but some mysterious *ESP* sensation led me in the direction of the five-dollar slot machines. 'I never play slots because the odds are highly against me and they are the casino industry's greatest revenue producers,' I remember generalizing. 'And five-dollar slots are usually out of the question,' my conscious mind determined. Despite my cynicism concerning high-stakes slot machines, I inserted three crisp one hundred dollar bills into the conversion slot and sixty five-dollar-tokens were automatically registered on the mechanism's impressive read-out display.

I experienced little initial luck but some remote force persuaded my will to persevere. 'There are only three tokens left!' I soon realized. 'Oh well, here's to Donald Trump!'

The reels rotated and halted and before I knew whatever was happening three handsome red sevens appeared in the triple windows with accompanying bells clanging and bright lights flashing. When I finally fathomed that I had hit the super progressive jackpot, my heart started pounding fiercely and I felt a rush of blood surging-up to my head, making me somewhat dizzy and giddy.

A casino cameraman rushed over to obtain pertinent newspaper publicity and the employee snapped my photograph standing next to the three majestic magic red sevens. Momentarily, I was in ecstasy at winning a cool million dollars. I am a very bashful person, felt grossly uncomfortable being in the center of a gaudy circus environment and almost fully resented all of the excessive adulation and exaggerated ballyhoo.

The casino's floor manager and three attendants then checked my driver's license, casino card and several credit cards to verify my identity. I was briskly escorted to a special room where in half an hour a wonderful check for $650,000.00 was graciously handed to me amidst flashing cameras and multiple questions from several shouting reporters. "The federal and state income tax money has been withheld and will be paid in your name to Uncle Sam and to the

Governor," the barrel-chested casino head official professionally and sanctimoniously revealed. "The rest is yours to keep and spend at your own volition."

My heart was wildly throbbing and I was in fear of having a major coronary right there on the spot. I refused an offer to notify my wife by phone, explaining to the casino managers that I preferred to surprise Joanne with the extraordinary bonanza. "I'll certainly buy her a mink coat and a new diamond ring," I prevaricated to my captive audience. "And then she's always wanted a white *Lexus* and a three-week Hawaiian vacation. Maybe she'll get those special rewards if she learns how to play the marriage game by *my* rules," I shrewdly announced. Everyone there in that well-guarded vaulted room laughed in response to my "unique sense of humor."

I drove from Atlantic City thirty miles west back to Hammonton in a state of wild exultation. Never before had I ever felt so exhilarating. Some impulsive internal force compelled me to pull into the Oak Grove Cemetery and to triumphantly walk the mile of twisting and looping asphalt lanes, something I had neglected to perform that morning in deference to my most fortuitous excursion to the bustling Atlantic City casino. 'I'll dedicate this happy victory stroll to Joanne's legendary temper!' I contemplated.

I found the venerable graveyard devoid of other living humans. My soul sought solitude and quietude to sufficiently evaluate and adequately appreciate my recent good fortune. 'Gambling is usually regarded as a self-defeating sin but today it ironically proved to be a marvelous blessing,' I conjectured as I parked my merlot *Maxima* under a tall shade tree. 'Ah, only a few gray squirrels darting around looking for last fall's remaining nuts!'

The casino check had been gently placed in my *Maxima's* glove compartment and then I carefully closed and locked the small door. I pressed an overhead button and closed the roof's sky-hatch, fearing that some wayward itinerant would enter the graveyard and dastardly climb into my automobile while I was strolling a half mile away. I then locked all doors with my electronic key device and distrustfully checked all four of them twice to make certain that the sedan was absolutely secure.

About a quarter mile into my trek I stopped at my father's grave-site and stared blankly at the headstone. I closed my eyes and quietly recited a brief prayer, thinking that my deceased Dad's intercession had something to do with my fantastic Atlantic City windfall. When I opened my lids, at least fifty brown acorns rained down from various oak trees in the vicinity and that sudden surprise instantly made me feel extremely nervous. 'That's awfully strange!' I thought. 'It's late spring and acorns have yet matured to their brown state where they could *fall* to the ground. That happens in autumn.'

My mind thought about my previous day's Libra horoscope advising that I identify and honor all signals for the next forty-eight hours. 'The casino payoff was the result of the newspaper signal I had intuitively obeyed, and now this Oak Grove Cemetery acorn aberration must be a definite harbinger of another event about to occur,' I restlessly hypothesized.

Next my pupils stared at my maternal grandmother's grave-site situated directly in front of my father's final resting place and the name and the dates of birth and death mystically vanished and then supernaturally reappeared three consecutive times at separate five-second intervals. I rubbed my eyes to ascertain that I was not imagining the implausible anomaly I had just witnessed. 'I suppose nothing is really carved in stone, not even granite headstones,' I remember rationalizing. My brain was in a state of flux and my jangled emotions were in a near state of panic.

My eyes then focused on my maternal grandfather's grave and the flowers all amazingly wilted, died and then came back to life in a most remarkable sequence of botanical resurrections. 'Even the plastic artificial flowers perished and then rejuvenated,' I marveled at what I considered a series of inexplicable 'miracles.' I resolved to abandon my deceased relatives' burial places and finish my mile-long haunting hike through the normally peaceful cemetery. 'My head must be so enthralled at winning the jackpot that it's playing devious tricks on my five senses,' I evaluated in a disguised vain effort at allaying my overall trepidation.

A half-mile further into my daily pilgrimage I stopped at my father-in-law's mausoleum on the Old Forks Road side of the hallowed cemetery. I glanced over at the modern high school building and felt some comfort while considering the notion that other living human beings were in close proximity.

Before I could finish my reverie, I was alarmed and staggered when my eyes perceived a long thick black snake emerge from behind my father-in-law's two-tier mausoleum and then slither across the grass into a thick tangle of tall yew bushes. 'My God!' I thought as my body trembled. 'That's another signal from the afterlife. I didn't heed the acorns falling, the tombstone acting like a classroom blackboard and the flowers dying and then self-resuscitating.'

My legs and knees felt rubbery, but without buckling, they somehow managed to sprint and carry my anatomy as quickly as they could back to my merlot-colored *Nissan*. Hastily I re-entered the car, turned on the ignition and then stepped heavily on the accelerator. The responsive vehicle's back wheels squealed as my tires made traction against the asphalt and the performance-oriented *Maxima* quickly responded to the transmission and drive train's synergy.

I abruptly turned left onto *Route 30* and then a quarter of a mile down the congested thoroughfare adroitly maneuvered the car into my driveway without the courtesy of using my right turn signal. The overhead automatic garage door button was pressed and the portal on the right ascended. I found Joanne lying unconscious on the cold cement but her pallid face, even with closed eyes, still showed an expression of ghastly horror.

I hurriedly exited my car. My eyes scanned the garage's shadowy interior and they immediately identified a black snake sliding its way towards a wall crevice where the clothes dryer vent's metal tube led from the laundry room to the exterior outside wall. My animosity towards the slinking sliding reptile enraged me and I instinctively picked-up the "death shovel" leaning against a stack of four cardboard boxes and then I crazily and mercilessly smashed and thrashed the creature's head and body with the improvised weapon. In fifteen seconds I had killed the vile-looking animal with a series of maniacal thrusts.

My unsettled mind still possessed a degree of rational problem solving-ability. My first impulse was to call *911* and have the Hammonton Rescue Squad's paramedics administer first aid and then transport my unconscious wife to Kessler Memorial Hospital. I next demonstrated good mental self-discipline and honored my second strategy. 'I can be at the hospital in just about the same time it takes the ambulance to get *here*,' I decided.

My arms lifted my wife's limp body from the cold cement and I frantically hustled her over to the *Maxima,* which was parked in the driveway. I managed to open the door and after placing Joanne inside, I harnessed her with the front passenger's seat-belt. I felt her pulse, which was weak and almost non-existent. Being in a virtual state of delirium, I pressed the electronic button that lowered the garage door and without any regard for traffic laws, I squealed my back wheels in reverse, halted, placed the gearshift in 'Drive' and soon sped out of my driveway onto busy *Route 30.* The four-mile nightmarish hospital drive seemed to take an hour as I discourteously wove in and out of intense highway congestion and luckily zipped past one yellow and four green traffic lights at seventy-to-eighty miles an hour.

The *Maxima* was steered into Kessler Hospital's back ambulance entrance and *that* split-second decision actually wound-up saving my wife's precious life, for if I had carried her into the emergency ward the apathetic by-the-book admissions' desk clerks would have insisted that I fill-out bureaucratic paperwork before Joanne could have been treated. The only thing I told the emergency room doctor and two nurses was that I believed that a poisonous snake had possibly bitten my wife.

As I impatiently waited for word of Joanne's condition in the small visitors' lounge, my disorganized mind reviewed the past two-month's highly-irregular events in a rather vivid mental newsreel. 'An excess of money is evil and leads to decadence,' I morally surmised and concluded. 'I was much happier *before* I became a filthy rich egomaniac!'

I then quietly prayed as I sat in the lounge and next vowed to donate the entire six-hundred-and-fifty-thousand-dollars to charity if Joanne were to survive her snakebite trauma. A half-hour later the physician in charge of the emergency room exited the suite and met me on the other side of the huge swinging doors. "Your wife was indeed bitten by a snake but I'm happy to report that it was non-poisonous," the surgeon calmly explained. "Your better half went into shock and soon fell unconscious from her most terrible ordeal. She's now fully awake and you'll be able to speak to her privately in about ten minutes."

I never told Joanne about the lost Atlantic City treasure-trove. I did donate the spectacular sum to various community charities and churches. 'My peace of mind and Joanne's life are worth far more than a mere six-hundred-and-fifty-thousand dollars!' I intelligently concluded.

"Drama and Trauma"

An unusual-but-welcomed lull existed that Thursday mid-November evening in the emergency rooms of Philadelphia's very reputable *Thomas Jefferson University Hospital*. Only five admissions had been recorded in the last hour and only one of them had been life-threatening, a policeman suffering a chest gunshot wound. The triage and trauma staffs on duty were discussing the upcoming *Thanksgiving* holiday, certain planned Caribbean tropical vacations, early *Christmas* shopping and anything else that would temporarily get their minds off of the high-pressure "life or death" responsibilities that dominated their professionalism and also incidentally superseded daily hospital rules and procedures.

"Has Ed proposed to you yet?" the head nurse asked her very reliable assistant. "Ginny, I'm glad I introduced you to him. I honestly believe he's the finest surgeon we have here at *Jeff*'. And if I'm not invited to the big wedding extravaganza, I promise *you're* not going to get a good recommendation on your next evaluation," jested Nurse Supervisor Anita Clark just outside the large swinging doors of the hospital's emergency operating suite.

"He's going to get around to it, sooner or later," R.N. Ginny Clemm sincerely answered. "I have to confess Eddie's so busy and so ambitious that work often takes priority over everything else, even marriage," the pretty brunette added. "He's always lecturing, traveling to seminars or reading professional journals, and we hardly ever have time to go out to dinner or to a show. What should I get Eddie for *Christmas*?"

"How about two tickets to *Sandals Resort* down in Jamaica," Anita Clark imaginatively suggested. "You both need some *r and r* and a beautiful setting to spark your romance, and then you two can take your passion to a higher level. I think a picturesque tropical island would be the ideal solution to your emotional dilemma."

"You're perfectly right as usual," Ginny Clemm readily agreed. "We're both slaves to our jobs. Eddie is so dedicated to this famous hospital that settling-down and having children are now very remote goals in his mind. Anita, I'm going shopping tomorrow morning to *The Gallery* and buying a few skimpy bikinis for *our* future Montego Bay get-away. If I can't find what I want there, I'll go across the river and shop at one of the large Jersey malls."

"You don't have to drive over to Jersey," Anita Clark cheerfully reminded her amiable subordinate. "The Philly'-Lindenwold High

Speed Line takes you pretty close to the *Echelon Mall*. It's within walking distance from the terminal platform and it's safe too!"

"That's right!" the proficient O.R. nurse replied to her superior. "I can just hop onto the subway train at Tenth and Locust Station and ride across the Delaware via the *Ben Franklin Bridge*. Forget *The Gallery*! I'll be heading straight over to New Jersey first chance I get. Anita, I think you should write a syndicated advice column for the newspapers!"

The casual conversation between the two competent nurses was interrupted by a city ambulance's shrill siren and red flashing lights. The emergency vehicle screeched to a halt outside the building's pane-glass windows. This all-too-familiar scenario was Anita Clark and Ginny Clemm's signal to forget prattling about the generally predictable outside world and to focus *their* energies on the next vital medical challenge at hand.

Two paramedics hastily rolled *Thomas Jefferson University Hospital's* latest patient into the Emergency Room's side-entrance and immediately and adroitly transferred the unconscious elderly man from the ambulance stretcher onto a gurney. The injured gentleman was then quickly wheeled through another set of large swinging doors into one of the medical center's operating rooms.

"What happened to the old man?" the ambitious-but-fatigued chief surgeon on duty asked the paramedics.

"He was hit by someone driving a speeding motorcycle at 7th and Walnut, just four blocks from here," the first rescue squad attendant volunteered. "The man had no ID on him. Some slick city vagrant or small-time heartless petty thief must have grabbed *his* wallet before the cops and us arrived at the scene."

"He looks well-dressed in a business suit," the head surgeon noticed and shared. "I don't think this man is a vagabond. And look!" the doctor exclaimed. "He has two-hundred and twenty-five dollars in his pocket. Anita, please see that this man's money and all of his other personal belongings are put into the standard plastic bag, temporarily labeled and then placed in the vault until the hospital admissions staff' learns exactly who he is."

"Yes, I'll do that right away as soon as we finish scissoring off his clothes," Nurse Supervisor Clark promised. "My word, this is an expensive suit we're cutting!"

"And Nurse Clemm," the harried chief surgeon professionally commanded, "let's get this patient prepped for surgery right away. I want to see if he has any internal bleeding in addition to the obvious broken left femur, multiple lacerations and fractured left wrist I've already examined. He appears to be in his seventies and his general condition seems to be rather weak."

"Sure thing Dr.," Nurse Ginny Clemm professionally warranted to her future fiance. "I'll get the *I.V.* set up and have your gloves ready after you scrub."

"We'll check with the police to see if they found any wallet at the accident scene," the second paramedic indicated. "The credit cards and any additional cash will probably be missing but other things like a Social Security Card, Red Cross Card or organization membership card can help both the authorities and the hospital identify this man. We'll see what we can find out."

"That's a good idea," the chief surgeon concurred. "The hospital doesn't like performing operations without permission or notification of the next of kin. Medical lawsuits are a dime-a-dozen in this day and age! But as far as I'm concerned, a person's bodily health takes priority over everything else!"

No sooner had the elderly victim been prepped for surgery that *he* began mumbling some strange indiscernible words. The old man's monologue would continue throughout the series of incisions and sutures his body would soon endure. Soon his gibberish became louder and presented itself as a distracting annoyance to the already under-duress *O.R.* medical team.

"What's he mumbling?" Ginny Clemm asked before passing a requested scalpel to the chief surgeon. "It sounds like he's hallucinating in his sleep!"

"The man has a ruptured spleen and we'll have to remove it," the doctor observed and articulated while inadvertently ignoring the assistant nurse's inquiry. "That's the extent of his internal injuries. I hope *we* can save him."

"He does look distinguished with that gray mustache," Nurse Clark described as she indirectly acknowledged and addressed her subordinate's curiosity. "He's probably a retired *University of Penn* professor judging from his formal appearance. Will he regain consciousness doctor?"

"Let's see if he survives his trauma first," the assistant surgeon Dr. James Ryan sternly demanded. "His advanced age and internal bleeding do *not* put the odds in *his* favor! Ginny, pass me a clean sponge while Ed begins removing the spleen! This man is bleeding from cuts and scrapes all over his body! He'll definitely require at least two pints of blood!"

The old man lay stiff as a board on the operating table and continued his dumbfounded mumbling. At first the highly-focused doctors and nurses ignored *his* incessant babbling, which to them was completely irrelevant to their attempt at saving a human life. But then the patient's words became more audible.

"Georg Znaeym, you vile obnoxious scoundrel, I loathe the very thought of your name," the old man jabbered from his unconscious state. "You and your pathetic heirs are not good enough for the scavengers to devour!"

"Doctor," R.N. Ginny Clemm noted, "I believe the patient is desperately attempting to communicate with us or with someone. Should we try asking him a few simple questions that might make him tell us who he is?"

"No!" the preoccupied chief surgeon emphatically responded. "He's evidently in a state of shock and anything he thinks or says will be hazy and inaccurate. Now please don't disturb me while I finish removing his damaged spleen."

"Georg, I despise your shiny boots and everything else about you," the old unconscious fellow strangely uttered as if immersed in a powerful trance. "My men will free me from *our* dilemma and then I will see that they murder you before my very eyes. This snag will only be temporary for me, Georg Znaeym, you rotten disgusting vermin! May the damned vultures feast on you!"

"I believe this George person must be someone who has wronged the old man," Anita Clark whispered to her underling at the *O.R.'s* equipment table. "Probably a greedy brother-in-law, a devious uncle or a wayward son."

"The last name *he* is uttering is not a common one and is too hard to even spell," Nurse Clemm noted and said. "I wouldn't even know where or how to begin spelling it! If we could obtain the name and write it down, the hospital or the police could then trace who this man is!"

"This George individual might not even be a relative!" the nursing supervisor speculated and declared. "My impression is that this George is an enemy and probably not a close friend of this old man. For all *we* know this George, whoever he is, might even be an imaginary name!"

"Nurses, we need your help right away!" the chief surgeon commanded. "Let's leave mysteries and melodrama to the afternoon soap operas! Our concentration should be on surgery and medicine."

The old man then proceeded to further describe his great enmity for Georg Znaeym. "Georg, don't you ever trespass into my forest again!" he oddly ranted. "Hunt only on your own accursed property, you uncivilized skunk! Georg, would you like a gulp of wine from my flask? We might be trapped here for hours! Wolf did you say! Wolf did you say!"

"This man is having delusions," the chief surgeon determined. "His talk is nonsensical! His ideas are not consistent and they contradict one another! I've read journal articles where this type of behavior is quite common during near-death experiences!"

A five-minute cessation of the elderly victim's weird drivel was followed with more indecipherable blabber. "I'm really not feeling that well right now, General Zaroff. I cannot possibly go hunting with you tomorrow morning. I plan to be leaving your residence soon and be away from your *hospital*ity," the elderly unconscious patient peculiarly babbled.

"The man is obviously linking remote ideas and people," the second doctor on *O.R.* duty declared. "Georg and General Zaroff are probably hunting friends of this old man. Nurse Reynolds," Dr. Ryan ordered to the third female inside the operating room, "go and see if the main desk can get any information on a General Zaroff! Contact the military if necessary! And please come right back here afterwords. We need all the help we can get!"

"I must swim and escape your evil treachery," the anonymous old gentleman mumbled from his deep state of shock. "I will escape all of your wild dogs and all of your other ferocious loose animals. I assure you I will not be your prisoner much longer!"

"He's definitely mixing vague ideas and making no logical sense whatsoever," the chief Surgeon further determined. "I wouldn't place too much credence in anything he says in his pitiful state of mind! We're hearing notions originating only from *his* lower mind and not from his learned behavior. I guarantee that anything this poor suffering soul says will be muddled and chaotic!"

"I should've stayed with Whitney! I should've stayed on the boat with Whitney!" the aged man bizarrely repeated from his horizontal position on the operating table. "There's that pistol shot again!" the old patient exclaimed as his body jerked and partially twisted on the operating table. "Where did the discharge come from and who fired the gun? Ivan no! No Ivan! Don't do that to me!"

The distressed patient suddenly changed his thought patterns and then mentioned the familiar historic name Simon Bolivar. "The *Spanish Main* is quite far from England, and I've never been to the South American coast before. Captain," the old man prattled, "and beware of the devious Spanish native pilot. He has evil eyes and I don't trust him as much as I would trust the Devil!"

"Now *he* thinks he's a sailor in another century fighting in a foreign war," the chief doctor said to support his "delusion theory." "Nurse Clemm, we'll have to use more sutures in this final area to the left."

"Ed, he probably thinks he's some sort of British mercenary," the second surgeon added, "and Simon Bolivar had liberated South America from Spain's colonial dominion. I remember that fact from a college history course. Maybe General Zaroff is somehow connected to the famous General Bolivar?"

"Jim, if the old man's involved in a big war right now, I don't think he has time to be going hunting with George and General Zaroff!" the head surgeon politely admonished. "Now let's fully detach and remove the spleen and sew-up the remaining tissue! This old man is in a war all right. He's battling for his life!"

"Captain, the native pilot we took aboard wants to blow-up the ship using its explosive cargo!" the old fellow distinctly articulated. "I'll never see Lizzie again! We'll all die before our time when those powder kegs go off! I'll never see my dear Lizzie again!"

"Who on Earth is Lizzie?" Nurse Clemm wanted to know. "This man's subconscious mind is more interesting than any noontime television soap opera!"

"Probably a former girlfriend in England that jilted him back in *World War II*," Dr. James Ryan surmised and related. "After we get the spleen problem rectified we'll concentrate on the man's broken bones and then clean-up the rest of his superficial skin wounds. We'll take one priority at a time going from most major down to least minor."

The aged patient was encountering severe breathing difficulties and regrettably his vital signs were waning. The doctors and nurses worked feverishly to stabilize the elderly fellow's heartbeat, oxygen intake and vacillating blood pressure. All the while the unconscious old man was making more enigmatic recitations.

"Major Morris, that is quite an interesting souvenir that you have there, I must admit," the man lying prone on the operating table mumbled. "You say you obtained the strange object in India! Why won't you sell it to me? Why can't you sell it to me?"

Several seconds later more arcane words emerged from the old man's lips. "Herbert, my dear Herbert! Crushed in the factory wheels at such a tender age! My heart is disconsolate! My mood is one of despondency! My tortured spirit has been devastated!"

"What in the world is he talking about now?" Nurse Clark nervously inquired. "This is rather abnormal and borderline insane, to say the least. Who do you suppose this Herbert is?"

"I've heard those words before somewhere but there are bits and pieces missing between the *object* part and the Herbert part. I remember from a college literature course a certain Herbert involved in some kind of horrible painful terrible death," Dr. James Ryan revealed. "But right this moment my mind can't connect the dots!"

"Where Jim? Try to remember!" the chief surgeon asked. "Those odd words do sound somewhat familiar now that you've mentioned it. Oh Nurse Reynolds, welcome back to the operating room. Hand me the smaller scalpel so that I can contour this remaining muscle tissue better."

"Who is Herbert?" Nurse Ginny Clemm re-actively asked. "And I wish Herbert had a last name. There must be ten thousand Herberts listed just in the Philadelphia phone book!"

"I know that I've heard those general words before," Dr. James Ryan insisted, "and I believe they have something to do with my undergraduate academic preparation before I entered *Jeff'* Med' School! I wish I had paid better attention in class so that I could recall exactly what the old man is alluding to and recollect what college course I had heard them!"

"The patient's blood pressure is decreasing to a very dangerous level, 100 over 50," the chief surgeon anxiously pointed out. "The old man's life is definitely in jeopardy, hanging on a thread. Let's concentrate our skills on salvaging him!"

"Ed, should we contact a priest?" Anita Clark reflexively asked. "Circumstances can't get any more critical for him than they are right now."

"Not yet," the head doctor answered. "Go see if you can find Dr. Crane. If he's not busy, ask him to come here immediately," the main surgeon ordered through his surgical mask. "Crane was a literature professor before he opted to attend med' school. This man seems to be referring to sophisticated literary dialogue that's very intriguing to say the least."

"Maybe he's melding stories and his subconscious mind is attempting to symbolically convey some important information to us," Dr. James Ryan suggested. "He's definitely linking formerly unconnected personalities and persons."

"If our literature premise is correct," the chief surgeon proposed, "I think Dr. Crane is the most qualified person on our staff to interpret this fellow's baffling ramblings."

"Bill, don't abandon me!" the old man slurred and ranted aloud. "Our gold sacks are too heavy. I beg you, let's discard half our gold! I say, let's leave our booty here for the wolves. Only man has a need and a lust for gold! Our gold is worthless out here!"

"He actually thinks he's now somebody else," Nurse Clemm said. "I think this man must have a multiple-personality syndrome. He keeps changing his identity to a new character, does not identify his fictional person but conversely, he does not remember who he himself' is!"

"Ed, you need a break! Let me help you sew-up the incision," Dr. Ryan offered. "Every second counts. I'm fascinated by this old gent and want to go to medical extremes and do everything humanly possible to save his life. What's *he* muttering now?"

"Those bones are Bill's, eaten by wolves the same as Georg had been," the old man concluded in a subconscious flashback that had mysteriously surfaced. "And now that sick infected wolf is craving me for its next meal!"

The old gentleman gasped on the table and everyone trying to keep him alive momentarily held their breaths. Fortunately *he* did not expire and then renewed his erratic sentences just as Dr. Joshua Crane entered the operating room.

"Dr. Crane," Dr. Ryan greeted, "I'd like you to listen to this man's utterances and determine what he's describing. We believe he's reciting, or should I say 'paraphrasing' certain passages from literature and that he might be substituting the fictional personality for that of his own," Dr. Ryan accurately explained. "It's a very fascinating phenomenon indeed and you're the most qualified person on the staff to recognize literary passages!"

"Okay Jim," Dr. Joshua Crane acknowledged. "I'll try and lend my literary knowledge although it's been over twenty years since I quit my mundane teaching post at *Villanova* and entered prestigious *Jeff' Medical School*."

Several minutes had elapsed without any distinguishable verbalization coming from the old gentleman's mouth. Then finally he slowly stated without any emotion evident in his weak voice, "Strike me a savage blow with your battle-ax, you craven fool. And after you do I shall lift my head up from the floor and screw it back onto my head. And then you'll have to journey to the Green Chapel a year hence so that I may have the pleasure of decapitating you. You have indeed met your equal."

"It sounds like he's reciting the text from one of the Arthurian legends," Dr. Crane realized and described. "If I remember correctly some offensive monster invaded Camelot and one of King Arthur's knights had accepted *his* challenge. Now the brave knight is doomed to perish at the hands of the supernatural ogre, who had just received the knight's strongest blow. But who the knight is or who the giant villain is presently eludes my memory."

"And Katrina, I love you so and hope that someday I can be your faithful husband," the old man slowly enunciated from his still-horizontal position upon the operating table. "I don't know too much about farming but I can learn quite quickly if I have to. And the view of the Hudson from here is quite spectacular! Where are old Nicholas Vedder and my dear friend Van Bummel? Where is Wolf?"

"Dr. Crane," Head Nurse Anita Clark spoke after the old man had stopped reciting, "he was speaking a half-hour ago of someone he held dearly named Lizzie and now he's speaking fondly of a lady named Katrina. And this is the third time he's mentioned *wolf.*"

"It could be Katrina from a popular Russian novel but my wild hunch is that he's referring to Katrina Van Tassel in Washington Irving's classic novella 'Legend of Sleepy Hollow'," Dr. Crane hypothesized and stated. "However, he'll have to provide more story details for me to be certain!"

"I have to get Gunpowder back to Hans Van Ripper soon," the old man prattled. "Gunpowder's no match for any Daredevil, that's for sure!"

"That's the second time he's referred to *gunpowder*," Ginny Clemm declared.

"Okay now, Gunpowder and Daredevil were two horses in Washington Irving's Sleepy Hollow story," Dr. Crane authoritatively announced to his puzzled audience. "Gunpowder was a slow about-to-die gray plow-horse that Ichabod had ridden to Katrina Van Tassel's party and Daredevil was the horse ridden to the affair by Brom Bones, Ichabod's chief rival for Katrina's hand in marriage," Dr. Joshua Crane related. "But the old man seems to also be combining some characters like Van Bummel the schoolmaster and Nicolas Vedder the inn owner from the story 'Rip Van Winkle' with particular people like Brom Bones and Katrina Van Tassel from the tale 'Legend of Sleepy Hollow.' And Wolf was Rip Van Winkle's hunting dog. And I remember Washington Irving's Ichabod very well because *his* last name happens to be the same as mine, Crane!"

"Dr. Crane, we're glad you've arrived to help us interpret all of this," Nurse Ginny Clemm commended. "I would've thought that 'gunpowder' was an explosive material and that 'the daredevil' the old man was recognizing was an enemy putting the old man's literary character in jeopardy! I think he's relating to near-death experiences in literature because his subconscious is aware that *his* own death might be imminent!"

Then the old man again proceeded with his random literary revelations. "May has locked Agatha in the vault! I must do something quickly because Ben Price is hot on my trail. If I set Agatha free," the old man softly disclosed, "I'll never be able to marry Annabel Adams."

"That's a rather familiar statement, but now I'll have to take an educated guess," Dr. Crane informed his medical colleagues. "It's got the makings of a surprise ending story with the bank vault scenario, and my mind seems to think the writer would most likely be Saki, Mark Twain or O. Henry. All three authors were fond of writing surprise-ending stories and all three writers had unique pseudonyms," the former literature professor maintained. "O. Henry was William Sydney Porter, Mark Twain's real name was Samuel Langhorne Clemens and Saki's actual name was H.H. Munro. But as for the exact title of the story, it completely escapes my recollection at the moment. Perhaps if I could hear a little more."

Dr. Crane stayed and decoded some other literary allusions that the old man muttered and mumbled. He expertly identified lines from Mark Twain's classic short story "The Jumping Frog" and another narrative association from one of Arthur Conan Doyle's Sherlock Holmes detective adventures. Finally, when Joshua Crane heard the names "Maken of the Blue Boar Inn" and "David of Doncaster," he automatically knew that those two characters exclusively belonged in a *Robin Hood* tale.

Suddenly all of the patient's vital signs ceased. Dr. Crane assisted his two colleagues and their nurses in a valiant-but-vain attempt at resuscitating the motorcycle accident victim back to life, but the *O.R.* heart monitor's waves soon collapsed into a "flat-line."

"No readings indicated! He's not responding!" Dr. Ryan yelled in frustration. "Let's try the defibrillator and see if we can shock *his* heart back into a rhythm!"

The medical team's heroic efforts were to no avail. The old man's heart chambers no longer throbbed, his lungs no longer yearned for oxygen and his eloquent literary words and ideas no longer escaped from *his* pallid lips. The battered body was respectfully covered with a white sheet and the three doctors and three nurses shook their heads in disappointment at their joint failure.

Ten minutes later in the busy hallway outside the *Jeff'* O.R. suite the three surgeons and their respective nurses were confronted with

100

the same paramedics that had transported the old man to the hospital from 7th and Walnut Street. "Doctors, I had found this book at the scene of the accident," the very honest ambulance driver excitedly said, "and some lady testified to the police that the old man was standing next to the curb reading the book when the motorcycle hit-and-run took place. I forgot to give one of your nurses the literary work in all the confusion upon delivering the old man!"

Dr. Ryan accepted the paperback book from the short burly ambulance driver and read the cover aloud: "*An Anthology of Twelve Novellas*." Much to the amazement of the others on the *O.R.* medical team surrounding him, Dr. James Ryan very slowly and deliberately recited from the collection's index the twelve titles represented. "The Interlopers" by Saki, "The Most Dangerous Game" by Richard Connell, "Blow Up with the Brig" by Wilkie Collins, "Love of Life" by Jack London, "The Monkey's Paw" by W.W. Jacobs, "Sir Gawain and the Green Knight, Arthurian Legend," "Legend of Sleepy Hollow" by Washington Irving, "Rip Van Winkle" by Washington Irving, "A Retrieved Reformation" by O. Henry, "The Adventure of the Speckled Band" by Sir Arthur Conan Doyle, "The Celebrated Jumping Frog of Calavaras County" by Mark Twain and "Will Stuteley's Rescue, A Robin Hood Tale."

"This is absolutely mind-boggling and rather incredible!" Dr. Joshua Crane exclaimed to his stunned colleagues. "The man obviously was vicariously believing and role-playing that he was a main character in each of the twelve stories in this short fiction anthology book."

"And his mind remarkably remembered almost every story in the exact chronological sequence from one to twelve!" Dr. Ryan declared in a very astounded and excited tone of voice.

Just then a Philadelphia police officer showed-up at the *Thomas Jefferson University Hospital* Emergency Desk and was directed by the clerk on duty to the area where the six operating room associates had just performed their unsuccessful surgery.

"Are you Dr. Edgar Poe?" the patrolman inquired.

"Why yes," the head surgeon politely answered. "What can I do for you Officer?"

"I'm Corporal Banks," the policeman matter-of-factly introduced himself. "The department just captured the guy on the motorcycle that had crushed the old man at 7th and Walnut," Patrolman Banks informed. "He was higher than a kite on drugs when they pulled him over on Roosevelt Boulevard. What a loser!"

"And is that the old man's wallet you have in your hand?" Nurse Virginia Clemm alertly asked the blue-uniformed keeper of the peace.

"Yes it is," Officer Banks confirmed. "The credit cards were stolen and all cash had been removed. We apprehended the petty thief six blocks away at Broad and Market on the other side of *City Hall*." Then the policeman handed the black leather wallet to Dr. Poe. "The handwritten *ID* that the old man had kept in the wallet is still inside! The old man did fill out his name! We now have his name and address!"

Dr. Edgar Poe opened the dead man's wallet and inspected the owner's name. "M. Valdemar!" he said as his bride-to-be Virginia Clemm looked on with a confused-but-grim expression on her countenance.

"Dr. Crane, why is your face so pale?" Dr. Poe anxiously asked. "Did you know this character named M. Valdemar somewhere in your past? Joshua, please say something! Does the name M. Valdemar ring a bell?"

"Red, White and Blue America"

The attractive svelte secretary showed the enthusiastic novice journalist into the prominent politician's walnut-paneled office. "Congressman Ennis," the young *Tulsa Free Press* reporter greeted. "My name is Jackson Lee and I'm here to do a big feature story on what America used to be like before the dramatic emergence of the *Heartland.*"

"That will be all Miss Burger," the sagacious government official imperatively stated. "Mr. Jackson Lee, I'd like to introduce you to my longtime confidante General Mitchell Lassiter. I was telling the Army General about your scheduled visit and since we're both old-timers, my military companion reckoned he would stay around and reminisce the past with me," Congressman Bertram Ennis said. "Mitch and I both go back a long way before the year 2070, I can guarantee you that!"

"Pleasure to make your acquaintance General," reporter Lee said as he vigorously shook both elderly officials' hands. "I'm really quite thrilled to be getting this huge assignment. It could represent a major breakthrough in my budding journalistic career. I hope I'm equal to the task. It's my biggest challenge at the *Free Press* by far."

"I think we'll get started with the business at hand," Congressman Bertram Ennis indicated while reaching into his top drawer and then removing and unfolding an enlarged-but-aged tarnished photograph showing a rather huge red and blue map of the continental United States. "I'll let General Lassiter provide you with a little background and then I'll monopolize the discussion from there on out."

"In all due respect Congressman Ennis," General Lassiter interrupted in deference to his longtime acquaintance, "you ought to go first so that this thing could have a sort of organized chronological time line, if you know what I mean."

"Thank you kindly Mitch!" the glib Oklahoma federal legislator replied. "Now Jackson, here's a very interesting blown-up photo' of a red and white map with *me* as a young boy standing beside the illustration. It was snapped in the year 2000 on the morning following that year's November Presidential election. Does it look at all familiar to you?"

"I've seen that same map before and I had studied it in a political science class at *Oklahoma University*," the callow reporter eagerly injected into the exchange. "I can spout-off a lot of interesting figures from that troubling era. Republican George W. Bush won the Presidency over Senator Al Gore of Tennessee although Democrat

Gore had gotten over five-hundred-thousand more popular votes than Bush had received."

"You must have been on the Dean's List all four years at *Sooner University!*" lawmaker Bertram Ennis commended. "You're smart enough Mr. Lee to address the Senate up on *Capitol Hill*. And please notice General," the Congressman embellished, "the Electoral College statistics show at the bottom of the picture that Bush received 271 electoral votes and Gore accumulated only 266, even though the Democrat decisively won the popular count! The Founding Fathers knew exactly what they were doing when they created the Electoral College," Ennis opined with a smile. "Sometimes the popular vote is quite fallible and the masses, or should I use the euphemism *public,* can make the wrong choice."

General Mitchell Lassiter cleared his throat to signal that he wished to contribute something relevant to the conversation. "And the red on the Year 2000 map is mostly southern and mid-western United States and what is now in 2070 affectionately called *Heartland America.* The red areas show the states carried by Republican Bush, and the blue areas represent the more industrialized urban states plagued with minorities that were won by Democrat Gore."

"That must have caused quite a bit of turmoil and controversy back at the turn of the century!" Jackson Lee observed and commented as he vigorously jotted down some vital notes relevant to his future article. "Everyone today knows that the terms Democrats and Democracy at the turn of the century meant socialistic welfare along with radical change and that the words Republic and Republican basically translated into respect for law and order, tradition and property."

Congressman Ennis paused, scratched his chin and pensively considered organizing all the associated ideas floating around in his head into a logical progression. "The most astonishing irony to me is the fact that the red and blue states appearing on the Year 2000 map are almost identical to the geo-political configuration of the United States today in 2070!" the statesman marveled and stated. "It's really rather remarkable when you weigh the similarity between that Year 2000 election results and the way the United States today is demographically arranged!"

"Yes Congressman," Jackson Lee impetuously acknowledged. "But Florida and Texas are now Blue States just like California, New Mexico and Arizona are. How did that all happen?" the fledgling reporter inquired, feigning complete ignorance on the subject. "I mean Gentlemen, I know how it generally happened but I need some hardcore direct quotes from you two distinguished citizens to give my article some real sizzle."

"Well young man, perhaps I can hit the ball into the general's court for a brief description of how security had changed in the dreadful Year 2001," the Congressman deferred. "That's what really tipped the scales and made the country sober-up in a hurry."

"Well Mr. Lee," General Lassiter declared with a slightly hoarse voice, "September 11, 2001 changed the mood and the focus of the country altogether. Actually, it was a blessing in disguise, a jolting wake-up call so to speak. Al Qaeda and the Taliban in Afghanistan and that tyrant Saddam Hussein in Iraq had to be dealt with. And because of economic necessity and cultural preservation the Red States today are still Republican conservative strongholds and the less-prosperous and highly-populated Blue States remain Democratic bastions of mediocrity." The General lit a cigar to signify to Bertram Ennis that *his* initial oratory had terminated.

Jackson Lee ceased his intense scribbling for a moment and begged for clarification. Congressman Ennis was more than glad to oblige. "After 9-11 Jackson, politicians began realizing our national security priorities and dropped their need to always be politically correct. Of course, two severe economic recessions, a major crippling depression, unprecedented stock market instability and the bankruptcies of California, Texas and Florida drastically accelerated matters to finally come to a dramatic head."

"Didn't all of the illegal aliens help cause the *Second Great Depression of 2031?*" the highly-motivated and alert reporter asked. "Exactly how did that debacle happen? You two Gentlemen had experienced the financial disaster first hand!"

"Productive white workers in the computer and microchip high tech' industries led the way by first evacuating California in droves because of mammoth state deficits and over-taxation without adequate taxpayer representation," Bertram Ennis explained. "In 2025 there were over twenty million illegal Mexican aliens living across the country and an estimated ten million were residing in California alone. And that's not counting the twenty million Mexicans that had already become legal because of ultra-liberal amnesty laws. That's when the crap really hit the fan!"

"And California alone had over four million illegal Mexicans driving around without motor vehicle licenses or automobile insurance," the General chimed-in before strongly puffing on *his* big cigar. Then the military official gathered his thoughts for a second and soon continued his interpretation of post-2000 history. "And Hispanics in California, Florida, Texas, Arizona and New Mexico were all-too-generously given state welfare and federal government benefits so that ambitious devious Democrats could win *their* favor. The leeching illegal Mexicans also would get free education for their children and job training for themselves even though they weren't naturalized citizens," Lassiter recollected and disclosed. "It got to the point where illegal aliens had equal if not superior rights under the *Constitution* and under our federal and state employment laws than *our* regular citizens did. And then, besides medical care welfare rights, the idiotic Democrats were proposing giving all Mexicans, either legal green card holders or illegal aliens the right to vote!"

"What a complicated political and economic travesty!" Jackson Lee concluded as he eagerly jotted-down more notes. "The whole country was being convoluted!" the rookie journalist deftly commiserated. "America was in a devastating self-destruct mode!"

"And also, just as an example," General Lassiter grunted with his raspy voice, "my uncle's car back in 2019 was hit by an illegal alien Mexican driver transporting twenty California farm workers in a dilapidated van. All twenty-one Mexicans automatically got free hospital benefits while my uncle's insurance company had to compensate *him* for injuries he had sustained and for massive damage done to *his* vehicle," the General recalled and balked. "The white flight to other states and the cost of benefits for illegal aliens eventually caused the sun-belt Mexican-infested states to all go bankrupt. And the federal government, in all its defective wisdom, then called upon the taxpayers in other already-struggling states to bail their warm-climate counterparts out!"

"And once the federal government began cracking-down on hundreds of Arab terrorists," Bertram Ennis articulated, "the Muslim religious fanatics all fled to the ultra-liberal Democratic Blue Sanctuary States where security was more lax and where prospective targets were softer. Terrorism was flourishing in Blue America."

"Please don't forget the three key New England *White States*, Vermont, New Hampshire and Maine," General Lassiter reminded his two attentive listeners. "They're right now about to secede from the *Union* and the Red States are going to follow suit. The second American *Civil War* is imminent and this next time around *we* rebels are going to win and re-establish this nation's original way of life based on solid Christian values, on obedience of law and on the *Protestant Work Ethic*. Lincoln never imagined the can of worms he had opened with that regrettable first *Civil War*," the General enunciated very clearly. "This time around we're gonna' eliminate the ugly perversions connected with the parasitic *mongrel welfare ethnics*," the high-ranking military man emphasized in what he considered a humorous play-on-homophones with his use of "ethics" and "ethnics."

The two older gentlemen then reviewed the argument that cultures like the Japanese and the Chinese had a distinct advantage over the United States' "salad mix population." The two Oriental countries each had a fixed people base that shared a common culture, history, national identity, language, sense of purpose and a protected gene pool. Those particular strengths allowed the Japanese and the Red Chinese nations to flourish while America was in a state of decline and losing its fundamental Christian heritage, its free enterprise system and its pioneering spirit. According to Ennis and Lassiter, the *United States Constitution* was undermining and subverting the *Declaration of Independence's* moral base that had given blessed Americans a "common free will Christian direction."

"Social issues like gay rights and gay marriage, a woman's right to choose abortion, and the 'red herring issue' of alleged white discrimination towards minorities eventually incensed even the most tolerant whites," Bertram Ennis elaborated, "and when the recessions and the calamitous depression came along the exploited whites automatically rebelled against harsh government mandates, formed town and state militias and chased the parasitic minorities into the already failing Democratic Blue States, which in turn could not economically support the great largesse of parasitic Hispanics, blacks and Arabs."

Jackson Lee then unilaterally discussed that *he* had studied in college how the original European immigrants had instinctively settled in geographic regions of America that were comparable to the climates they had experienced in Europe. "The British settled from Virginia up to *New England*, and the Poles, Swedes and Norwegians migrated to cold-winter states Michigan, Minnesota and Wisconsin, which all reminded them of life back in Scandinavia and in Warsaw," the young reporter voluntarily contributed. "And the Spanish sought warmer temperatures that are now emblematic of California, Texas, New Mexico, Arizona and Florida. And isn't it a strange coincidence," Jackson Lee academically generalized and stressed, "that Hispanics had in the early 2000s once again taken over the warm sun-belt states by default after productive free-enterprise whites had abandoned those bankrupt political entities and fled to the safety of *Heartland America.*"

The young reporter knew quite well that the Congressman had granted *him* the exclusive interview and had invited General Lassiter to sit in only as a courtesy to the journalist's wealthy father, influential computer entrepreneur Emerson Lee, who like the Congressman and the General wanted the Red and White elements of the United States to return to the pre-1950s political philosophy of "separate but *un*-equal." Minorities like blacks, Hispanics, Arabs and New Age Orientals were now free to live in the American Red and White regions, but *they* were compelled to be producers and not simply consumers living off the generosity of the government in a "despicable welfare nanny state." Also, those three minority ethnic groups were soon to be reduced to the *class*ification of "semi-citizens" with whites having ten votes in any given *Heartland* election and blacks, migrant Hispanics and itinerant Orientals having just one vote per individual.

"The fanciful impractical idea of America being a melting pot of many nationalities has in the last century proven to be a dismal canard," the Congressman prattled. "At one time up to the year 1950 *it* had been a worthy ideal. Irish, Italians, Germans, Poles, Swedes, French, British and Norwegians all shared two necessary characteristics. They were essentially Caucasians and they were also mostly industrious Christians having a desire to better themselves by means of their own labor and sacrifice. The European immigrants desired to be self-sufficient, wanted to learn English and had too much pride to be dependent on the government dole. After the detrimental *Civil Rights Act* of 1964," Bertram Ennis further mentioned, "the entire country began going haywire and started drifting away from fundamental Christian morality with lawyers, judges and politically correct politicians rewriting the *U.S. Constitution* through distorted interpretations and coincidentally and consequently, changing the general fabric of American civilization for the worse. That's precisely when this great nation along with American exceptionalism began becoming contaminated!"

"My friend Congressman Ennis is absolutely correct in his very vivid evaluation," General Lassiter told young Jackson Lee. "The new cosmopolitan mix in urban areas soon threatened the suburbs, poisoning the minds of young white people with things like rap music, baggy pants, tattoos, male earrings and sadistic body piercing. White teenagers soon looked like and imitated urban derelicts, and as you know Jackson," Mitchell Lassiter pontificated, "the way you look often reflects the way you think. If you look like a cannibal you're gonna' think and eventually act like a savage. Anyway, white suburban kids were coming under a very bad influence, an influence that preached idleness, laziness and rebellion against God, against adults, against laws, against culture and against country. All of this social disorganization was done under the guise of *democracy* and then the first *Ten Amendments of the Constitution* were being maliciously and egregiously used to dismantle the basic teachings of the very essential *Ten Commandments*."

"I really get the vital message now!" an animated Jackson Lee exclaimed. "Christian morality was being savagely attacked by the lawyers, judges and politicians arguing that the separation of church and state was quite consistent with the *Constitution* and that moral and racial discrimination were fundamentally unconstitutional. How insidious! The government itself' along with harmful *ACLU* policies was crazily tearing the fiber of Christian morality, of American free enterprise and of the Protestant work ethic apart."

"Exactly Jackson, and all of *that* ugly societal disgrace was being done in the name of democracy and liberty," General Lassiter angrily declared. "Freedom and rights for minorities started to redefine and then erode indispensable American qualities such as individual responsibility, courtesy towards others, hard work, family unity and basic Christian values. Congressman Ennis, please tell Jackson Lee here what you had so sagely related to me just before our young friend entered your office."

"Gladly General Lassiter," the gray-haired chubby orator somberly answered. "American lawyers, judges, civil rights leaders and politicians soon became what the ancient Greek philosopher Plato called 'Sophists'. The American villains were clever demagogues that persuasively used language to destroy the traditional American way of life. The obnoxious liberal cult would convincingly argue that black was white and that there were no differences between the two, and *their* totally naïve gullible audiences believed their hollow statements and their shallow perceptions. But *their* arguments lacked one vital ingredient?"

"What was that?" young Jackson Lee impulsively and succinctly asked.

"Their ideas were ethically empty. Their words were hollow and they had little grounding in morals, in ethics or in hard work. Their propaganda speeches and faulty assumptions were fundamentally valueless, or should I say American *value*less, ha, ha, ha!"

"Yes Jackson," the military expert inflexibly agreed with his philosophical political acquaintance. "When the charlatan lawyers, judges and politicians gave lazy non-productive consumers the same rights and privileges as ambitious producers enjoyed, the whole country went topsy-turvy. And when the millions of illegal aliens were granted the right to vote in 2033 by a new detrimental *Constitutional Amendment*, then *that* chicanery was the straw that broke the proverbial camel's back," General Lassiter insisted. "Not only did the government put a strain and a drain on the free enterprise economy with free education for illegal aliens, free hospitalization, social security benefits and loose national borders, it also opened the doors for the *Second Great Depression*, which eventually organized productive whites to assert their power in what has now graphically evolved into the separate Red and White States," the knowledgeable General explained. "This dichotomy left the pathetic Blue States with few alternatives. Even today the liberal Blue States continue to decline; their buildings, parks and monuments are virtually in ruin and *their* morality has decayed into rampant random crime and widespread social chaos. Decadence has become the Blue States' hallmark. Gentlemen, the *Second Civil War* is at hand, and this time the right side is going to emerge victorious!"

"You must understand dear Jackson that discrimination could actually be a good thing!" Congressman Bertram Ennis maintained. "If good did not discriminate against evil, there would be no difference between the two poles. That was the objective of the liberal left-wing lawyers, judges and legislators. They wanted to erase all noticeable differences between good and evil so that it would be difficult for the average American to effectively *discriminate* between the diverse moral and immoral values' terminals. The liberal stooges desired to get rid of black and while absolutes and replace them with arbitrary gray areas, thus making all social matters relative in nature!"

"Now I believe I understand completely," Jackson Lee affirmed. "That's when powerful conservative groups in the *Heartland* began buying black homes and property and paying minorities modest sums to move to the debt-ridden Blue States. Since the Blue Areas of the country were crumbling in the midst of its *Second Great Depression*, it was easy to entice most of the few blacks living in the *Heartland* to migrate to the large morally and economically bankrupt cities in the financially doomed Blue Zones. What a brilliant strategy! Social engineering at its best!"

"And now the urban areas in the Blue Regions are more like war zones instead of crime zones!" Congressman Ennis concluded and lectured. "Democracy carried out to its maximum extent amounts to anarchy! And that's exactly what the liberals have created for themselves so let them live and die with absolute democracy I say! I mean," the florid-faced corpulent Congressman paused to chuckle, "whoever thought that Tulsa, Oklahoma in the middle of the productive *Red Heartland* would grow into a flourishing modern slum-less city of ten million ambitious people and that our great metropolis would be destined to become the next federal *Capital of the United States.*"

"Let the terrorists and the minorities now blame, crucify and torture the liberal lawyers, legislators and politically correct judges that caused the second great societal catastrophe," General Lassiter proclaimed. "Let the Blue Welfare States be damned! And there are many disgusted formerly liberal patriotic revolutionaries in places like New York and Pennsylvania that are eager to ally with the *Red Heartland* and with the *White New England Patriot Movement* as soon as the next civil war breaks out! The Congressman and I are both impatiently waiting for the second Ft. Sumter to happen!"

"Thank you Gentlemen for the very enlightening interview!" the aspiring and perspiring journalist ecstatically exclaimed. "I believe I now have sufficient documentation to author a really terrific and truly accurate breakthrough article! Who knows? I might become the next Thomas Paine leading the *Second Revolutionary War!*"

Jackson Lee had plenty to contemplate on his pleasant drive back to his suburban townhouse on the outskirts of Tulsa. He was the main heir to his father's massive computer networking empire. His ongoing love affair with Melanie Collier was going full tilt. And the fortunate upstart reporter lived in a safe Red State where strict punishments were given to chronic offenders and to recalcitrant riffraff, and instead of penitentiaries, the government saved money by deporting its "maximum three-felony criminal element" to the chaotic Blue States by means of the *Second Underground Railroad.*

'I can play a big role in the upcoming *Second Civil War,* or should I more definitively say the *Second Revolutionary War!*' Jackson contemplated as he drove his expensive red sports car out of the city toward Claremore on old reliable *Interstate-44.* 'And now because the *Heartland's* economy is booming all the way from Denver to Virginia Beach, our no-nonsense conservative coalition states can now efficiently patrol all borders and keep illegal aliens and international criminals out,' the young fellow seriously evaluated. 'And the *Heartland* has much to be thankful for. Our schools are morally sound academic institutions that do not tolerate annoying discipline problems, and the urban ghetto decadence is rapidly bringing the liberal Blue States to impotency and self-implosion. A

Second Revolutionary War might be averted if the Blue States suddenly disintegrate, but that's highly unlikely and it actually constitutes wishful thinking on my part. But *that* remote prospect will never happen because of dangerous rabble factions fighting each other for power and because of corrupt police and government officials antagonizing the good citizens by catering to the corrupt special interest groups that have gained dominance all over the doomed Blue Regions. Another *Civil War* is inevitable!'

After Jackson Lee entered his deluxe townhouse, he immediately stepped to his desktop computer, sat down in his swivel chair and predictably checked his e-mail correspondence. 'Melanie usually e-mails me every morning,' he thought with a blithe heart. 'I wonder what flowery language she's concocted today? Quite honestly, she's a little too altruistic for her own good!'

The happy young man cheerfully opened his e-mail box and conscientiously read his girlfriend's letter, which was accompanied by an e-mail attachment in the form of a horrendous-looking photograph of one Melanie Collier. 'My God! She's got horrible black and blue marks and cuts all over her face! What on Earth has happened to her?'

Jackson,

Please help me, Jackson! Late last night, Blue renegades had captured and beaten me outside my Tulsa home and the evil spies have transported me in a stolen plane from Oklahoma to Kentucky, and then across the Ohio River into Cincinnati.

In exchange for my safe return, the kidnappers are demanding a large ransom of 5 million dollars within forty-eight hours or else they plan to immediately execute me.

Here are the instructions that the Blue criminals have permitted me to e-mail to you. First take a plane into Louisville. Then Travel to Newport, Kentucky, which is a town several miles east of Covington. Drive to the end of Monmouth Street where a twenty-foot-long blue motorboat will be waiting to cross you into Cincinnati on the Ohio side of the river.

112

You will be conducted to an abandoned warehouse at the corner of Lawrence and Arch Streets, just off the *I-71* exit ramp. My abductors are ruthless black ghetto delinquents that have threatened to rape me before executing me if you attempt any trickery. I beg you to be here with the money on the 23rd at 7 p.m. prompt.

Please be careful.

Love always,

Melanie

Several tears formed and glistened in the e-mail recipient's eyes, for he truly loved Melanie Collier, a quixotic middle-class *University of Oklahoma* senior that Emerson Lee absolutely loathed. 'I would always warn Melanie not to trust anyone, especially strangers,' Jackson lamented. 'She's been entirely too idealistic and too sympathetic towards the lower classes for her own good ever since I've known her. I wish she wouldn't try and help those that would take advantage of her innocence and ultimately harm her!'

The harried junior reporter exited his townhouse, hastily locked the front door and next frantically dashed to his speedy red sports car. He motored to downtown Tulsa where he would seek help and guidance from his filthy rich multimillionaire father. Young Jackson's breathing was labored and his heart was pounding heavily in his chest as his speedy automobile neared the revered *Lee Computer Corporation Headquarters*.

Very distressed, Jackson Lee motored into *his* designated parking spot in the corporation's high-rise garage and soon took the elevator up to the penthouse suite on the thirty-fifth floor. The flustered young man hurriedly bypassed the preoccupied receptionist and the *CEO's* main secretary and then the on-a-mission vernal visitor startled Emerson Lee as *he* burst into his father's luxuriously furnished office unannounced. The elder Lee was casually conversing on the wide screen "speaker-video-conference-phone" with his fellow *Heartland* advocate, the ultra-conservative Congressman Bertram Ennis.

"Dad! I gotta' speak to you right now!" the disturbed son exclaimed. "It's a dire emergency!"

"I'll talk to you later Bert! I have to do some family business!" Emerson awkwardly finished on the telephone before hanging up.

"Did something traumatic happen to your mother?" the father anxiously asked.

"No, Dad! Mom is fine!" the son replied.

"Now, Jackson, I know you're intensely excited about getting the coveted newspaper story and the special interview with the Congressman and with General Lassiter. I just want to show you Son something rather interesting that I've been keeping for decades in my office desk!"

"Dad! This is very important!" the young reporter pleaded. "I've gotta' ask an extremely big favor of you!"

"First Son, let me show you this old literature textbook I've pilfered and saved from *my* eighth grade English class," Emerson Lee implored as he opened a bottom desk drawer. "It was published way back in the year 2003. My father was livid when he read the literary selections and your grandfather vehemently protested to the politically correct school board about the quality of the lousy stories represented."

"Dad, I want to tell you something that's of urgent importance to *me* right now!" Jackson nervously protested. "Something's happened to..."

"I'll hear your problem after I finish saying what *I* started!" Emerson Lee egotistically admonished and overruled. "Now Jackson, just listen to this litany of authors that appears in this propaganda-oriented eighth grade literature textbook. 'Gloria Gonzalez, Yoshika Uchida, Gwendolyn Brooks, Maya Angelou, Julio Noboa Polanco, Martin Luther King, Judith Ortiz Cofer, Langston Hughes, Julia Alverez, Ophelia Rivas, Nereida Roman, Rudolpho A. Anaya'....don't you see what I'm driving at Son?" the thoroughly disgusted father boomed. "This atrocious index of authors was out-and-out standard brainwashing and it was attempting to send white America's children on a terrible guilt trip! Whatever happened to great white authors like William Shakespeare, Poe, London, Irving, Twain, Dumas, O. Henry, Doyle and H.G. Wells? The greatest authors in Western Civilization were being demoted in our American public schools to play second string to these obscure black and Hispanic wannabes'! What an academic disgrace that was!"

"Dad, I have to talk to you about Melanie!" the son loudly-but-politely interrupted. "She's been kidnapped by Blue renegades and taken all the way to Cincinnati. And now the lousy thugs want a five-million-dollar ransom!"

"Son, that's the best thing that could have ever happened!" the father haughtily bellowed in a rare emotional outburst. "Good bye

114

and good riddance to that good-for-nothing humanitarian bleeding-heart girlfriend of yours! I wish you had never met that untrustworthy radical-minded tramp in the first place!"

"But Dad, I love her!" Jackson begged. "She's asked me for my help. How could I possibly refuse?" The son then reached into his pocket and gave his wealthy father a copy of the urgent e-mail *he* had recently received and printed. The *CEO* of *Emerson Enterprises* and its six subsidiaries quickly scanned the short "emergency *SOS* letter."

"I'll tell you what, Son!" Emerson calmly responded. "The *Second Civil War* is about to commence next Friday. Most of the *Red Heartland States* and the three *White New England States* have secretly agreed to cut off all funding to Washington. Many disgruntled white *IRS, CIA* and *FBI* agents have already conspired to come over to our side and join our noble cause to liberate our race from social slavery and from an endless national debt," the father confidentially divulged. "This recent development could be the crucial incident that triggers off the impending war a few days earlier than intended! This could be the Ft. Sumter moment we've been waiting for! I'll call General Lassiter immediately and explain your delicate situation. We'll get back to you with the particulars after *he* confers with his army colleagues and with Bertram Ennis! If we can't implode *Blue America,* we'll then have to explode it into oblivion!"

That night, Jackson Lee received a top-priority phone call from General Lassiter, who outlined *his* "well-conceived blueprint" for retrieving Melanie Collier and for also deliberately destroying several arms' warehouses "controlled by Cincinnati ghetto scum" along the Ohio River waterfront. "Your father has agreed to provide two black suitcases full of hundred dollar bills to cover the five million ransom. Now listen carefully Jackson," the high-ranking military man proceeded, "the money will be valueless in a week or so because the *Heartland Red States* will be printing our own paper currency based on *our* vibrant economy and we'll also be minting our own coins. That's why your father has agreed to go along with the plan with the soon-to-be-worthless ransom money idea!"

"Okay, General, what else do I need to know?" the heartbroken young man asked. "I'll do anything to get Melanie back safe and sound!"

"Follow to the letter the exact directions stipulated in Melanie's e-mail," the veteran General advised. "We'll dispatch three combat-ready Comanche attack helicopters from *Fort Knox* and have them available at the Louisville airport when your flight on your father's private corporate jet arrives from Tulsa. After you turn over the money and exit the abandoned Cincinnati warehouse with Melanie," the General further directed, "a hit team of crack Army commandos will land and swiftly recover you and her! Then they'll quickly fly you and Miss Collier in a Comanche over the Ohio River back into the safety of *Red Kentucky*."

"Thanks a lot for your fantastic assistance General Lassiter!" the grateful heir answered. "Your clever plan seems to be well-conceived and foolproof!"

"And there's one final detail," the General commented. "We'll be inserting a microchip into your right leg so that the Army can monitor your passage into Cincinnati. After you've crossed the river in the blue boat, we'll shut the microchip down by remote control so that the enemy won't be able to intercept any suspicious signals. Two doctors are on their way to your townhouse right now to perform the minor surgical implant procedure."

"Thanks again for your help, General! I really appreciate it! I'll be waiting for the doctors! And may God bless Red and White America!" Click.

'Maybe Dad is right and Melanie is wrong about minorities and illegal aliens!' Jackson pensively considered. 'Liberal revisionists are still attempting to rewrite history. Liberty, justice and prosperity *for all* translate into white tax dollars subsidizing health, education and welfare programs for lazy non-productive blacks and Hispanics. How could George Washington Carver experimenting with peanuts and Martin Luther King complaining about unequal rights for lazy Americans be placed on the same accomplishment scale as the remarkable achievements of Washington, Jefferson, Twain, Darwin, Einstein, Shakespeare and Sir Isaac Newton?' Jackson Lee pondered. 'Melanie definitely needs a reality check about human nature once I get her safely back to good old Oklahoma.'

On the bumpy flight from Tulsa to Louisville, the computer heir considered the falsity of "phony indoctrination ethics" that had been pounded into his brain by overprotective teachers and politically correct adults ever since pre-kindergarten. 'The General, the Congressman and Dad are right. Militant ghetto blacks, Hispanics, Arabs and White Trash populate the urban areas of *Blue America*,' he considered. 'They plan to use the extortion money from Dad to buy guns and weapons to conduct their destruction of the remaining white society in neighboring *Blue States*. WASP culture is doomed in *Blue America*. The underground economy of the *Blue States* has led to severe economic depression, to racial turmoil and to social disorganization,' Lee concluded. '*Blue State* liberal government officials have become mere puppets of vigilante street gangs and intimidating mobsters that have taken over the already-corrupt sanctuary cities. Drugs, crime and sexual perversion now dominate the ever-expanding urban zones of the diabolical *Blue States!* And chaotic Cincinnati is no exception to that very distressing rule!'

Everything in the elaborate clandestine Army commando raid was smoothly progressing as scheduled. Jackson's father's private jet landed at the newly constructed *Louisville International Airport* at 4:15 on the 23rd of the October. Captain Blake Jennison was assigned to lead the elite Comanche helicopter patrol across the river into Cincinnati. The combat-ready officer was waiting for Jackson to descend from the corporate jet, and then introduce himself and his crew to the newly arrived money messenger.

"These Comanches are much better equipped than the old Apaches ever were, even the modified upgraded version," Captain Jennison told Jackson Lee on the airport tarmac. "These babies are the finest chopper flying machines the military has to offer."

"Captain Jennison, let's discuss exactly how the rescue plan is going to unfold in the *VIP Lounge*," the concerned money courier suggested. "These suitcases are getting rather heavy."

"Good idea, Mr. Lee!" the Army Captain complimented. "Do you know the exact directions on how to get to the riverfront in Newport? I mean has General Lassiter told those details to you?"

"Yes, I've studied the road maps contained in my *National Geographic Street Finder* disk on my laptop computer at least a hundred times," the neurotic-but-determined young man answered. "It's all memorized and cataloged in my head, every single aspect."

An hour later, Jackson Lee drove an airport rental car to the end of Monmouth Street in Newport, Kentucky to have his "secret rendezvous" with the radical occupants of the twenty-foot-long blue boat. He reviewed in his mind how the current cultural pattern in *Red Heartland America* had mimicked the former social fabric of the 1950s. Blacks went to black schools and churches and only married blacks. The same held true for Hispanics. Most everyone living in *Red Heartland America* openly respected the region's no-nonsense laws and established social mores and the loyal citizens obediently stayed within their own social compartments. Blacks and Hispanics were accepted and treated courteously as long as they remained within the expectations of *their* rigid behavioral parameters. 'I'm really glad Dad has advanced me the ransom money!' the young man thought. 'Little do the greedy thugs taking me to Melanie know that the cash will be absolutely useless in less than a week!'

Jackson parked his standard four-door silver rental car at the end of Monmouth Street and quickly met the blue boat Cincinnati gangsters at the riverbank. The money carrier was nervous but tried acting nonchalant.

"Got the bread?" a tough-looking black street-wise hooligan with tattoos all over his bald head nastily asked. "That's the reason for us home boys bein' here in Red Kentucky!"

"Right here in these two suitcases," Jackson indicated. "Where's Melanie?"

"We wanna' take ya' to the gang's warehouse and count the loot first," a second punk with earrings in both lobes and a pierced nose with a diamond stud in the left nostril gruffly answered. "Then ya' could have the dumb chick if she wants to go back to Oklahoma with ya'!" the fierce-looking product from the 'hood directed.

'The microchip in my leg will soon stop functioning,' Jackson imagined as the tarnished blue motorboat propelled across the murky Ohio River toward Blue Cincinnati. 'Wait a minute! We aren't heading toward the Lawrence and Arch Street warehouse! We're going much further up river!'

The four urban guerrilla guards stared at Jackson menacingly, as the boat's navigator zipped the craft across the Ohio towards a secret destination. The passenger/courier then realized that the three attack helicopters would accidentally raid the wrong enemy stronghold situated at Lawrence and Arch. "Why aren't we going to the warehouse that was specified in Melanie's e-mail?" the young hostage inquired with a degree of alarm evident in his tone of voice. "Why a change in plans?"

"Because, Whitey. Let's now say there's been *a radical* change in plans," the bald-headed militant replied and qualified. "We wanna' make sure that you ain't bein' tailed by some honky crackers with rifles, machine guns and grenades!"

After the blue boat was stealthily docked next to a well-concealed, shadowy Cincinnati pier, Jackson's eyes gazed-up into the dusky late October sky and witnessed three Army Comanche helicopters heading across the river, twelve or so blocks away. 'The computer chip has ceased functioning and now Captain Jennison and his elite squad will never be able to track me!' the suddenly terrified money-courier realized. 'Oh well, I'll simply trade the ransom cash for Melanie and then *we'll* be taken back to the Kentucky side in the blue boat once the deal is consummated.'

A loud explosion was heard in the twilight sky and Jackson and his five escorts stared-up toward the southern horizon. One of the three choppers had been hit by a *Stinger III* shoulder-mounted missile. Seconds later the second helicopter flying in tandem also burst into flames. Without hesitation the third Comanche performed a one-hundred-eighty-degree maneuver and zoomed back toward the opposite riverbank, going full throttle.

"Ha, ha, ha!" the head black hostage-taker snidely laughed. "Brother Arab terrorists shot down two honky choppers with rockets. Ha, ha, ha! This is hilarious! That'll teach those stupid honky pecker-woods not to fly stupid reconnaissance missions over Cincinnati! This is *our* turf dudes! Ha, ha, ha!"

Jackson was then blindfolded, roughly shoved into a blue-paneled van and transported four blocks north to the radical urban gang's secret hideout. The hostage was violently lifted out of the vehicle's back cargo area and then forcefully led into an old brick storage building's interior. Young Lee's blindfold was then removed and he voluntarily inspected the form and features of a familiar curvaceous female standing directly before him. The hostage's first instinct was to embrace his soon-to-be-fiancee.

"Melanie!" Jackson exclaimed in a somewhat doubtful tone of voice. "Why are you wearing that camouflage paramilitary uniform and black combat boots? And what has happened to all of the nasty cuts and bruises on you face?"

"Jackson, you're such a rich foolish imbecile!" Melanie Collier sarcastically criticized her hoodwinked boyfriend. "That was just a good makeup job you saw in the e-mail photo attachment. And as you can plainly see I'm a high-ranking member of the *Urban Revolutionary Army* and I'm sworn to destroy all that is evil in capitalistic *White Corporate America!* And that includes your old man's exploiting imperialistic greedy computer company! "

"But you've betrayed me!" Jackson indignantly squawked to no avail. "I loved you Melanie and risked my life to come here to ransom and save you, and now you've virtually stabbed me in the back. Why have you aligned yourself with this urban scum?"

"Ha, ha, ha!" the five treacherous minority hoods mocked and laughed at their captive. "Ha, ha, ha!"

"You and your avaricious father take advantage of innocent and poor people, and then always profit from the labors of others," Melanie smugly replied. "You and your heartless old man use people that must suffer and slave for *your* bloodsucking corporation and its greedy banal stockholders' prosperity. A revolution is coming Jackson," Melanie predicted, "a rebellion so great in magnitude that it is going to topple all of the decadent WASP trash occupying high places from New York to San Francisco. *Blue America* will rise above social injustice! Power to the people!"

Melanie Collier proudly raised her clenched right fist, and her symbolic and defiant power-gesture was quickly imitated by the seven urban gangsters surrounding Jackson Lee. The neophyte reporter was temporarily flabbergasted.

"I should've listened to father's sage wisdom," the gullible hostage regretfully returned. "He advised me to stay away from middle-class girls that seek improving the living conditions of lazy urban lowlife. Dad warned me that women who are dedicated to causes are incapable of having loving relationships and are bent on establishing a hedonistic revisionist culture in America," Jackson woefully stated. "Their radical *cause* eventually supersedes everything else of meaningful importance in their lives! Absolute freedom without responsibility means nothing more than mass anarchy and the eventual ruination of civilization."

"You're a demented white capitalistic romanticist Jackson!" Melanie depicted her former male friend. "You're opposed to human rights for everyone, including gays, minorities and militant bisexual intellectuals like myself!"

"All *you* want to do is grab what father and I have earned without ever working for it!" Jackson accused his former lover with blazing bloodshot eyes. "You've become just like the repugnant ghetto maggots standing around us! You want to destroy the world Melanie, without a clue about how to rebuild it into a better place!"

"Ha, ha, ha!" the seven black urban warriors simultaneously laughed at their prisoner's futility. "Ha, ha, ha!"

"And furthermore, my dear Jackson Lee," Melanie very seriously resumed her angry narrative. "Thanks for participating in my little kidnapping scheme!"

"What do you mean?" the jilted and now-jaded former boyfriend incredulously asked.

"I mean that the five-million-dollar-ransom was only a little bait to get *you* here for the privilege of rescuing me," Melanie revealed with a snicker. "Now we're gonna' put makeup cuts and exaggerated bruises on *your* face and e-mail the photo' to your very generous doting father. Emerson Lee will gladly pay twenty-five-million-bucks to get his spoiled pampered little son back from a pack of out-of-control psychopathic urban guerillas! How do you like my imaginative ingenious strategy? Ha, ha, ha! Power to the people Jackson! Ha, ha, ha! Power to the people!"

120

"The Power of Suggestion"

Personal Record

Monday, October 6, 2003

I, Peter Simon, Dr. of Psychiatry have been assigned to study and hypnotize a certain Martin Quade, an inmate at the United States Federal Penitentiary, Lewisburg, Pennsylvania. The subject has been convicted of using a butcher knife to brutally murder Richard Anderson, *his* dormitory roommate at the *University of Pennsylvania*, Philadelphia.

The felony had occurred on the evening of Friday, September 13th, 2002 near the Memorial Tower Archway, not far from the prestigious *Ivy League* campus's famous *Ben Franklin Statue*. Dr. Eugene Fischer, a prominent psychiatrist and colleague, desired to have an independent study undertaken so he had requested for me to psychoanalyze Martin Quade while the prisoner would be under hypnosis. My inquiry's purpose is to determine if the subject had indeed been sufficiently criminally insane when he had committed the heinous murder. Execution by lethal injection is scheduled for Monday, November 17, 2003. All defense appeals have been exhausted and the prison authorities strongly believe that a reprieve from the state governor will not be forthcoming unless new relevant information can be obtained.

This afternoon, I had the opportunity to interview the Death Row convict under hypnosis to assess if any negative event from Martin Quade's past had contributed to the perpetrator's motivation to kill his former friend and roommate, Richard Anderson. I must confess that I an a staunch advocate of the Penitentiary System and I endorse the principle that murderers should become remorseful and subsequently pursue "self-reformation" after admitting guilt to a major felony involving human death. However I am not in any way a supporter of the death penalty. I think that only the Almighty should have *that* divine privilege, and I have always maintained that incarceration in the form of a life sentence constitutes far more punishment than execution would subsequently effect. Indeed, etymologically speaking, the word "penitentiary" derives its origin from the adjective *penitent.*

After I had placed Martin Quade under the influence of my verbal suggestion, my design was to keep the experiment confidential so I gestured with my hand and immediately dismissed *his* two guards to an adjoining area outside his cell. I had effectively put the subject (who was lying in his prison cell on his bed) under hypnosis and then I comprehensively interrogated him. I found Martin Quade to be cooperative in both his conscious and subconscious existence, but most of the convict's answers were delusional and his psyche appeared plagued with paranoia and also with denial of guilt. I took accurate notes during the entire analysis, and here is the essence of *our* spontaneous question and answer session.

"Martin, please state your full name, age, hometown address and place of birth," I prudently commenced with my interview.

"My name is Martin Quade, and I am twenty-two years old. My family and I live at 423 Park Drive, Willow Grove, Pennsylvania," the subject very clearly stated. "I have lived at that residence all my life prior to attending college."

"What prompted you to viciously attack and murder your college roommate, Richard Anderson on the night of Friday, September 13th, 2002?" I bluntly proceeded. "The police report indicates that Richard had been savagely stabbed forty-seven times in the chest, abdomen, arms and shoulders."

"Richard was always making unnecessary demands upon me, forcing me to write his term papers and to help him study for *his* major tests and for his first semester courses' final exams," Martin explained. "He would borrow money from me every week, usually a hundred dollars at a clip and then never pay me back. Richard would constantly intimidate me and push me around because the brute was nearly twice my size. I saw the butcher's knife as a great equalizer the next time he would badger me and shove me around. The relentless bully took me to the brink."

"I see, but your court trial defense was that you had *only* claimed you were being *verbally* and not physically abused," I indicated, "but the jury was not convinced since you had maliciously stabbed the victim forty-seven times."

"I admit I do have a fairly nasty temper at certain times," Quade conceded under hypnosis. "But when I learned that Richard was having a love affair with my girlfriend Lori, I lost it and went off the deep end! And besides that situation, my strange roommate had ambitions of becoming a sadistic Fascist dictator!"

"Why didn't you tell the story about the love triangle to the jury?" I curiously asked while completely ignoring the ridiculous Fascist comment. "Your legal defense could have been that you had murdered Richard Anderson out of sheer jealousy!"

"I didn't want the jury to know I was jealous," Martin revealed. "I have always felt inferior to other more aggressive men because of my short height and my light weight. I've always tried to consciously conceal that disturbing fact from the public's view and that's why I have a sort of *Napoleon Complex*, acting cocky and arrogant, obviously to compensate for my diminutive size."

"Had you ever committed a major crime before you had savagely assaulted Richard Anderson on Friday night, September 13th, 2002?" I asked as I feverishly jotted down notations.

"Yes, Sir, in another life, in a previous life," Quade surprisingly replied without any trace of emotion. "I certainly had committed another murder in a previous life!"

"And exactly what did you do? On what date did you perform the previous crime and where did it occur?" I most curiously inquired.

"Forty years ago, at 12:30 in the afternoon I had assassinated President John F. Kennedy. The date was November 22, 1963. The crime had been done in Dallas, Texas," the patient/inmate incredibly disclosed in a monotone voice. "I was an expert marksman and had shot bullets from an Italian scoped-rifle. My position was a sixth floor window of the Texas School Book Depository. I especially aimed at Kennedy, who was in a motorcade on its way to the Dallas Trade Mart. It's well-documented that John Fitzgerald Kennedy died a half hour later at Parkland Hospital."

"How could you have done such a deed as Martin Quade, a 2002 senior at the *University of Pennsylvania* in Philadelphia? You weren't even born yet in 1963!" I further interrogated.

"I was not Martin Quade on November 22, 1963," the interviewee under deep hypnosis calmly emphasized. "My identity at the time was Lee Harvey Oswald. After I had assassinated the President, forty-five minutes later I then shot a Dallas policeman that had attempted to arrest me. I was finally apprehended by the cops in a movie theater that same eventful afternoon."

"What was the name of the Dallas policeman you had also shot?" I anxiously asked, for I myself' was well-versed on *that* particular historic assassination detail and *this* astute researcher was quite cognizant of the answer.

"I heard other cops at the scene yell out the name Tidbit or Tippit or something like that," Quade recalled and answered, "but I was more concerned about the news of the President's death than learning that the life of a mere Dallas cop had been snuffed-out!"

'This young man is definitely suffering from an advanced latent and suppressed case of schizophrenia,' I logically suspected. 'He has a most complex multiple-personality-syndrome and Quade probably psychologically identifies with Lee Harvey Oswald, also a short man that wanted to make a sensational impact statement on the world.'

I was quite fascinated with Martin Quade's confident oral responses, which appeared to be genuine along with being both distorted and unrealistic. My fundamental intent at that moment was to delve deeper into the controversial Lee Harvey Oswald' relationship. I felt compelled to ask Martin Quade about Lee Harvey Oswald's widely publicized Marxist ties, about the political dissident's connection with Fidel Castro and about a possible assassination conspiracy (organized with Oswald principally involved, or government-inspired with Oswald as the designated scapegoat) but then I observed that the subject was beginning to squirm under duress so I immediately terminated the trance.

"Martin, you may wake up now!" I sternly instructed. "I'm going to count backwards from ten down to one, and when you hear the number *two* you may passively wake up and return to Monday, October 6, 2003."

Personal Record

Monday, October 13, 2003

Only Hindus, quacks and charlatans profess a belief in reincarnation, and I presently contend that Martin Quade falls within the second and third more ignoble categories. He has subconsciously experienced "delusions of vicarious grandeur" in a most nefarious way, gaining satisfaction and a sense of accomplishment in enacting negative villainous misdeeds both in reality and in fantasy. This I suspected was the truth but I required additional information to verify my hypothesis. The fanciful reincarnation manifestation had been invented by the subject's imagination to camouflage his basic feelings of inadequacy about his puny body size and strength.

I am a cynic by nature and generally regard skepticism as an excellent counterbalance to a patient's euphoria or to his or her emotional despair. I am certain of one axiom of modern-day psychology and that one indisputable truth is that individuals are *driven* to perform an act (whether it be murder or societal achievement) to satisfy an emotional need (gratification, honor, recognition, infamy, greed). In Martin Quade's case the subject feels a need to alleviate his myriad shortcomings and insecurities.

Consequently Martin's subconscious mind imaginatively fabricated the Lee Harvey Oswald story to mesh and identify with John F. Kennedy's assassin's confused and somewhat neurotic personality. At least this is what my professional opinion and impression happen to be this bright Monday morning, October 13th at *Lewisburg Federal Penitentiary.*

After I again had put Martin Quade into a relaxed mental state, and thus rendered him harmless, I casually signaled for his jailers to depart the examination sector, which doubled as *his* prison cell. I had had a bout with insomnia the entire past week and was quite anxious to hypnotize my newest patient and then enthusiastically initiate the second meeting with the convicted killer.

"Martin, do you still believe that you are Lee Harvey Oswald?" I asked after I had ascertained that the subject was ready for his new series of questions. To my amazement Quade insisted that he was someone else other than Oswald, a person named Johann Georg Elser, and then the subject mysteriously continued answering my interrogatives in a distinct German dialect. I was absolutely dumbfounded by the whole bizarre phenomenon.

"Martin, excuse me, Johann. I am not that proficient in German so please speak English if you possibly could," I had the wherewithal to formally request while my reasoning was temporarily trapped in a mild state of shock. "Now allow me to rephrase my question," I persisted. "Do you think that justice has been served with the jury finding you guilty of murdering your dormitory roommate Richard Anderson? Was justice served?" I reiterated.

"Who is Richard Anderson?" my state-assigned client inquired from his deep trance. "Richard Anderson sounds like a Swede. Where in Germany does *he* live? English is such a barbaric language. Please speak in German."

"Aren't you Martin Quade?" I incredulously asked. "Everyone knows you as Martin Quade!"

"No, Sir. My full name is Johann Georg Elser. That filthy Nazi Heinrich Himmler has ordered the Gestapo to execute me in one hour," Quade nervously informed.

"What is today's date?" I neurotically questioned with my mind accelerating into an advanced state of bewilderment. "Try to be as specific as you can."

"It is the morning of April 9, 1945," Quade remarkably described. "I will soon be executed as scheduled at *their* whim and volition! It's supposed to be a Nazi secret order, but I have heard of it from other condemned prisoners. Hitler, Himmler, Goering, Rommel and the rest of their putrid ilk are avowed human butchers. To call them cannibals would be too great a compliment!"

"Why have you been sentenced to death?" I nervously prompted. "Specifically, what have you done that warrants that extreme punishment?"

"I am accused of attempting to assassinate Adolph Hitler on November 8, 1939," Quade said from his deep trance. "My elaborate plot fell short of its goal!"

"Then, this failed attempt you allude to was not the famous conspiracy organized by Hitler's generals to dispose of him in 1944 when a time-bomb had exploded inside the Fuehrer's camp headquarters!" I proceeded.

"No, that was another separate incident altogether!" Quade maintained. "I had *his* explosives attached to a timing devise behind the rostrum at the Buergerbraeukeller on November 8, 1939. Hitler was about to address some of his most dedicated veteran fighters in the enormous Munich beer hall."

"For my records, let's go back a page or two!" I recommended while under intensified emotional duress. "Johann Georg Elser, where were you born?" I awkwardly flipped back pages in my notebook.

"In the village of Hermaringen, in 1903," Quade disclosed. "In 1917 I was apprenticed as a lathe operator in an iron works. I later became a skilled cabinet builder."

"Why had you attempted to kill Adolph Hitler?" I probed. "What was your motive?"

"I strongly despised the dictator's political philosophy and his cruel methods of obtaining and keeping power," Martin Quade very plausibly replied. "I had belonged to the Rotfrontkaemferbund, a Communist organization opposed to Nazi right-wing militancy. I wholeheartedly believed that the people should have governmental power and coincidentally share the country's wealth."

I was quite captivated by Quade's mammoth claim. My mind conjectured that the subject I had been interrogating under hypnosis couldn't be all that evil if he had planned to eliminate the epitome of twentieth century brutality, Adolph Hitler. But how Quade knew so many obscure details about this hardly known man Johann Georg Elser's life presented itself to me as a distinct mystery. Lee Harvey Oswald's biography is well-documented and could have been easily studied in high school or at *Penn*, but how could the subject be knowledgeable about a remote insignificant historical figure such as

Elser? I then very carefully and meticulously resumed my comprehensive psychological investigation.

"Tell me more about this Socialist, or should I say Communist organization that you had joined?" I promptly asked. "What did it aspire to achieve?"

"The underground Rotfrontkaemferbund stood for the *Red Fighters' Association*, but I was not a leader and was content taking a subordinate role by playing a trumpet in the organization's brass band," Martin Quade, now alias Johann Georg Elser elaborated. "As an impressionable youth I had seen the devastation and the havoc that *World War I* had had on both Germany and on Europe," my extraordinary subject elaborated. "I did not wish to have the civilized world experience a second atrocious war where armies were equipped with sophisticated weapons produced by advancements in science and technology! And the Nazis, as despicable as they were, had developed missiles and military equipment that could potentially bring massive death and destruction to all cultures on all continents," Quade added. "I felt that I had to act and terminate a demented madman bent on dismantling western civilization and then diabolically rewriting history and culture in *his* vile name!"

I promptly ended Quade's second session and must indicate that my opinion of this complicated man has been drastically altered. Quade is amazingly retreating further back into history going from October 6, 2003 to September 13th, 2002 to November 22, 1963 to November 8, 1939. I am certain that the subject is sincere in his declarations and that he is incapable of deliberately deceiving me while in his controlled hypnotic condition.

This ardent truth-seeker has gone home, and I have thoroughly researched Johann Georg Elser on the *Internet* and have discovered substantial documentation on *his* here-to-fore unknown life. I am eagerly anticipating my next engagement with Martin Quade's exceptional and somewhat-addled psyche. What has intrigued me the most is the fact that Martin Quade claims to be several different people from the past that had opposing political ideologies to the men that happened to be in political power at the time. But Quade seems incapable of distinguishing between the act of assassinating good men and the art of assassinating evil men. I find this poignant distinction (or lack of it on Quade's part) to be most fascinating.

Personal Record

Monday, October 20, 2003

I honestly think that when Martin Quade had been under hypnosis, he actually believed that he had been in previous lives Lee Harvey Oswald and the less notorious Johann Georg Elser. I wondered if indeed my subject would again regress further into the past and take responsibility for committing a third act that had gained national notoriety or had had significant international impact. During my third visit I found Martin to be in a very genial mood in spite of the fact that his court ordered execution was to be less than a month away. Upon getting the subject comfortably relaxed into *his* hypnotic state, I then endeavored to have the unconscious convict connect with his true identity as Martin Quade.

"Martin, would you care to describe how Richard Anderson showed evidence of Fascist objectives?" I tersely inquired. "Was your college roommate a neo-Nazi, a Ku Klux Klan leader or right-wing militia sympathizer, or was he a white supremacist pushing for Master Race world domination? Possibly your dorm' roommate Richard Anderson was a combination of several of those factors."

"My name is not Martin, and I cannot fathom why *you* refer to me as such!" Quade adamantly and restively declared. "Why do you speak to me in English? I am Gavrilo Princip, assassin of Archduke Francis Ferdinand, heir to the Austro-Hungary throne. Is that fact perfectly clear to you?"

"Where and when did the surprise assault of the Archduke take place?" I excitedly and incisively urged.

"In the Serbian city of Sarajevo, in 1914," Quade blandly responded. "I jumped onto the automobile's running board and fired the shots that killed the Archduke. It was incredibly easy and required more audacity than actual skill!"

"Now, I remember the event you're describing from high school sophomore history," I purposely interrupted, fully desiring to encourage and not excoriate my fragile-minded subject. "Tell me Gavrilo, why did you want to trigger-off *World War I?* Upon first impression you look very much like a peace-loving pacifist!"

The convict paused to thoroughly fathom the substance of my inquiry and then he gave a weak flinch. I had trouble understanding how Martin Quade was so well-versed in history, particularly in European history. I knew that an assassination had sparked the *First World War* but the exact circumstances surrounding the incident were not stored in my brain's information file cabinet. "What caused you to shoot the vulnerable Archduke? Why did you do it?" I persisted in asking.

128

"A patriotic group of Bosnian Serbs had formed a secret society we called 'Union or Death'," the reclined patient recollected and then slowly communicated. "The Serbs wanted Bosnia and Hercegovina liberated from Austro-Hungarian control and then fully reunited with Serbia, whose history and traditions were more aligned with *our* cultural heritage. Since Francis Ferdinand was the favorite nephew of Austrian Emperor Francis Joseph and since *we* had learned through *our* reliable intelligence sources that the Archduke was to be riding in an automobile through Sarajevo," the amazing patient sedately uttered, "the royal snob became a prime assassination candidate, an obvious target for the noble Union or Death' Society."

"Do you regret what you had done?" I questioned. "Do you feel any guilt or remorse?"

"Not at all," the patient firmly returned in his subconscious state. "My people had to be reunited and I wanted to send a strong message to the Emperor that his forced reign would not be tolerated! Serbia had to be emancipated from the pompous Emperor's control! That's why the society strategically targeted *his* nephew, the Archduke."

"Did you ever think that your action would instigate *World War I*?" I volleyed. "*That* was really a horrendous and merciless conflict!"

"No, I thought that the act was simply an isolated incident to demonstrate Serbian contempt for Austro-Hungarian tyranny," the man lying on his jail cell's bed slowly and methodically uttered. "I would not in good conscience hesitate doing it a second time. In fact I know I would do the exact same thing again if given the command and the opportunity!"

"One final question for today," I slyly announced. "Do you know any of the following men? Lee Harvey Oswald, Johann Georg Elser or Richard Anderson?"

"I am not acquainted or familiar in any way with any of those persons," Martin Quade (a.k.a. Gavrilo Princip) articulated. "The name Elser sounds German in origin and the other two individuals sound as if they are foreigners."

My mind was in flux, as if contemplating a great labyrinth-type conundrum, for I felt as if I was being exposed to and was being administered a tremendous hoax that ironically, I myself' had generated. My instincts tell me not to divulge the essence of my studies to my honorable mentor Dr. Eugene Fischer or to any other distinguished consultant in the elite psychiatric world out of fear of being ridiculed in academic circles and then being labeled a hypocrite or a pretender.

I am conscientiously keeping this personal record as valid and reliable documentation of my research and plan to create a fictional account of my professional interactions with the inimitable Martin Quade to later present *that* contrived fabrication to Dr. Fischer. Nevertheless I must confess that I am so engrossed and so immersed in this most-intriguing case that the project has indeed transcended all other appointments and interests in my already busy life. I can hardly wait until next Monday to hear whose identity the inimitable Martin Quade will assume next.

My career and my professional learning at first made me consider discarding Martin Quade's testimonies as 'rubbish', but I still remained quite introspective and receptive to *his* outlandish commentaries concerning his litany of past lives. Chronologically the young man's meshing of murder stories made sense ranging backwards from 2002-to-1962-to-1938-to-1914. But Johann Georg Elser and Gavrilo Princip had to be both living in Europe at the same time, which would negate any rational validity to the lame *invalid* reincarnation theory.

The subconscious mind is indeed quite frightening because scientists know so little about its function or about its dysfunction. The conscious mind (what psychology refers to as the superego) is a combination of learned and socially expected behavior patterns that are predictable and acceptable by public standards. The converse holds *only partially true* for what lurks and lies below the conscious surface, and that direction was precisely where my intensive probing of Martin Quade's heart and soul was heading.

Personal Record

Monday, October 27, 2003

After I had again gotten Martin Quade into his relaxed hypnotic state, I motioned for the cooperative guards to quietly exit the penitentiary cell. I was ready to hear additional attestations from the convicted criminal's lips. Today his disposition seemed to be both pleasant and candid. I then commenced with my inquiry.

"To whom am I speaking?" I diplomatically began. "Please give your name and occupation."

"I am Aaron Burr, former United States Vice-President under Thomas Jefferson from 1801 to 1805," Quade firmly and dispassionately claimed. "My political career became endangered when I violently and intentionally shot Alexander Hamilton in a pistol duel on July 11, 1804 at Weehawken, New Jersey."

"What did you have against Hamilton?" I cautiously queried. "Why was he your adversary?"

"Hamilton and I had our basic political differences," the subject vicariously and almost persuasively stated. "Hamilton threw his support to Jefferson at the end of the presidential election debate and that deliberate action on *his* part betrayed my trust. Alexander Hamilton abandoned me so I had to settle for the Vice-Presidency and had to play second fiddle to that devious scoundrel Jefferson. Those four inglorious years of my life as Vice-President were rather humiliating for a man of my great pride and ambition to endure!"

"I recall reading a magazine article about you Aaron Burr being tried for treason," I carefully added. "What was that controversy all about?" I probed, since I academically wanted to test Quade's knowledge foundation on whom he claimed to be.

"I was set up by the frivolous political establishment, all of whom were allies and friends of that devious rogue Hamilton. My patriotism was as solid as a rock but I was ruined by ruthless power-hungry lie-perpetrators in *Congress,*" Quade elucidated. "Many political opponents alleged that I wanted to make Mexico into a U.S. Territory and other prominent enemies accused me of trying to get the developing western territories to secede from the Federal Union. Politics is the most formidable game on this damned planet," the prone, horizontally-lying patient editorialized. "The stakes are high and the avaricious vipers are just waiting to condemn a good man's aspirations and wickedly sully his good reputation. I found that I was surrounded by countless envious political vultures!"

"Have you ever heard of Franklin Delano Roosevelt, Thomas Alva Edison, Henry Ford or Sigmund Freud?" I asked, for I wanted to determine some definite time-line consistency to either support or refute the man's most recent assertion of being the notorious infamous rogue Aaron Burr.

"No, those names are alien to me," Martin answered. "They do not connect anywhere in my memory."

"Did you ever hear of a famous literary story titled 'The Man without a Country' written by Edward Everett Hale?" I advanced. "Your name Aaron Burr is mentioned in the work several times."

"No, both the story and the author are unfamiliar to me," Quade confidently replied from his trance. "I have always viewed literature and fiction as the politics of ludicrous fools! Literature is usually invented fiction! It's not pragmatic and that is why I loathe it and basically abhor its dreaming creators!"

"What about a person named Philip Nolan?" I pressed on. "Have you ever heard that name before?"

"He sounds like a fictitious person or an author or a worthless whimsical philosopher to me," Quade aptly declared. "Surely I would remember a queer name like that one if I had ever been introduced to the gentleman!"

I was at wit's end. The entire sequence of interviews made perfect historical sense but yet lacked fundamental plausibility and credibility when scrutinized through the prism of scientific analysis. I rejected the absurd 'reincarnation explanation' in favor of the more feasible 'multiple-personality-disorder hypothesis'. But if Martin Quade was not a serious student at *Penn*, how could he ever have formulated such an intricate-yet-flawless string of murderers' lives without possessing an adequate knowledge base?

Personal Record

Monday, November 3, 2003

Today, I became very disenchanted with Martin Quade. He was moody and more dramatic than he had demonstrated in past comprehensive interview sessions. My hunch is that the subject is undergoing internal turmoil as a result of his rapidly approaching execution date (Monday, November 17). Quade meticulously keeps a calendar on his cell wall and marks a large X for each successive day that has expired.

Martin today professed to be Jonathan Small, an unimportant pirate lost somewhere in early 1700s' micro-history oblivion. According to Quade's strange statements, Jonathan Small was conspiring to kill the ruthless Blackbeard and was soon betrayed and reported for his treachery. Small was brutally tortured and then horribly decapitated by the heartless seafaring swashbuckling monster, Blackbeard himself.

And then Quade began speaking in what sounded like some archaic Oriental language, and after I directed him to converse in English, the subject insisted that in 1225 A.D. he had been a constant companion of the infamous Genghis Khan and that he later double-crossed the Asian conqueror and was ultimately punished for his

132

insubordination with a death sentence that had been carried-out by the chief Mongol himself.

I am not looking forward to next week's visitation. Both Martin and I are lapsing into melancholy and show symptoms of depression as *his* measured time on this Earth is reaching an end. I will have to really motivate myself to be able to finish what has evolved into a most preposterous project in terms of its overall psychological justification. I feel as if my personal journal simply contains an offbeat bizarre murder/homicide story of questionable merit, even by recognized contemporary liberal literary pulp-fiction standards.

Personal Record

Monday, November 10, 2003

I am now feeling and showing symptoms of despondency. I presently and unprofessionally feel genuine compassion for Martin Quade. I realize that a sea of erratic turbulence is eddying around and swirling about inside his hyperactive subconscious mind. I am presently organizing and falsifying a second more "professional study," which I intend to submit to Dr. Eugene Fischer. Even though I have learned to care greatly for the subject, I must still protect my untarnished psychiatry reputation among my judgmental peers. The principal aspect that greatly disturbs me about Martin Quade is that (in his mind) he indiscriminately betrays those individuals that trust him and feels no obvious guilt or compunction about his very evident lack of loyalty. Martin seems much more loyal to *causes* than to people, and *this* very evident reality might explain his rather noticeable guilt deficiency. Thank God I only have today's final session to record, for next week my focus of study (Martin Quade) will be cruelly eradicated from earthly existence.

As I entered the man's solitary confinement penitentiary cell, I expected to find a fellow with a dismal and negative perspective regarding his absolute fate. Instead, Martin was in a jovial and almost buoyant frame of mind and he couldn't waste any valuable time and requested that *this* researcher immediately place him under hypnosis, which quite frankly was beginning to also mesmerize *my* sanity.

The inmate lay in his bed and I dangled the usual fob chain and gold watch before his eyes and spoke the monotonous soothing words and phrases that gradually dulled his eager senses. Then upon counting backwards Quade was finally under the dominion of my suggestion and had compromised all external features of his mercurial conscious demeanor. I then motioned for the vigilant guards to again depart the cell.

Under deep hypnosis, Quade was more rational but also quite ambivalent in terms of his new identity. However the subject's volition was not weakened and he was now a prime candidate for my next (for me) unorthodox interrogation.

One thing was for sure: I had to find out if Quade was going to continue his reverse chronology regression from the age of abominable Mongol conquests that paralleled the European Medieval Period, or would he retreat into the *Dark Ages* or even take an ambiguous mental journey into ancient history?

"What is your name and where do you live?" I objectively asked, while thinking that *this* would be an extended session in that it was to be *our* last encounter.

"My name is John Wilkes Booth and I used to reside in Washington, the nation's capital," my extremely unique subject mechanically stated.

I felt I knew plenty of information from reading magazine articles about the Lincoln assassination so that I was sufficiently qualified to find a weak point in Quade's direct responses and then I'd be enabled to exploit *that* special vulnerability. I was so enthused about Quade's new identity that I had overlooked the essential fact that *he* was no longer journeying further into the past but conversely, had accelerated from the Age of Genghis Khan forward to the *Civil War* era, a more than six century leap. "Who is your father? Why did you assassinate President Abraham Lincoln? What was the date and hour of the assassination?" I verbally fired back in rapid succession.

"My father's full name was Junius Brutus Booth," Quade very soberly replied. "My sympathies during the *War between the States* were with *the South* so naturally I detested Lincoln and his traitorous ideas on changing a traditional set way of plantation life in *Dixie*. The assassination took place at just past 10 p.m. on the evening of April, 14, 1865."

'Remarkable!' I thought and concluded. 'Every detail is accurate and all of *his* facts are valid.' I needed to compose myself to further quiz the young man, who must have exclusively read and studied the *Encyclopedia Britannica* for the past several years while pretending to be an authentic C student at the *University of Pennsylvania*. But during that final fascinating interview I felt an urgent compulsion to disprove *his* up-to-that-time very audacious and ostensibly intimidating historically accurate knowledge.

"At what Washington theater did you perform the deed and what play was in progress?" I curtly demanded from the imposter who was pretending to be a very iniquitous *Civil War* era actor/murderer.

"I enacted the noble accomplishment at Ford's Theatre while the play 'Our American Cousin' was in progress," the sage subject appropriately answered. "I knew the theater well because I myself had often performed on stage as an accomplished actor there. I surreptitiously entered Lincoln's private box and then wounded the traitor in the head. Next I leaped from the elevated box and landed poorly on the stage, breaking my leg in the process."

My memory recalled something salient from past textbook and magazine readings that only a true-blue history buff would remember or know. "What Latin phrase did *you* proclaim to the shocked Ford's Theatre audience and what does it mean when translated into English?" I zealously insisted on finding out from *my* patient.

"I shouted 'Sic semper tyrannis!' which means in English 'Thus always to tyrants'!" the subject astoundingly conveyed. "Sic semper tyrannis!" Martin Quade hauntingly repeated.

"What actually happened when you fled the theater?" I queried. "Were you immediately pursued?"

"Despite my broken leg, I rode a swift horse and fled the city and after a series of misadventures, at night I secretly crossed the *Potomac* by boat from Maryland into Virginia," Martin Quade mentally masquerading as John Wilkes Booth communicated. "I was later captured at a barn outside the town of Port Royal where I was hunted down and shot."

I was so exasperated and so spooked upon hearing his remarkably accurate testimony that I inadvertently abandoned my next question and repeated, "Who was your father?"

"Junius Brutus Booth," Martin stated for the second time. And with the utterance of *that* name from his lips, Quade began to shake and quake upon his cell bed as if afflicted with a sudden palsy attack. I grabbed his trembling hands and folded his arms over his chest as best as I could. Fortunately the subject gradually evolved out of his frightening and quite turbulent self-destruct mode. Three minutes later the patient's breathing and pulse rate returned to medically acceptable levels. "I must kill Gaius Julius Caesar! I must kill Gaius Julius Caesar!" Quade eerily yelled and reiterated. "He plans to declare himself a god! His dictatorship is a threat to the Republic! That vile tyrant Caesar must die!"

Obviously, the aforementioned pronouncement of John Wilkes Booth's father's middle name *Brutus* had sent the subject's subconscious mental dynamics back into the rudimentary days of the Roman Republic. I couldn't think of anything pertinent to say so I mentioned the first vague idea that flashed across my mind. "What day is it? What year is it?" I ranted like a raving maniac.

"It's the ominous *Ides,* which is celebrated according to Roman tradition on March 15th on the Julian calendar," the Brutus impersonator almost magically imparted. "The year is what you now know of on the Gregorian calendar as 44 B.C."

"Who were some of your accomplices?" I prodded. "What were their names?"

"Gaius Cassius Longinus and Marcus Lucinius Crassus were my principal conspirators," Quade (alias Brutus) divulged, "and other noblemen from the Senate assisted us in clandestinely carrying out *our* foolproof plot! Death to tyrants I say! Sic semper tyrannis!"

Then frightfully, without warning Martin Quade commenced shivering and radically tossing about on his jail cell bed. Soon the delusional young man was going into wild convulsions and foaming at the mouth while still remaining in his unpredictable unconscious state. I panicked and hastily summoned the assigned guards, who immediately returned with several very alarmed prison physicians. The spectacle had chills running up-and-down my spine for I fearfully thought that Mr. Martin Quade's spirit was at that precise place and time in actual communion with the Devil (if such a supernatural beast exists). His final incongruous words during his erratic frenzy on the cell's sturdy bed were, "I am the betrayer Judas! I am the betrayer Judas!"

'He'll be stone-cold dead next week so then why has everyone including myself tried to save *his* life?' I questioned my heart in a very perplexing self-examination of conscience. 'The doctors, the penitentiary guards and I are all hypocrites living totally fake quack lives!' I further critically evaluated. 'A human death now, next week or next year has miniscule significance in relation to the complex operations of an infinite and eternal universe! Just look into an ordinary telescope and view the complex night sky to comprehend exactly what I mean!'

Personal Report

Friday, November 21, 2003

Martin Quade was finally executed by lethal injection at 9 a.m., Monday, November 17, 2003. He showed no repentance for murdering his college roommate Richard Anderson, who the now-deceased subject had thought was a future dangerous Nazi tyrant. 'Since man loves and values freedom, Quade was no exception,' I theorized. In each autobiographical case, right or wrong, whether he believed he was Johann Georg Elser, John Wilkes Booth or Marcus Junius Brutus, Martin Quade shared one common denominator with those historical characters he had astonishingly pretended to be: he deeply felt that *his* personal freedom was being diminished or was being jeopardized. Consciously Martin Quade was a stalking spotted leopard, and his bullying adversary roommate Richard Anderson ultimately became *his* unfortunate prey. But subconsciously the unstable volatile subject was (in my estimation) an amoral guiltless human chameleon.

As for my humble self, I have become quite insecure and jittery ever since I read graphic accounts of Martin Quade's execution in the Tuesday morning newspapers. I had developed a certain endearing attachment to the young man, and I firmly believe that the *University of Pennsylvania* student in *his* heart felt that he had assassinated a ferocious future dictator (Richard Anderson) that represented a great potential threat to the world's prominent civilizations.

The Friday after the *Thanksgiving* holiday (November 28th), I presented my thick falsified typed report in a fancy black leather portfolio to Dr. Eugene Fischer. Visiting at the eminent professor's Philadelphia office at the time was Dr. Charles Garrison, an internationally acclaimed foremost authority on hypnosis. Dr. Fischer noticed my nervous deportment and suggested that Dr. Garrison be permitted to place me under hypnosis to alleviate my apparent stress. I was suffering from such acute anxiety that I foolishly consented to *his* rather irregular request. My delicate subconscious had been penetrated for a full two hours when I finally became aware that Dr. Garrison's experiment had finally been completed.

Dr. Fischer's revelations about my "inner sunken mind" both staggered and dismayed me. My ears and brain wanted to instantly reject his and Dr. Garrison's insistence that I had indeed vociferated the peculiar claims I purportedly had made.

"Peter, you had said the most incredible things while under hypnosis," Dr. Fischer lucidly began his review. "For instance, you first maintained that you were a young German named Gunther Schmidt who had failed in assassinating Adolph Hitler in Munich in 1938. Next Peter, you stubbornly argued that you were Jack

Rubinstein, who the public knows as Jack Ruby," my distinguished mentor lectured. "You then said you had been selected by the *Almighty* to exterminate John F. Kennedy's assassin. I don't quite know how *you* managed to trick Dr. Garrison and me with your remarkably facetious statements, but you had done a very competent and undeniably enviable job at doing so! You appeared to have been completely independent of the power of suggestion!"

"And furthermore, Peter," the revered Dr. Garrison injected, "you then jumped two thousand years into the past. You insisted that you were Simon Peter, the frugal-minded apostle that bought the food and provisions for the *Last Supper*. You even went as far as elaborating that the word par*simon*ious comes from *your* name, because you Simon Peter were a very shrewd and stingy shopper and a clever money trader for Jesus Christ's traveling entourage. Ha, ha, ha," my venerable and world-renowned fellow hypnotist cackled. "And besides *that* rather incredible oddity my dear Peter Simon, you insist you have felt extremely guilty for not killing your despised enemy Judas Iscariot when *you* had the opportunity! And as you well-know Peter, a very innocent Jew died on a cross outside Jerusalem because of *your* failure to act! Ha, ha, ha! Peter Simon, Simon Peter, what a marvelous play on words! Ha, ha, ha!"

Monday, December 8, 2003

After my ears had heard Dr. Fischer and Dr. Garrison's startling summary presentations, my knees buckled and I soon staggered and then collapsed to the office's blue carpeted floor. An ambulance was summoned and the dispatched paramedics speedily transported me to the *University of Pennsylvania Hospital* where I was immediately admitted to the facility's Intensive Care Unit.

I am encouraged to positively report that I have almost completely recuperated from what Dr. Eugene Fischer and Dr. Charles Garrison have authoritatively described as "a minor nervous breakdown." Two days ago I had been transferred to a semi-private hospital room. I was released from the acclaimed Philadelphia medical institution on Friday because my *HMO* hospital-stay insurance coverage had expired. Despite the overall adversity I have endured and suffered, I, Peter Simon, Licensed Psychiatrist, hope to still have a wonderful and joyous *Christmas*.

138

"June 30, 1956"

Samuel James Parsons led a happy life living with wife Linda and children Bobby and Carolyn on 228 Francisca Avenue just off the Pacific Coastal Highway, Redondo Beach, California. The medical supplies salesman had earned a company promotion to District Sales Manager beginning February 1st, 1956. Bobby was a fifth grader playing *Little League Baseball* and Carolyn was a studious fourth grade honor student. Linda Louise Parsons was pregnant and expecting in early October, and Sam's neighbor Craig Armstrong and he often went fishing out in the Pacific in Craig's small motorboat. But on the afternoon of Friday, February 10, 1956 Samuel Parson's entire life quickly transformed from dull-predictable to extremely bizarre.

'Life is good!' Sam thought as he was returning home from work on West Imperial Highway in his green and cream '55 Chevy Bel Air coupe. 'Linda and I live just four blocks from the ocean, I'm scheduled for another big pay raise in September and our third child is due in October. Craig's gonna' soon get a bigger fishing boat so we'll be able to go out as far as Santa Catalina Island on future Pacific excursions! I'm living the American Dream!'

Samuel James Parsons reverie was rudely interrupted at the busy Imperial Highway and Hawthorne Boulevard intersection. A drunk driver in a red and white '55 Ford Crown Victoria ran the Hawthorne Boulevard red light and then smashed directly into Parson's right front fender. The '55 Bel Air flipped over twice from the jolting impact.

Paramedics found Sam unconscious and they rushed the injured man in an ambulance to the California Medical Center where the "accident victim" remained in intensive care for four days. After Sam's broken right wrist had been set in a plaster cast, Parsons was released from the hospital on Tuesday, February 21st, and loyal Craig Armstrong visited the very lucky medical sales manager's home the following evening.

"Those drunk drivers should all lose their licenses for five years and spend at least six months in jail," Armstrong began in criticism of the negligent motorist that had nearly killed *his* best friend. "That wrist will soon mend and we'll be goin' out into the Pacific and reeling in some real whoppers! Say Sam, Sarah tells me Linda's due in October. What are ya' hopin' for, a boy or a girl?"

"It's going to be *our* second girl and Linda's goin' to name her Jill," Sam answered quite matter-of-factly. "The baby's goin' to be healthy and will some day graduate with honors from the *University of Michigan.*"

"You gotta' be kidding!" Craig indulgently laughed. "What's wrong with *UCLA* or *Southern Cal*? How could you possibly know those things?"

"I can't explain it, but I just know them!" Sam adamantly insisted. "I think the automobile collision must have affected my brain. I now sometimes have visions that belong in the future. But Jill's goin' to come into the world on Wednesday, October 3rd. And that's no silly educated guess either!"

"Maybe you need to see a brain doctor or something," Armstrong honestly suggested. "You might have some tissue that needs to be re-attached inside your head."

"No, Craig, x-rays show that there's been no brain damage," the slightly injured man maintained. "I only have to heal this broken right wrist and also a half dozen lacerations in delicate places and then I'll be a hundred percent again. And these annoying skin cuts actually hurt more than the broken wrist does."

"Okay, Sam, if that's what the doctors told you," Craig diplomatically replied. "Say, where's Linda right now? Doin' some last-minute grocery shopping or getting a new hairdo at the corner beauty parlor?"

"She's using *our* rented car to pick up Bobby over at his friend's house and also to transport Carolyn over to the school play practice," Sam remembered and said. "My daughter's the co-star in a *St. Patrick's Day* play her teacher's directing. The big production is slated for about four weeks from now."

"When will you be getting your green and cream Chevy back?" Craig innocently inquired. "That neat coupe model is gonna' be regarded as a classic car some day."

"It's been totaled!" Sam disgustingly exclaimed. "I'll have to wait and see what sum the insurance adjuster gives me and then buy a new practical means of transportation. One thing's for damned sure Craig. My next vehicle's not going to be a red and white Ford Crown Victoria!"

"Whatever you say," the jovial neighbor agreed. "And now that it's all over with, I must tell you that you're a fortunate pup escaping that terrible accident with minimal injuries."

"It's really pretty ironic, isn't it?" Sam responded with a rhetorical question. "I'm a hospital supplies district manager and I wind-up in the California Medical Center requiring the services of products I just happen to distribute! What a weird coincidence! It just doesn't get any stranger!"

"Yes, it does!" Craig challenged. "You thinking that you know the sex of the baby Linda will be having next October!"

"On Wednesday, October 3rd!" Sam clarified and reiterated. "Jill will be born at exactly 5:15 a.m. See you' tomorrow, Craig! And stay out of hospitals too! See ya' good buddy!"

On Wednesday afternoon March 21st, the auto parts distributor received a call from the almost fully recuperated medical supplies district manager. "Craig, how about you and Sarah goin' out to the movies with Linda and me tonight. We got my talkative nosy mother-in-law on babysittin' patrol this evening."

"No thanks, Sam," the normally jolly neighbor replied. "Sarah wants to stay home and view the *Academy Awards* on TV. She says the suspense is better than that of any of the melodramatic soap operas my wife habitually watches."

"Why waste your time on something that is so predictable?" "Swami Parsons" questioned his close acquaintance. "*Marty* is goin' to get the outstanding movie award and its star Earnest Borgnine is goin' to win the Best Actor Oscar."

"I think *East of Eden* is goin' to get the Best Picture Award and James Dean is gonna' get the Best Actor for his role in *Rebel without a Cause,*" Armstrong maintained.

"You're all wrong, Craig; wrong as usual," Sam jokingly objected. "Close but still wrong."

"What do ya' mean?" Armstrong mildly protested. "I do have a brain, ya' know!"

"James Dean was in *East of Eden* but Jo Van Fleet is goin' to get the Best Supporting Actress Oscar for her part in that fantastic film," Sam stubbornly persisted. "And Anna Magnani will earn the Best Actress gold statue for her role in *Rose Tattoo*! What a terrific performance!"

"You're crazy! Gone off your long pier into the deep end!" Craig accused. "How can you be so confident about future things nobody really knows about! Are you psychic or something?"

"Well yes, I guess I am," Parsons modestly answered. "I just have a peculiar gut instinct that I can't rightly explain about a lot of upcoming future events."

"Maybe the car accident has rearranged your cerebral activity and made you psychic while coincidentally destroyin' some major brain cells," Sam's humorous neighbor whimsically theorized and expressed. "I happen to think and believe Natalie Wood is gonna' get the Best Actress Award."

"Not a chance! She's too young to win it," Sam answered with absolute certainty. "And Jack Lemmon is gonna' surprise everyone by getting the Best Supporting Actor presentation for his stellar performance in *Mr. Roberts.*"

"If you're right, I'll let you pilot my new boat with your one good arm out to *Santa Catalina Island* on its first fishing expedition!" Craig promised. "I'm getting it tomorrow!"

"The neat song 'Santa Catalina, 26 Miles Out to Sea' by the Four Preps will be coming out two years from now on March 3rd, 1958," Sam informed his confused listener over the phone.

"I think you need to go back into the hospital!" Craig jested. "But this time it oughta' be inside a mental institution. Say, how was Carolyn in the *St. Patrick's Day* play?"

"Now my daughter's the one that really deserves an Oscar," Parsons joked. "Se ya' tomorrow, Craig!" Click.

The following afternoon, Sam visited his loyal neighbor, who was totally stunned by the accuracy of Parsons's Academy Awards predictions. "I don't know how ya' did it, but all five of your crystal ball prognostications came true. Do you have any other future news to report?" Craig asked his amazing friend. "With you around I'll never have to buy another newspaper as long as I live."

"I'll tell you all about it if you take me out to Santa Catalina on your new *yacht,*" Sam jested.

"Okay, but I'm a guy that keeps his promises," Craig volleyed. "You're gonna be the first captain on my new yacht's maiden voyage, broken right wrist and all."

Craig drove his fishing buddy out to the local marina's parking lot in *his* new blue and white '56 Pontiac sedan. Soon the men hopped into Armstrong's "new nautical toy" and Parsons proudly took over the helm.

"Well, good buddy," Craig said, as "Sam the man" steered Armstrong's new outboard out of the Redondo Beach Marina in the direction of Santa Catalina, "only twenty-six miles and we'll' finally get to *our* heavenly destination. Now tell me," the curious man continued, "what's gonna' happen in the form of major news that the reporters haven't learned yet?"

"National or international news?" Parsons defensively qualified. "Please be more specific and discriminate better when you ask me random questions."

"National issues would be just fine!" Armstrong apprehensively answered.

"Well, a series of catastrophic tornadoes will pound the Midwest April 2nd and 3rd," Sam indicated with a degree of body animation, "and unfortunately forty-five people will be killed and over fifteen million dollars in property damage will occur in the states of Mississippi, Wisconsin, Kansas, Tennessee, Michigan, Oklahoma and Arkansas. I tried calling the weather bureau and warn them but the guy on the other end called me a 'crackpot' and hung-up before I could finish telling him the remainder of the vital information! This psychic ability I possess does have its credibility problems with the rest of our species!"

"And what other important news is about to happen?" Craig inquired. "I always say that no news is good news! That mantra is my favorite credo."

"Yes Craig, now I fully remember. On Sunday, April 8th six Parris Island Marine recruits will unfortunately drown while on a platoon disciplinary march," Sam matter-of-factly related. "A man named Sergeant Matthew C. McKeon will be convicted later this year for causing the unnecessary tragedy. McKeon will be found to be drunk while on duty and guilty of negligent homicide," Sam predicted. "He will be disgraced and demoted to a private," Parson's elaborated, "and he'll also spend three months rotting away in the brig'!"

"April's too far ahead to even think or worry about. I have trouble just making it through March. Any good news to balance out the bad?" Craig incredulously asked his enigmatic friend. "I mean what's gonna' happen soon in the ever-competitive sports world? Now the *NCAA Basketball Championship* game is scheduled for tomorrow, Friday March 23rd. What team do ya' think is gonna' emerge victorious?"

"I'm not an avid college basketball fan," Sam humbly apologized, "but I'm quite positive that *San Francisco* is gonna' beat *Iowa* to win the big tournament and the score is gonna' be 83-71! Yes, that's what my mental vibrations are tellin' me! 83-71!"

"If you get the score exactly correct," the auto parts distributor chuckled, "you can be my sports adviser forever, that is as long as your forecasts are on target!"

"No problem, Craig!" Sam amiably agreed. "You don't even have to waste your time watching the game on TV. I guarantee that the outcome's a lead pipe cinch!"

San Francisco starring Bill Russell did capture the college basketball crown and the final score was exactly what Sam Parsons had amazingly augured. Craig decided he would start making sports bets on Sam's uncanny knack of perceiving future events. When Parsons stated that the *Philadelphia Warriors* would defeat the *Fort Wayne Pistons* for the *NBA* championship four games to one on April 7, Armstrong contacted a local bookie without his best friend's knowledge and soon thereafter collected three times *his* original wager. And when the medical supplies district manager foretold that on Tuesday, April 10th the *Montreal Canadiens* would vanquish the *Detroit Red Wings* four games to one for the coveted *NHL Stanley Cup* trophy, Craig contacted his bookie and got a thirty-five-dollar return on his ten-dollar investment.

"Well Sam," Craig said with admiration as Parsons again steered with one arm Armstrong's new outboard out of the Redondo Beach Marina in the direction of scenic Santa Catalina, "only twenty-six miles and we'll finally get to *our* heavenly destination. Now tell me," the curious man continued his inquiry, "there aren't any important sports events until the big 60th *Boston Marathon* on April 19th. What's gonna' happen there?"

"Somebody named Antti Viskari from Finland is gonna' win the marathon with a record time of two hours, fourteen minutes and fourteen seconds," the temporary boat captain revealed. "You can bet your house on it!"

"How do you spell that name?" Armstrong asked as the fellow rapidly searched and soon found a pencil and memo' pad in a side compartment of his new blue and white twenty-foot-long motorboat. "Spell it out Sam."

"A-n-t-t-i V-i-s-k-a-r-i!" the pilot returned. "He's definitely from Finland!"

"Sounds like the guy has wings instead of *fins*!" Craig laughed. "And ya' say his time is gonna' be two hours, fourteen minutes and fourteen seconds?"

"That's right!" the navigator answered in a distinct melancholy apathetic voice. "Say Craig, I should have called the forty-five people that had died in the Midwest tornadoes on the telephone. I knew their names and numbers but never even once picked up the phone. I feel really guilty about it now!"

"It was an Act of God!" Armstrong sympathized. "And neither you nor I can do anything to change God's will! And besides that, those forty-five people would call you a quack and then give you a tin ear to match your hard plaster-right-wrist."

"Thanks for the encouragement," the boat guider readily acknowledged. "But I shoulda' also called and notified the six recruits that needlessly drowned at Parris Island. What a horrible preventable tragedy!"

"The recruits and their bosses would have accused you of being a nuisance or a weirdo and would have then angrily hung-up on you too!" Parsons' supportive fishing companion insistently argued. "Now just get your mind focused on catching some striped sea bass. Remember this is a fishing trip and not a guilt trip!"

"Our luck's gonna' be weak today. We're just goin' to reel in a couple of small sand sharks and toss them back into the blue Pacific," Sam predicted. "Knowin' what's goin' to happen next takes all the fun out of life! The present can become pretty boring if you know all about it beforehand."

"I can't be too skeptical of reality!" Craig promptly responded. "Who'd ever think that a guy from Finland is gonna' be triumphant in the *Boston Marathon*? And one more thing pal and this is really important."

"What's that?" Sam facetiously asked while knowing exactly what was on his buddy's puzzled mind.

"Yesterday, I listened to the radio all day long and never once heard that tune 'Twenty, Six Miles Out to Sea' by the Four Preps! You said it was due out March 3rd."

"You'd better get the wax unclogged from your ears!" Parsons genially criticized his forgetful fishing partner. "The Santa Catalina Island song will first hit the music charts on March 3rd, 1958. We're still living in April, 1956!"

Antti Viskari did win the April 19th *Boston Marathon* and Craig Armstrong had converted his hundred-dollar bet into a handsome two thousand bucks. 'My bookie is getting mighty suspicious of my good luck streak,' Armstrong realized the next morning while shaving in the master bathroom. 'I'm gonna' switch to another guy that Jim Reynolds at work has recommended. I can't wait for the 82nd *Kentucky Derby* on Saturday, May 5th. Sam says Needles is gonna' win in two minutes and three and two-fifths seconds with Dave Erb aboard as the jockey. I've parlayed the two thousand bananas I won on the Bean Town marathon and if I hit again on the *Derby* my return will be ten grand. Sam better be right on this one!'

Craig did hit the horse race jackpot with his ten-thousand-dollar *Kentucky Derby* bonanza. He kept his winnings a secret from his "honest gifted neighbor" and hoped that Sam wouldn't shortly receive a second blow to the cranium that might return him back to normalcy. A delighted Armstrong called his chum on the phone about Needles and jockey Dave Erb taking the Churchill Downs Winners Circle photo-shoot.

"Sam, you were right on the money with Needles coming in first in the Derby!" Craig characteristically praised. "Is Needles gonna' win the *Triple Crown?*"

"No sir, Craig," Parsons calmly-but-emphatically answered. "The May 19th 81ˢᵗ *Preakness Stakes* will be won by Fabius in one minute, fifty-eight and two-fifths seconds with Bill Hartack as the jockey. And then," Sam quite naturally proceeded, "Needles with Dave Erb in the saddle will come back and take the big *Belmont Stakes* on Saturday, June 16ᵗʰ with a great time of two minutes, twenty-nine and four-fifths seconds."

"I have a terrific idea," Craig declared. "Why don't we both quit our monotonous jobs and go into the entertainment industry. Sam, you could be a mentalist or magician or someone famous like that and I'll tour the country as your grateful manager. I'll even introduce you on stage."

"Thanks, but no thanks," the humble neighbor said over the phone. "I'm basically very shy and have a dreadful phobia about appearing or speaking in front of large audiences. Performing in show business is not exactly my cup of tea! I prefer demonstrating my mental magic in private and exclusively to my closest friend. See ya' later good neighbor!" Click.

Craig Armstrong was really acquiring the gambling fever, especially with the odds drastically tilted in *his* favor. 'I can't go back to the local bookies because they're beginnin' to gossip about my good luck skein,' the wannabe' entertainment manager thought. 'I'll have to fly or drive out to Vegas where the big betting action is. Even when I win thirty-thousand that's gonna' be just small potatoes to those big operators practicin' their fine art on *The Strip*.'

Craig accumulated a stupendous sum for his *Kentucky Derby*, *Preakness* and *Belmont Stakes* winners and never disclosed his new-found prosperity to his shy good neighbor. And after Sam predicted that Patrick Francis Flaherty from Chicago was destined to win the 40ᵗʰ *Indianapolis 500 Auto Race* in three hours, fifty-three minutes and fifty-nine second at an average speed of one hundred twenty-eight and a half miles an hour, Armstrong anxiously caught quick back-and-forth commercial airplane shuttles from Los Angeles to Las Vegas and then back to L.A. His colossal winnings came to over fifty thousand dollars and "a buzz" was rapidly circulating up and down Fremont Street and around the flashy illuminated Vegas strip casinos about the "lucky guy from L.A."

Early Sunday morning, June 3rd a rather euphoric Craig Armstrong visited Sam's place for coffee and doughnuts. "Say Sam, Linda and the kids still in bed?"

"No, she's getting Bobby and Carolyn ready for church," the introverted mentalist turned clairvoyant answered. "Here, have a doughnut. They're only a day old."

"Thanks a lot," the visitor gratefully accepted. "I'm only gonna' stay for about ten minutes. I got plenty of yard work to catch up on and Sarah is in one of those erratic tyrannical woman moods, if ya' know what I mean. She's ready to start chewin' nails and then spittin' sharp metal chunks in my face if I don't get motivated and begin mowin' the lawn."

"Did you have anything particular or special in mind you wanted to discuss?" Sam perceptively queried. "Usually you sleep late on Sunday mornings."

Craig wanted to share some of his secret gambling profits with his astounding neighbor and he finally figured out a way *he* could do it. Armstrong proposed that Sam and he and their wives take a week-long vacation starting Saturday, July 7th in Atlantic City. "The treat will be on me!" Craig offered. "And you've often confided that you'd like to stroll the world-famous boardwalk. I'll arrange all of the details with my travel agent."

"You must be unaware of one important date and fact," Sam responded before taking another sip of black coffee. "Your second cousin Jerry Gares is getting married on Saturday, July 7th up in San Francisco. Sarah is gonna' insist that you both attend the ceremony and reception so you'd better cancel any plans you have for Atlantic City. You're gonna' be spending most of your vacation time up in Frisco'. Don't forget to visit *Alcatraz*!"

"But Sarah and I haven't received any invitation to any wedding yet?" the prospective guest exclaimed. "And how do you know that my wife's second cousin's name is Jerry Gares? I've never mentioned *that* nutcase to you before anywhere!"

"The printer had a delay in running off the invitations," Sam rationally explained. "You'll be receiving the wedding notification in tomorrow's mail."

"Okay, but I want to establish a rain check vacation date with you and Linda sometime in the early fall," Craig regretfully uttered. "Perhaps the four of us can do a four day Las Vegas pleasure junket instead of Atlantic City. And speaking of *Alcatraz*, sometimes I think I'm living there with Sarah as the warden!"

The postman did deliver the fancy wedding invitation to the Armstrong's mailbox and that evening the gambling addict opened the elaborate envelope and silently read the notice, feeling great disappointment. 'Well, there goes the fabulous Jersey shore trip,' the unlucky recipient of the San Francisco bad news lamented. 'I suppose Atlantic City boardwalk thrills will have to be postponed until late next summer.'

On Sunday afternoon June 10th, Sam accompanied Craig on what had become their weekly fishing pilgrimage to Santa Catalina. "I'll be doin' about twenty knots so we'll be at the island in a little more than an hour," Armstrong told a temporarily aloof Parsons. "This new boat really has some acceleration when I open it full throttle. Say Sam," the weekend mariner articulated, "how about providin' some juicy futuristic news. My imagination is starvin' for some extraordinary ideas to consider."

The boat passenger was passively gnawing away on a peanut butter and strawberry jam sandwich that Linda had considerately prepared in a brown paper bag, and after swallowing a tasty well-chewed mouthful the "nautical guru" then expressed several sensational prophecies to his very alert fishing mate. "On July 10th the *National League* is goin' to win the 23rd annual *All-Star Game*, 7 to 3," Sam almost lethargically uttered.

"That's too bad!" Craig replied as he made a mental note of the yearly baseball contest. "I've always been an *American League* fan and I love the *Red Sox* and Ted Williams. Did you know that I was born and raised in Boston?"

"Why yes!" Sam Parsons automatically answered. "I've been cognizant of that remote fact ever since I came out of unconsciousness after the auto' accident."

"And while we're on the subject of baseball," Craig resumed as the blue and white motorboat exited San Pedro Channel and entered the dark blue Pacific heading southwest, "what about the *Fall Classic*. Who's gonna' win the *World Series*?"

The up-to-then listless *ESP* practitioner paused momentarily and closely examined the cast on his fractured right wrist to dramatically enhance his careful response. He drank two ounces of orange juice from a bottle with his good left hand and then said, "The *Yankees* are gonna' beat the *Dodgers* four games to three. On Monday October 8th Don Larsen will pitch a fantastic no-hitter and the *Yanks* will win that game two to nothing. That exceptional accomplishment will represent the first no hitter in *World Series* history."

"Don Larsen!" Craig bellowed with an attendant laugh. "He's the worst pitcher on the entire *Yankee* staff. You gotta' be wrong and have your wires crossed on that one!"

"Well, you oughta' be glad an *American League* team is gonna' win the *Series*," the mentalist concluded and nonchalantly stated. "But Craig, you're gonna' have to become a *National League* fan because the *Dodgers* are gonna' move from Brooklyn to L.A. in 1959 and the *New York Giants* are gonna' come out west to San Francisco a short time later."

Craig Armstrong's stimulated mind was in a quandary trying to assess and record the series of startling revelations. He asked his incredible friend about what was going to transpire in the rough and tumble political arena. 'They take political election bets in Las Vegas too!' he greedily contemplated.

"On November 6th Dwight David Eisenhower will be re-elected to a second term winning over Democrat Adlai Stevenson, 475 electoral votes to 74," Sam Parsons incidentally communicated. "Eisenhower will get 35,387,015 popular votes to Stevenson's 25,875,408. And on *Election Day* the Democrats will gain one seat in the Senate giving them a 49-47 majority over the Republicans, and the Dems' will also gain an additional seat in the *House,* affording them a 233 to 200 advantage."

"Eisenhower's okay, but I don't trust his running mate, that Nixon guy!" the boat navigator opined.

"Richard M. Nixon is going to one day be the *President of the United States* and involved in an immense scandal that'll be called *Watergate*!" Sam disclosed.

"I hope I'm dead and buried when that happens!" Armstrong verbally rendered. "I don't like that guy's small beady eyes and his broad sneaky smile! Say Sam, are ya' feelin' all right? You look a little despondent and green in the face!"

The listener hesitated for a moment to further garner his sensitive thoughts. Then he asked his friend "the Skipper" for help in undertaking a most dangerous enterprise. Craig Armstrong was spellbound as he listened with his mouth agape to his companion's remarkable tale. Then the good-natured fellow responded to his friend's inordinate request for assistance. "Look Sam, I trust your integrity and your honesty more than anyone else's!" Armstrong supportively verbalized. "I'm with you on this project a hundred percent as long as no one gets hurt or killed, especially me!"

Sam's fertile mind had had a terrible psychic manifestation that his second cousin, a brilliant electronics engineer was going to perish in a tragic airplane disaster. Parsons had visited his relative living in nearby Hawthorne, explained the situation, and was thanked for his concern. However the endangered cousin placed little credence in the predictor's warning saying, "You should have been an *Old Testament* prophet preaching the end of the world. You *were* named after the prophet Samuel in the *Bible*, you know!" the psychic's fated cousin said and chuckled.

"Exactly how and where will this airline calamity occur?" Craig asked as the blue and white boat reached the eastern tip of Santa Catalina. Parsons quickly recovered from having his almost-hypnotic daydreaming interrupted.

"Over the *Grand Canyon* on the morning of June 30th!" Sam informed his most-trusted friend. "My cousin will be aboard a *TWA Super-Constellation* and the other plane involved in the midair collision will be a *United DC-7*. The irony is that both planes will be taking off about the same time from *Los Angeles International Airport* and then flying east at different altitudes of 21,000 and 19,000 feet."

"Then, how are they gonna' smash into each other?" Craig queried as he momentarily became distracted and forgot about steering the boat. "That's quite an altitude gap even by large airplane standards, about a half a mile!"

"From what my psychic impressions suggest," Sam very deliberately said, "the *TWA Super-Constellation* will be assigned to 19,000 feet and the *DC-7* to 21,000. The *TWA* captain will request a clearance to ascend to a higher altitude to avoid turbulence while the *DC-7* cockpit crew was probably showing its passengers a glimpse of the *Painted Desert* and then planned to view the *Grand Canyon*."

The boat Skipper next made a sage observation and deduction. "Then the *TWA* crew probably knew about the *DC-7* being in the vicinity but the *United Airlines* plane was unaware of the *Super-Constellation* penetrating into its air space!" Craig declared.

"That conclusion is correct," Sam confirmed. "Both four-propeller planes will leave the air traffic control that's maintained by the *Los Angeles International Airport* tower. They're each basically on their own, thinking that they have been separated from one another by sufficient time and space."

"But how are we gonna' survive, if we're both riding on one of the ill-fated planes?" Craig finally asked. "Isn't this putting both of us in jeopardy if the air accident is inevitable? I think *that* one little overlooked matter should be of paramount importance to the both of us!"

150

"Craig, *we'll* be passengers on the *United DC-7* so that my cousin won't recognize me because he'll be on the *TWA Super-Constellation,"* Sam methodically explained. "We'll enter the cockpit and draw pistols to make the *United* pilot change course and avoid the midair collision. I'll use my powers and make sure the odds for survival are in *our* favor."

"Why are you so fond of this special cousin, the electronics engineer?" Craig curiously inquired. "Is he worth us risking *our* lives for?"

"The guy's an absolute genius," the boat passenger related. "If he lives he'll meet a guy named Bill Gates and then go into something that will in the future be called the computer industry. They'll both become multi-billionaires and you and me will have cake executive positions in the massive corporation."

"Keep talking!" the boat captain urged. "This wild story is getting mighty interesting!"

Sam hastily described the future computer industry and told his companion all about desktops, laptops, hand-held devices and the *Internet*. Suddenly Craig Armstrong stopped the boat, shut off the motor, dropped anchor and sat mesmerized listening to his friend's intriguing exposition.

"How we gonna' board the *DC-7* and get by airport security and ticket takers?" Craig asked. "It seems that too many things have to go perfectly right for your plan to succeed."

"I have a friend working in security at the airport who owes me a big favor," Sam conveyed to his captivated but slightly dubious listener. "We'll be able to slip onto the *DC-7* from the tarmac. The plane will only have sixty people aboard including the three-crew-members and *us*. There will be seats available in the back, and since we're not riding in a train, no conductor is gonna' come down the aisle and check out tickets."

"How many people will be on the *TWA Super-Constellation?"* Craig wanted to know.

"A total of seventy!" Parsons excitedly exclaimed as he saw he was convincing Craig to go along with his bold strategy. "Just think. We'll be revered heroes in every big city newspaper if we can save a hundred and twenty-eight innocent lives in a near-miss accident!"

"Okay, Sam. But can you just tell me how we're gonna' get into the cockpit to give directions to the flight crew!" Craig demanded. "That point needs some clarification."

"That's easy!" Parsons enunciated with a grim expression on his almost-pallid face. "Listen carefully! Here's how it's all gonna' be done!"

Early Saturday morning, June 30th, 1956 Sam ambled over to Craig's kitchen door and then the two "Good Samaritans" walked to a popular Redondo Beach coffee and doughnut shop and had a brief breakfast. The dual adventurers next ambled three blocks and caught a northbound bus that would drop them off near the bustling *Los Angeles International Airport*. Sam and Craig met-up with Jake Ryan as scheduled in a terminal Men's Room. Ryan then inconspicuously led the two through an unmanned door reserved for transcontinental airliner crew-members and onto the tarmac where they casually boarded the *DC-7* ten minutes before the regular passengers had been allowed admission through the airline's assigned loading gate.

"That exercise was a breeze!" Sam confidently commented to his fidgety accomplice from *his DC-7* seat. "Let's pretend to be reading these newspapers I've brought along until we're finally rolling down the runway."

Everything went according to plan. The other passengers entered and occupied their assigned seats listed on their ticket stubs. The stewardesses were so preoccupied with their myriad loading responsibilities that they failed to recognize that two well-dressed stowaways in business suits were on board, sitting quietly in rear unsold seats. Soon the *United DC-7* was taxiing to the end of the runway and in another five minutes the enormous four-propeller plane was off the ground and heading into the clear blue sky.

The "UnFasten Seat Belt" signs began blinking fifteen minutes after takeoff and the two plotters heeded the flashing instructions. The *United* flight had already circled over the Pacific and then headed inland toward the California and Arizona deserts. Soon the Los Angeles metropolitan area below gave way to towns and farms and then to vast arid wasteland. Sam had little time to initiate the next phase of his grandiose scheme.

"Stewardess, could you tell the captain that his favorite cousins Tom Wells and this fellow, Ray Cross are surprise passengers on this flight?" Sam requested. "I know he'll be happy to see Ray and me!"

"Certainly, Mr. Wells," the accommodating and alert attendant agreed. "I'll do that right now!"

"Soon, we'll be flying over the *Painted Desert* and then keep your eyes open for a spectacular view of the *Grand Canyon,*" the public-relations-minded captain stated over the airliner's intercom.

Five minutes later, the pretty brunette stewardess gingerly stepped down the aisle and approached the two illegal anonymous passengers. "The captain says he'll be glad to show you gentlemen the plane's sophisticated instrument panel," she cordially informed. "Please follow me to the front cabin entry door."

After Sam and Craig entered the cockpit, Armstrong slammed the portal shut. The captain turned his head and said, "Hello….say, you're not Tom and Ray!" as he noticed the pair of drawn handguns pointed directly at *him* and his exasperated copilot.

"This is not a hijacking or a holdup!" Sam apologetically yelled with a pistol in his shaking left hand. "There's gonna' be a fatal midair collision with a *TWA Super-Constellation* over the *Grand Canyon* so we've got no time to explain how I know this! Just please steer the plane south to avoid going over the canyon and then we'll surrender our weapons and do whatever you tell us. Captain, we mean you no harm and only want to avert a major disaster!"

The very rattled captain gestured to the *DC-7's* nervous copilot to cooperate and to follow the intruders' strange commands. A minute later a loud shout was emitted from the already-disturbed copilot's lips. "Watch out captain! An unidentified aircraft is closing in on us from the right at an altitude of twenty-one thousand. It's not a *Super-Constellation!* My God! It's circular! It's one of those *UFOs!"*

The captain quickly rotated the steering control to the left and the interplanetary near-air collision was skillfully averted. "What was that thing doing? Sightseeing over the *Grand Canyon*?" the pilot angrily squawked. "Anyway, we're now fully out of *Los Angeles International's* air control. We're on our own!"

"Maybe the saucer was on a secret government reconnaissance mission," Sam speculated and then uttered. "Oh my God captain! We've changed course and are heading north again! Quick captain! Turn this airplane south right now! Turn it south or we're all doomed to die!"

"Captain," the panicky copilot shouted, "we're in a dense cloud cover and oh my God, I think I see the gleam from another large plane heading right….."

The midair collision between the *TWA Super-Constellation* and the *United DC-7* occurred directly over the *Grand Canyon.* All one hundred and thirty people aboard the two prop' liners died. Swiss mountain climbers were flown in from Europe to attempt recovering the victims' bodies, but many were never found.

Jake Ryan never mentioned a word about his collaboration with Sam Parsons and Craig Armstrong being smuggled aboard the *DC-7* out of fear of losing *his* airport position, and also then worrying about going to prison for being a participant in a major manslaughter case involving a possible failed hijacking. According to Los Angeles police reports, Parsons and Armstrong were officially placed on the area "Missing Persons' List."

Addendum Note: The author's wife's second cousin Thomas Sulipuzio was a passenger on the ill-fated *United DC-7*. Tom was thirty years old at the time of the accident and was a brilliant electronics engineer working out of Philadelphia for the *Rheem Corporation.* Ironically my wife's cousin died in the air catastrophe. Oddly enough, his purpose in traveling from Philadelphia to Los Angeles was to present plans to corporate and government officials for developing a "Collision Avoidance System" to prevent midair commercial plane disasters.

The great air calamity shocked and alarmed the American public. As a result of the horrible air tragedy of June 30, 1956 the government laid the groundwork for what eventually materialized into the *Federal Aviation Administration*, which now in our "jet age" is responsible for monitoring air traffic control on all flights from coast to coast.

About the Author

Jay Dubya is author John Wiessner's initials (J.W.) and also his pen name.   John is a retired New Jersey public school English teacher and he has taught the subject for thirty-four years. John lives in southern New Jersey with wife Joanne and the couple has three grown sons.

Jay Dubya has written other adult literature besides *Nine New Novellas*. *So Ya' Wanna' Be A Teacher*, *The Wholly Book of Genesis*, *Black Leather and Blue Denim, A '50s Novel* and its sequel, *The Great Teen Fruit War, A 1960' Novel* are humorous literary endeavors. *Pieces of Eight*, *Pieces of Eight, Part II*, *Pieces of Eight Part III* and *Pieces of Eight, Part IV* are' short story/novella' collections featuring science fiction, paranormal and humorous plots and themes. *So Ya' Wanna' Be A Teacher* is a satirical autobiography describing the author's thirty-four-year educational career in American public schools.

Ron Coyote, Man of La Mangia is adult humor and the work is an imaginative satire/parody on Miguel Cervantes' *Don Quixote*, published in 1605. *The Wholly Book of Exodus* is also adult satirical humor. *Thirteen Sick Tasteless Classics*, *Thirteen Sick Tasteless Classics, Part II*, *Thirteen Sick Tasteless Classics, Part III* and *Thirteen Sick Tasteless Classics, Part IV* are adult satirical rewrites of famous literary short fiction.

John has also authored a trilogy of young adult fantasy novels, *Enchanta*, *Pot of Gold* and *Space Bugs, Earth Invasion*. *The Eighteen' Story Gingerbread House* is a new collection of eighteen diverse and creative children's stories.

Jay Dubya likes '50s rock and roll music, and he also enjoys pop' songs by the Beach Boys, Fleetwood Mac, the Eagles, the Rolling Stones, *ELO* and by John Fogerty. When not writing or listening to music, Jay Dubya likes watching *76ers* basketball and *Phillies* and *Yankees* television baseball games.

Author Biography

Born in Hammonton, NJ in 1942, John Wiessner had attended St. Joseph School up to and including Grade 5. After his family moved from Hammonton to Levittown, Pa in 1954, John attended St. Mark School in Bristol, Pa. for Grade 6, St. Michael the Archangel School in Levittown for Grades 7 and 8 and then Immaculate Conception School, Levittown, Pa. for Grade 9. Bishop Egan High School, Levittown Pa was John's educational base for Grades 10 and 11, and later in 1960, the aspiring author graduated from Edgewood Regional High, Tansboro, NJ. John then next attended Glassboro State College, where he was an announcer for the school's baseball games and also read the nightly news and sports over WGLS, GSC's radio station.

John Wiessner had been primarily an English teacher in the Hammonton Public School System for 34 years, specializing in the instruction of middle school language arts. Mr. Wiessner was quite active in the Hammonton Education Association, serving in the capacities of Vice-President, building representative and finally, teachers' head negotiator for 7 years. During his lengthy teaching career, John had been nominated into "Who's Who Among American Teachers" three times. He also was quite active giving professional workshops at schools around South Jersey on the subjects of creative writing and the use of movie videos to motivate students to organize their classroom theme compositions.

John Wiessner was very active in community service, being a past President of the Hammonton Lions Club, where he also functioned for many years as the club's Tail-Twister, Vice-President and Liontamer. John had been named Hammonton Lion of the Year in 1979 and in 2009 received the prestigious Melvin Jones Fellow Award, the highest honor a Lion can receive.

John also was a successful businessman, starting with being a Philadelphia Bulletin newspaper delivery boy for two years in the late 1950s in Levittown, Pennsylvania. After his family moved back to New Jersey in 1959, John worked at his grandparents and his parents' farm markets, Square Deal Farm (now Ron's Gardens in Hammonton) and Pete's Farm Market in Elm, respectively. He later managed his wife's parents' farm market, White Horse Farms in Elm for three summers.

Also, in a business capacity, for 16 summers starting in 1967 John Wiessner had co-owned Dealers Choice Amusement Arcade on the Ocean City, Maryland boardwalk and also co-owned the New

Horizon Tee-Shirt Store for eight summers (1973-'81) on the Rehoboth Beach, Delaware boardwalk. In addition, "Jay Dubya" was a co-owner of Wheel and Deal Amusement Arcade, Missouri Avenue and Boardwalk, Atlantic City. And then, for 18 summers beginning in 1986, John had been the Field Manager in charge of crew-leaders for Atlantic Blueberry Company (the world's largest cultivated blueberry farm), both the Weymouth and Mays Landing Divisions.

After retiring from teaching in 1999, writing under the pen name Jay Dubya (his initials), John Wiessner became the author of 75 books in the genre Action/Adventure Novels, Sci-Fi/Paranormal Story Collections, Adult Satire, Young Adult Fantasy Novels and Non-Fiction Books. His books exist in hardcover, in paperback and in popular Kindle and Nook e-book formats.

In January of 2022, John Wiessner (Jay Dubya) was nominated into Marquis Who's Who in America, and in April of that same year, was one of nine distinguished Who's Who in America members honored with receiving Lifetime Achievement Awards, all nine sharing a news article of recognition appearing in the Wall Street Journal.

Google: Jay Dubya, books
Google: Walmart, Jay Dubya